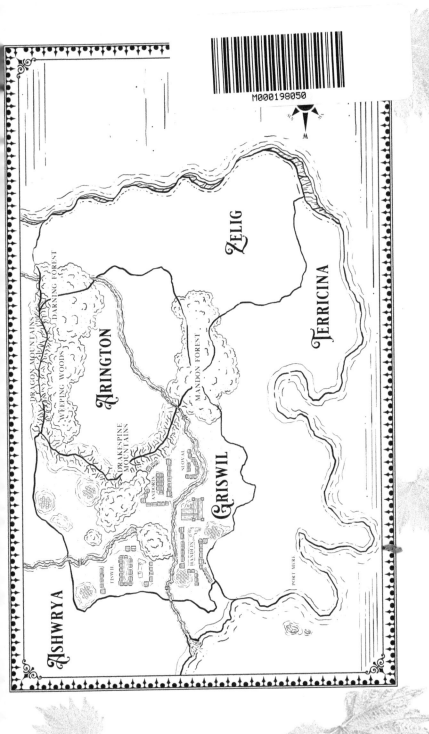

Edited by Maria Rosera of The Paisley Editor
editor.paisleypressbooks.com
Interior Design and Formatting by Melissa Stevens of The Illustrated Author Design Services
Cover Design by Melissa Stevens of The Illustrated Author Design Services

theillustratedauthor.net

To Christina Walker
Without you, I wouldn't be on this great adventure!

ONE

My roar echoed into a scream.

Cold sweat dampened my shirt, and I jolted upright in my bed. Quickly, I searched my body with clammy hands. I pressed my hands against my face, patting each detail, smoothed the hair of my eyebrows, felt the scar on my cheek from when I'd fallen as a child. Next: arms, legs, breasts, toes. Even in the pre-dawn light filtering through a gap in the curtain, I could see nothing had changed.

I was still me.

Still human.

I'd survived another night without turning into a dragon. The nightmares always got worse the nearer I drew to my birthday, and this was the dawn of my seventeenth.

1

I flopped back onto my pillows and let out my bottled-up breath. "Five … four … three …"

My bedroom door flew open, as it had every dawn of every birthday since I could remember, and my father rushed in with a sword in hand.

I tossed my arm over my eyes.

"*Allul!*" he shouted.

The torches on either side of my bed crackled as they lit.

"I'm fine," I said. "Still not a dragon."

He heaved a sigh of relief.

Being cursed to become a dragon was worse than finding myself standing in a pile of horse manure in the middle of summer.

I couldn't fully blame my father and mother for overreacting. After all, I didn't know what I would do if I had a daughter cursed by a sorceress to become a dragon by her eighteenth birthday. I imagined I, too, would try to protect her. I didn't, however, think I would keep her locked in the castle every day.

"Are you certain you're all right?" Father pressed.

I nodded. "See?" I held up both hands and turned them to show him the backs as well. "Toes too." I pulled the blankets back to show him my feet.

"I'm relieved to see you're safe." He lingered and calmly walked over to my side. My bed shifted under my father's weight as he leaned down and kissed my head. "Happy Birthday. I'm certain your sisters have every moment planned."

"They usually do." I lowered my arm from over my eyes and gave him a faint grin.

He straightened. "I'll see you at breakfast."

When I heard the door shut, I reluctantly climbed out from under my covers, then pulled my nightgown down as I walked to the mirror. The crisp morning air nipped at my toes as I padded across the rug, then onto the polished wooden floor, but I ignored the air's frigid bite because I needed one final visual confirmation before I could definitively convince myself I was still human.

No dragon horns.

No tail.

No scales, teeth, or claws.

According to my reflection, my hair was still as yellow as the sun, my eyes were still blue, and my skin still pale. No hint of any dragon details.

I'd had nightmares since I was a child of transforming into a gigantic lizard with swords for teeth, red eyes, and vicious claws. As I grew older, the nightmares evolved from merely transforming to devouring my family and burning down the houses and forests of my kingdom. These nightmares had plagued me since I was first told the story of my curse. The curse that ran through my mind almost daily.

A curse upon her head I place,
that all will see her truest face.
The rage of a dragon shall grow inside
until, the truth, she can no longer hide.
When she reaches her eighteenth year,
her destiny will be made clear.

She will hear the dragon's call,
then she will come and destroy you all.

This was my last year before Selina's curse would take hold. No amount of pondering or worrying answered my biggest question of all: *Why had the sorceress chosen me to curse? What was so important about me that made her hate me so?*

I'd done my fair share of research about dragons, but the books I could find in the castle were ancient, and no one had seen a dragon in nearly a century. From what I gathered, dragons were essentially oversized lizards that could fly, and according to the stories, they only had one desire in the world: collect treasure.

The chair groaned softly as I slid it away from the carved vanity and sat to brush through my long blond hair then braided it down over my right shoulder. *It's possible the sorceress who gave me the curse said it wrong.* I thought. *She could have missed something. Or maybe the faeries have discovered a cure while I slept.* I didn't believe it even though I desperately wanted to.

I got up and opened the curtains to look out over my kingdom. Captured in a perpetual state of springtime, the weather always wavered between crisp mornings and sweltering afternoons. We hadn't had snowfall since long before my parents were born, and we never got as hot as Terricina.

As I gazed out over the wood-carved town, I knew the arborists would be awake by now. Many would be eating breakfast before going out to their walnut, pecan, or fruit orchards. Their spouses were also awake and fretting over breakfast, comforting a sick child, perhaps cuddling their new baby, or being grateful the kids were still asleep at this hour so they had some much needed time together as a couple.

The hole in my chest ached, and I stuffed it with more lies—someday. Someday, when I no longer had to worry about killing my potential friends, I might have some. Someday, when this curse was broken, I would find a husband who would love me. Someday, when I wasn't controlled by my fate, I might have children.

"Someday," I whispered.

The door flew open. I jumped and wheeled around, and my two sisters ran in, both still clad in their nightgowns.

Marigold, the youngest at nine, headed straight to my bed and started jumping up and down. Her charcoal pigtails bounced with her. "Happy Birthday, Elisa! You're still not a dragon!" Her eyes, the same brown as our mother's, sparkled with her excitement.

Dahlia could have been her twin, even though she was four years older. She walked over and locked her arms around me. "We weren't *expecting* you to or anything. Marigold just gets these ideas …" She threw Marigold a glare.

Marigold rolled her eyes and hopped off the bed.

"I'm excited I'm not a dragon too." I laughed.

"But it *is* a cool story," Marigold insisted. She hopped off the bed. "Even if nothing ends up happening. Do you feel any different at all?" She looked me over as if expecting to see horns protruding from my head.

I put my fingertip on her forehead and pushed her away gently. "No, I don't."

"Hey!" Marigold objected as she was forced to step back.

I suddenly scooped her up and promptly dropped her onto my pillows. "Maybe I'm a tickle dragon! Fear my claws!" I said in my deepest voice and showed her my fingers before tickling her.

"Elisa!" she screamed. She gasped for air between bursts of laughter and wiggled.

Dahlia jumped up beside us, a candlestick in her hand as if it were a sword. "I'll save you!" She jabbed the candlestick against my ribs, then in my armpit, causing me to instinctively tighten my arm to my side.

A familiar voice cleared her throat, and we all stopped to look at our mother standing in the doorway. Already in her dress, with her cheeks rouged and hair done up under her crown, she was every bit the regal queen of Griswil.

She raised her ebony brows in disapproval. "The guests will be arriving for your birthday celebration after breakfast," Mother said in a flat voice. "You should *all* be getting ready, not fooling around like children."

The familiar heat of shame crawled up the back of my neck and down my jaw. "Good morning, Mother," I greeted, sitting up.

Dahlia and Marigold reluctantly climbed off my bed, and Dahlia replaced the candlestick on my dresser where it belonged.

"But we were having fun," Marigold whined.

I knew what Mother would say before she said it. "The crown princess doesn't have fun. It isn't one of her duties."

"She never gets to have fun with us," Marigold mumbled as she marched out the door and down the hall.

"It's okay," Dahlia added, looking at me. "We get to have lots of fun today. It's your birthday after all." She gave me a smile and then also left to join Marigold in their shared room.

I gave the queen a smile of my own, straightened my spine, and held my arms out. "Well, I'm still not a dragon."

Her eyes moved down and back up, and I could have sworn there was a hint of disappointment in the corner of her cold eyes.

My heart sank.

She took a few steps nearer and sighed. "I know you're trying your hardest, Elisa. You're doing the best you can. We are too, you know."

"Any news about the faeries?" I asked, shifting the conversation. After I'd been cursed, the faeries had vowed to help break it. Yet faeries seemed to be just as scarce as dragons.

Mother shook her head. "The scouts haven't arrived yet. I was hoping before breakfast, but … it appears that won't happen." She reached out and put her hand on my cheek.

I immediately put my hand over hers and felt a rush of joy.

Her cool fingers reminded me of the fever I'd had as a child. She'd stroked my face with that same gentle touch, comforting me, insisting everything would be all right. I wanted her to whisper those words to me again. I wanted so desperately for her to tell me this would be the last day of worry.

Instead, she leaned forward and put her forehead against mine. "I know this is hard for you. No matter what happens, I promise your father and I have done everything we've thought of. There is an end in sight." She stepped back too soon. "We have something important to discuss at breakfast. Hurry up."

These moments of comfort were becoming rarer, and I longed to throw my arms around her and hold on as I did as a child. But I was growing into a woman. And crown princesses didn't ask for hugs.

"Get dressed and come down." Mother turned but paused and looked over her shoulder at me. "And, Elisa?"

"Yes?"

She smiled, but pain wrinkled the corners of her eyes. "You look beautiful."

I reached up and touched my hair as she left. I grinned broadly.

Whether or not it would be my last, it was still my birthday. I put on my favorite green dress, knowing I would receive a new ball gown that night for the celebration. I suspected it would be rather extravagant, more than any others had been. After all, if this truly *was* my last birthday, I needed to look smashing.

It wasn't like the curse clarified exactly when the big transformation would take place. Would it happen all at once the night before my birthday? The morning of? At sunset? While I slept?

I pushed the familiar questions aside—I'd never been able to answer them—and checked my reflection one last time before leaving my room.

I was still me.

I straightened my spine and looked once more at my hands. The pale blue veins stood out against the porcelain of my skin, and I had a small freckle on the middle knuckle of my left hand. My right middle finger had a scar across the first knuckle from when I'd tried to help in the kitchen and sliced it with a kitchen knife.

Selina's curse echoed in my head with each step I took. *The rage of a dragon shall grow inside until, the truth, she can no longer hide.*

TWO

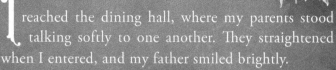

I reached the dining hall, where my parents stood talking softly to one another. They straightened when I entered, and my father smiled brightly.

"Good morning, again," I said, curtseying.

Dahlia entered right behind me, soon followed by Marigold.

"Have you heard from the faeries yet?" Marigold blurted. "Did we find one?"

"Hopefully, we'll know within the hour," Mother answered. I could see the tightness of worry at the corner of her lips as they tried to smile.

My father studied me with caution—ever-growing as my days wore on.

Marigold tugged on my hand, pulling me from my thoughts, and dragged me to a seat beside her. "What sorts of fun things do you want to do today? We could go out into the gardens!"

"Or maybe a horseback ride?" Dahlia asked, looking at our mother for permission.

Mother rarely allowed me to go on horseback rides. She wanted me in the castle, studying to be the queen, locked up where I would never be able to hurt someone. Both of my sisters knew my birthday and the spring ball, about two months later in March, were the only two days of the year my parents allowed me to go horseback riding. Even when we attended the seasonal celebrations of the other kingdoms, we rode in the carriage.

"And we can have a picnic in the forest!" Marigold gasped.

"I haven't had a picnic in a long time." I grinned. "I think those would be a lot of fun. Mother? Father?"

Father shrugged. "That's not a bad idea."

"We have your birthday celebration this evening," Mother reminded me as though I needed to be. "You'll need to be home in time to prepare around noon, so a picnic is really out of the question."

"It doesn't take me six hours to dress and do my makeup, Mother."

"I already told you no."

"Rachel, it's her birthday," Father said in a low voice.

My lips tightened, and my eyes scrunched. I didn't mean to glare and quickly looked away before my mother could see it.

"Which reminds me, there was something important we needed to discuss." Her gaze weighed heavily on me. "There will be a special guest at your party tonight."

Luckily the servants entered in the royal colors of green and yellow. I'd never been so grateful to see them in my life. They broke the uncomfortable moment, and their cheery uniforms helped brighten my mood a little.

I resisted the urge to lick my lips as the servants set down trays of delicious food, featuring all my favorites: eggs, bacon, steak, hash, and fresh vegetables.

With the servants in the room, Mother changed the discussion to plans for my celebration that evening. She'd invited many guests, ordered special decorations, planned loads of food, and even arranged special musicians to perform.

I knew she was doing such a big celebration because everything in my future was so uncertain. I didn't mind so long as I got to have some fun.

We were barely halfway through breakfast when the door swung open and our herald entered. I swallowed the chunk of meat in my mouth before I had properly chewed it and nearly choked.

"Your royal—"

"Skip the formalities," I blurted after a cough. "What did they find?"

He stepped aside and the head of the scouts entered.

The man bowed so low he swooped his hat across the stone floor. "Your Highnesses. We searched every inch of the kingdom ..." His brows were pinched, his face soft, his lips tight, and his eyelashes shifted as if he were trying to keep his gaze away from me.

My stomach dropped.

"The last known city of faeries was found destroyed, and lying in the center was a body with a note on it." He crossed to my mother and handed over a piece of parchment, dirtied with a dark red smear I knew to be blood. "I'm terribly sorry. It appears there are no faeries left in the land." His eyes finally settled on me, soft with pity.

The note trembled in my mother's hands.

I snatched the paper from her grasp and read it myself.

"Elisa, no!" she yelled.

I walked to the side of the room and looked down at the note. It was the curse, but at the bottom was a section I'd never heard before.

> *A curse upon her head, I place,*
> *that all will see her truest face.*
> *The rage of a dragon shall grow inside,*
> *until the truth, she can no longer hide.*
> *When she reaches her eighteenth year,*
> *her destiny will be made clear.*
> *She will hear the dragon's call,*
> *then she will come and destroy you all.*
> *But if a rose shall prick her finger,*
> *the spell will no longer linger.*
> *She will have a decision to make,*
> *and the kingdom of Griswil will be at stake.*

"Elisa, darling," I heard my mother say.

"Is this another part of the curse?" I wheeled around. "Or is this the cure we've been searching for all along?"

Mother's face paled, and my father slowly rose to his feet, but I didn't move my attention to him.

"What does it mean?" I demanded. "The spell will no longer linger?"

"Selina is playing games with you," Father said.

I finally looked at him. "Have you heard this before?"

He shook his head. "I don't know what you're referring to. I can't see the paper." He held his hand out, and I reluctantly took a few steps forward to hand it over.

My heart pounded so hard I could feel the pain in my throat, and more than once I rubbed my hands on my dress. "A rose? A prick of a rose?" I asked once I was certain he'd had time to read it. "There are no roses in Griswil, right? Do we need to find one?"

Father handed the parchment back to my mother, and they exchanged a look I couldn't read.

Mother gave a slight shake of her head and folded the poem in half. "It's your birthday. Let's not worry about this." With three steps, she was beside the fireplace.

"Don't," I snapped. My voice sounded … stronger. More demanding. "That's mine. Selina sent it for me."

"It's nonsense," Mother said. "Just something to get you riled. It's bad enough she's killed the last of the faeries." She flicked her hand, and the paper landed on top of the flames, which instantly seized upon the paper and burned it. "As I was saying earlier about this guest. I think it's time we discuss other options to hold your dragon curse at bay."

My eyesight grew red, and my nails bit into the palms of my hands.

"Your father and I have spoken about this a lot, and we both feel this is the best option."

I let out a growl from deep in my chest, and then a roar so loud the china on the table rattled. My father sprinted around to my side of the table, only to grab hold of my sisters and drag them away before I swooped my arm across the table. The china hit the stone floor and shattered. I rose to my feet and tore the room apart. The anger made my hands hot. Wood cracked, a window exploded, and finally I flung the entire table on its side.

"Elisa, breathe," my father's voice said, penetrating my blind anger. "Remember? Don't give in."

His voice was so calm and out of place from the rage in my mind. I faced him and saw my sisters clinging to his side, their blue eyes filled with panicked tears. I realized my father had his hand out toward me. No, it was stretched toward someone behind me. I turned and saw soldiers in the doorway with their swords drawn. He was telling them to wait.

I swallowed hard, the sensation cooling my burning throat. The heat of the dragon anger heated me from the inside as though I had a fever, but this was an illness with no easy antidote. I drew several deep breaths, through my nose and out of my mouth.

As a child, I had a short temper and my father taught me to count to ten. But I'd never had a tantrum like this.

I collapsed to my knees. My body trembled, and tears rolled down my flushed cheeks.

My father's stance relaxed, and he softly said, "Everything is fine. Go about your duties."

Marigold reached me first and threw her arms around my neck. I clutched her, sobbing into her small shoulder.

The last fae had been killed.

The faeries were the only hope I'd had of being saved from my curse. They were the ones who had arrived with a gift—a promise that one of them would rescue me from Selina's curse. They never said how they would save me. But Selina had made sure their promise would never come to pass. And with that teasing last phrase about a rose and the spell lingering … There was a part of my curse I didn't know, and now it had been destroyed.

The reality was that, in twelve months, I would be a dragon. It weighed on my chest heavier than anything else.

"Elisa, stop this nonsense," my mother scolded. "Princesses don't cry, and a princess certainly never shows her anger."

"Mother …" Dahlia's voice said softly.

I reluctantly pulled back from Marigold. Something about Dahlia's voice drew my attention to her. She stared at me but hadn't come any closer. She hadn't tried to hug me as Marigold had. I reached up

16

and wiped at my tears with rough fingers and took a big breath to suppress my emotions.

I gave Dahlia the biggest smile I could muster. "I'll be okay. It was just a fit of anger."

Her eyes were locked on my hands.

I lowered my gaze and found black scales covering my hands from fingertip to wrist. I gasped and recoiled from Marigold. I turned my hands over again and again. The palms of my hands had much smaller scales than those that had grown on the back, and my nails were black. I curled my fingers, expecting them to feel tight like gloves, but the scales moved without any friction.

Scales.

The transformation had begun.

I quickly climbed to my feet, my stomach churning, and assessed the damage in the dining hall. My mouth dried. Shards of white china, painted with spring flowers and green and yellow leaves, lay about the floor like an unsolvable jigsaw. My mother had proudly used them for special occasions since I was a child. Not one dish had survived my fit of anger. They had been a wedding gift from the queen of Zelig.

The cracking wood I'd heard had been the chairs. Most of the backs and legs were now broken beyond repair. The table didn't appear to be damaged. Then I saw the marks on the wood.

Claw marks.

Bile of panic rose in the back of my throat. I'd thrown the biggest tantrum of my life and destroyed the entire dining hall. Now I didn't know what to do.

Dahlia and Marigold clearly didn't want to be near me at that moment. Father was still standing protectively in front of them, and Mother had her back pressed against the wall. Neither of them seemed to know what to do either.

"I ... should go. I'm ... not feeling well." I curtsied and then ran from the room.

THREE

The sun warmed my back as I sat hunched forward on the bench in my little garden. This tiny garden on the western side of the castle had been mine since I first found it as a child. I used to ask for different plants to add to it, and now it was a thriving, magical place in spite of the high, curved wall around me.

I had no tears left to cry.

I felt numb with the realization I was indeed cursed. It was no longer something my parents told me. Sending scouts to find the cure had been part of life, being disappointed no fae were found just another piece to that, but now I *knew* I had a dragon waiting inside. The reality of my curse and lack of help sat heavily on my chest.

This I didn't want to accept.

I wished in my heart Dahlia or Marigold would come and comfort me. More than likely, they were still afraid, or Mother could have refused them to come to me.

I massaged my forehead where a small headache had begun festering.

The hinges of the wooden door groaned behind me, and I looked over my shoulder to see who it was. To my surprise, it was my mother. She'd never come to my secret place.

I found myself straightening and on my feet facing her in an instant. I hid my hideous hands behind my back. "Yes?"

"Your father and I want you to remember that, although some unfortunate events have happened today, it is still your birthday." Her voice was tight. She tried to keep her eyes on my face. It was all she could do to not look down at my arms and assess the scales, but I caught her gaze drift before it would snap back to my face. "You've been alone long enough. Hopefully you've got the tears out of your system. Your sisters are waiting by the stables to go on a horse ride and picnic." She gestured with her left hand.

"The crown princess doesn't cry," a voice in my head chided.

I bowed my head to her. "Certainly." I waited for her to plaster on a smile and step back.

Only, as I went to step past her, she held out her hand. Hanging from it was a pair of black, elbow-length gloves.

I didn't need her to tell me to take them. "Thank you, Mother." I felt obligated to say it even though embarrassment burned at my cheeks. I didn't look at her as I tugged the gloves over my new scales.

If these changes continued, would she eventually have me wear a dress to the floor and a veil to hide the monster I'd become?

I left my sanctuary and fell into a quick pace through the hallways, past the kitchen, and out the back door to the path that led to the stables. Philip, the stable boy, already had three horses saddled and ready. I'd always been fond of Philip. He was handsome and kind with dirt-brown hair and dark-brown eyes.

Dahlia and Marigold joyfully chatted as they stroked the eager horses' velvet noses while feeding them apples.

I fiddled with the fingertips of the gloves. I worried about how they would react. I could pretend nothing had happened, or I could apologize for terrifying them.

I barely got my mouth open before Philip greeted me. "Happy birthday, Your Highness. Your sisters told me you get to go on a ride today." When I didn't return his smile immediately, his own fell. "You're not excited?"

"No, of course I am," I scrambled to put on a smile. "I was just distracted. May I?" I held my hand out for the reins of the horse.

Philip handed them over. "This is Tao. He's my favorite. You've ridden him before."

I reached up and stroked Tao's nose with my gloved hand. "I remember him. He's rather charming."

He didn't seem bothered that a part of me had changed that day, and I would never be the same again. His big eyes almost looked empathetic as he nudged my hand and then arm.

"He's looking for a treat," Philip laughed. He reached into his pocket and produced a handful of grain, which he put in my free hand.

Even though Tao nibbled it, he leaned his head forward yet again and put his chin on my shoulder. He let out a soft snort.

I looked at his large eye and couldn't help but think he was comforting me.

My throat tightened. "Thank you," I whispered.

I hugged his neck and shared a moment of connection. Too many people thought animals weren't intelligent. I'd never felt that way, and this moment only confirmed my theory.

"Are you coming with us?" I asked, looking over at Philip before walking to Tao's side to climb up on the saddle. "You did last year."

Philip rubbed the back of his neck. "I don't know. I have a lot of chores today preparing for the birthday guests."

"Oh please!" Marigold jumped in. "It would be fun to have you."

"We aren't going far," Dahlia added. "Just the meadow down by the waterfall."

He shrugged. "I can ask."

As soon as Philip was out of sight, Dahlia leaned over to me. "Can I see them?" she whispered a little too loudly.

I shifted my gaze from her to Marigold. "You actually want to see? After frightening you earlier?"

"We don't care. I want to see too!" Marigold leaned to see past Dahlia.

"You aren't worried?" I asked, completely stunned.

Dahlia reached across the short distance between us and grabbed my arm. "Elisa, you're still our sister. If you turn into a dragon later, oh well. We'll figure it out then."

I hugged her.

Tao shifted his stance, and I squealed as I was pulled away from Dahlia and off-center on the saddle. Philip rushed over, but I managed to let go of Dahlia and right myself before he could help.

"You should be more careful, Your Highness," Philip said, heaving a sigh of relief. "Horses can be dangerous."

My cheeks flushed, and I fiddled with my braid. "Thank you."

"We haven't got all day!" Marigold complained. She nudged her horse into a walk. "Come on!"

"I won't be able to come," Philip said, patting Tao's neck. "There's too much work here. You have fun with your sisters." He bowed at the waist as he stepped back.

My heart dropped a bit. "Thank you for preparing the horses."

"Wait up!" Dahlia called after Marigold. "Hurry, Elisa!"

The ride to the waterfall could have taken all day and I would have been satisfied just being out of the castle walls. The canopy of leaves overhead filtered green and yellow light, creating a sun-splotched painting on the path. Birds chirped happily in a nearby tree, answered by another farther ahead in a short burst of trills. I watched two butterflies dance around each other, their black and white wings flittering silently over the flower-lined path. I drew a deep breath, savoring the smells of the forest. I could almost taste the rustic pine, sweet yellow honeysuckle, lush grass, and even the dirt. Bright orange and red poppies stood like soldiers on the right side of the path, their dark centers like helmets bowing to the princesses as they traveled to their destination.

The air grew more humid shortly before I heard and smelled the fresh water of the river and, a few minutes later, the waterfall rumbling in the distance.

"We're almost there!" Marigold announced.

"I'll beat you!" Delia challenged. She nudged her horse into a gallop.

"Hey, no fair! You got a head start!" Marigold took off after.

I didn't trust myself to burst into a gallop, but I gently struck Tao's sides with my heels, prodding him into a gentle trot. By the time I reached the clearing, Dahlia and Marigold were arguing over who won. I pulled Tao to a halt and slid off the saddle.

"You both win," I interjected.

My sisters turned to me.

Marigold had her small hands planted firmly on her hips. "I clearly won."

"I came last, so you both win. Help me set out our lunch."

Dahlia was the first off her horse and flipped open one of the saddlebags. She withdrew a blanket, and I took the opposite end so we could lay it down flat. Meanwhile, Marigold began taking cloth-wrapped food out and set them down on the center of the blanket.

"Oh yummy! Pecan pie!" Marigold excitedly held up the tins of individual pies.

"You shouldn't eat dessert first," Dahlia instructed. "We should eat our sandwiches first."

Marigold looked at me, her nose wrinkled.

I laughed. "It's my birthday. I say we have pie first."

We sat down around the food, and Marigold handed out the pies. Abby, the cook, must have known we would go on a ride today. She made the best pecan pie with just enough sweet and just enough pecans and just enough crust. The filling melted in my mouth, and the soft crunch of the pecans was the perfect accent.

"You should have seen your face when you destroyed the dining room this morning," Marigold said casually. "Your eyes were like glowing red."

I glanced at Dahlia.

She nodded. "It's true." She licked her thumb. "It was a little bit scary."

I unwrapped the crackers and opened the jars of filling: imported fish from Terricina or chicken with sundried tomatoes. "I really didn't mean to. The news that the faeries were gone for good, and that letter showing up ... I lost it. What if that last phrase really was a cure? What if I'm supposed to find a rose?"

"I think Mother was right. Surely, if you prick your thumb on a thorn, something bad will happen," Dahlia said. "Why else would Selina have left it for you to find?"

I spread some chicken on my cracker and took a bite. "But what if it wasn't?"

"But Mother wouldn't have burned it if it were a cure," Dahlia argued.

I nodded.

Marigold grabbed the jar with the fish and began loading up her crackers.

As we ate, I looked around the gentle slopes of the earth covered in vibrant green bushes, small pink and yellow flowers, and spotted with larger white ones now and then. The long necks of aspen trees rose above the pine trees, and we sat under one of the large maple trees ready to be tapped for syrup.

"Look," I whispered and pointed to the riverbank. A small brown rabbit with stark white feet lazily hopped to the river's edge to get a drink.

Marigold pulled her knees to her chest and covered her mouth as she giggled. "He's so cute!"

Being in the woods with my sisters was the best birthday present I could have ever asked for.

"Can we swim?" Marigold asked. She was already on her feet, unlacing the back of her dress.

I glanced at the gloves covering my hands and slowly pulled them off. "If this is my last birthday with you, let's make it count."

I jumped to my feet and helped Marigold pull her dress off. Dahlia helped me while Marigold helped her. Soon, the three of us were in nothing but our underclothing, and we ran down the grassy slope and into the icy river.

It was barely high enough to reach Dahlia's waist, and the current was lazy enough I didn't feel concerned at all as we swam and splashed around. I didn't care what our mother would say when we returned home sopping wet. It was my birthday, and I was going to enjoy every moment with my sisters.

FOUR

Clad in only my undergarments and a sheer slip, I released my long blond hair from its braid and shook it loose. I dipped my fingers in the small box of crushed lavender before running them through my hair to freshen it. The crimp settled beautifully on my bare shoulders.

Mother had thrown an absolute fit when we arrived back at the castle, Marigold covered in mud because she'd fallen on the banks. We'd laughed and tried to rinse it off to no avail. Mother told us how unladylike it was, and I'd let out a giggle when Dahlia made a mocking face behind her, which earned me a harsh glare from my mother.

My ears picked up the sound of footsteps, and my heart jumped into my throat. Instinctively, I grinned and got to my feet, knowing it had to be Mother with my birthday dress.

As predicted, there was a knock followed by my mother announcing, "I've got your dress!"

"Come in." I rushed over, but she pushed the door open before I could reach it.

"What do you think?" Mother raised her hands and, with them, my dress, showing it off.

My stomach sunk.

It was pink.

I expected green, the color of every previous birthday dress, the color that went with my hair and eyes, my *favorite* color. I told her I wanted it to fade from dark at the bottom to light up top. I'd asked for it to be decorated with rhinestones that would catch the light. I expected the dress of a woman.

Pink.

No rhinestones, no fancy lace, or even need for a petticoat. It was simple. Plain.

This was a dress for a child.

My mind scrambled to try and figure out why mother would arrange such a dress to be made for me. Had I done something to deserve a punishment? I'd never known Mother to joke. Did she intend this to be Dahlia's dress? She's the one who adored pink with all her heart. Or maybe this was the dress for the dinner and I'd get a proper ball gown for the celebration.

"You don't like it," Mother said, her voice flat. She lowered my dress and tossed it onto the bed. "I hoped I would surprise you with the latest fashion. Clearly I was wrong."

"It's pink," I blurted before I could bite my tongue.

Mother's brown eyes stared at me like the cold eyes of a painting. Her lips pinched.

"It's just not what I was expecting," I recovered quickly. "I do love it."

A lie.

"If you don't want it, don't wear it." Mother turned on her heel and marched out the door.

The tang of anger burned the back of my tongue.

Dahlia's birthday cake two summers ago was a lavender, six-tier, vanilla and raspberry cake. My dessert last year was a collection of bite-sized desserts, such as miniature pies, cookies, and brownies. Mother had insisted she'd ordered different kinds of desserts to give me a variety and to please all of the guests who visited the "crown princess." I'd made the mistake of asking where my cake was. I'd been politely removed, scolded for being ungrateful, and then locked in my room the week after my birthday celebration to read *Proper Behaviors of a Queen*.

Tonight, like many times before, I wondered if she knew I would never make it past my eighteenth year, never be the queen.

Her fears would be confirmed now that black scales adorned my hands.

I walked over to the dress and touched the fabric. Silk. I wondered if the silk had been imported from Zelig or the northern countries. Was it spider silk? Caterpillar silk? Or could it have come from the silk trees in the Weeping Woods of Arington?

Wherever Mother had purchased it, my black hand stood out starkly against the pink.

It's your last birthday. This is what she gives you?

I squeezed my lips together until they hurt. My heart twisted. I could wear my new dress and please my mother, as I had every day of the last seventeen years of life, or I could choose one of my previous dresses—a faux pas in any royal court.

Do what you want for once in your life.

I walked to my closet and whispered, "Allul."

The torches lit, showing the dresses that lined each wall. I wouldn't wear the dress I'd worn to the autumn or winter balls, it was too soon, and I couldn't wear the dress from the spring ball last year because certainly Princess Tavia, the princess of Zelig, would remember and make a comment. I needed something none of them would have seen before, or at least not in a while.

I ran my fingertips along the dresses, taking time to caress the fuzzy velvet, bumpy lace, cool cotton, and slippery silk until they rested on the lovely sensation of raised fabric. I pushed the dresses apart to reveal the most colorful dress I owned. Orange, yellow, and brown pieces of fabric gathered under the bodice and flowed outward. It wasn't at all what I expected to catch my eye. I'd wanted it made for the autumn ball in September, but Mother didn't want me to clash with Dahlia and Marigold's happy yellow dresses and had a different one made.

Without hesitation, I took it off the hanger and slipped it over my head. It was everything I never typically wore—no sleeves, layers of fabric that flowed and stretched to the ground, and no petticoat needed. Princess Ismae of Arington would have been very proud to have it in her court last year, and maybe I would have caught her brother Keltin's eye.

The thought made me blush.

Keltin would never throw a second glance at a cursed princess.

Perhaps Mother disapproved because it would draw too much attention, and attention meant a risk of people seeing my new hands. But I wanted something to catch everyone's attention tonight. I wanted to be different. For once, I wanted to find me.

I looked at myself in the mirror and grinned.

I heard a scoff. "You're not wearing *that* are you?"

I looked over my shoulder and put my hands on my hips. "I think I am, Marigold. Do me up, will you?" I moved my hair out of the way so she could button the back.

But she didn't move. "No way. That's not springy at all. You have to wear something bright and fun!"

I rolled my eyes. "This has orange and yellow."

"And *brown*. Gross." She made a gagging noise.

I rolled my eyes and faced her. "Well, it's barely January, and I'm not wearing pink!" I gestured dramatically to the dress lying on my bed.

Marigold gasped and ran over to it. "Why not? It's lovely!"

"Pink is Dahlia's color. Not mine." I glanced again at my reflection, my stomach sinking. Marigold was right. This dress would make me stand out for the wrong reason.

It was an autumn dress, not something appropriate for the crown princess of the spring kingdom.

I wiggled the dress over my head and replaced it where it belonged. *I'll never get to wear it,* I thought miserably.

"I've got an idea," Marigold said.

"What's that?" I didn't mean to sigh and sound annoyed, I just really didn't want to wear a pink dress with absolutely nothing charming about it.

Marigold walked over and held it up to me. "Put it on."

"Marigold …"

"Just do it!"

Once I had it on, even I had to admit it didn't look that bad. It hugged my body, but the material flowed beautifully. There was even a little bit of a train on it. Had it been any other color …

"What's your great idea?" I asked.

"Come on." She took my hand and dragged me through the castle, using the back hallways instead of the normal route. "We're going to take you to Jarrett."

"The old wizard? Why?"

"Just trust me, okay?"

"How are we going to get there? He lives at the edge of the city—"

Marigold halted. "Do you want to be stuck in a pink dress or not?"

"Well … no," I admitted.

She nodded once and confidently led me outside, right to Dahlia who stood with her arms folded and foot tapping, looking very much like our mother.

"And where are you two escaping off to?" She eyed my dress.

"None of your business." Marigold skirted around her.

"We're supposed to be preparing for the ball!" Dahlia snipped, trying to grab Marigold before she could escape.

Marigold easily darted away and hollered over her shoulder, "And we are! We'll be home in time for the celebration!"

Dahlia narrowed her eyes at me. Again, her gaze moved down and back up. "Well I'm going with you, or I'm telling Mother. Why are you wearing a pink dress?"

I sighed. "Mother had it made for me. It's to be my gown tonight." I ran my hand over the front and grimaced. I'd forgotten gloves. "Marigold thinks Jarrett will help."

"Ooh, that's a good idea." Dahlia relaxed and stepped aside so we could walk down to the stables together. "Didn't you tell Mother what you wanted in a dress?" She gave me a sideways glance. "She always asks us."

"Yes, I was very specific. I wanted flowers on it, layers of color, rhinestones, and no sleeves."

Dahlia nodded. After a brief moment of silence, she softly said, "I'm sorry Mother always treats you differently." Her words surprised me. I didn't know either of my sisters had noticed.

"What else would you expect for the crown princess?"

"I think it's also the curse. I think she's afraid and doesn't know what to do, so she thinks having higher expectations will prevent you from transforming."

We arrived at the stables, and Philip was already walking out with a single horse-drawn carriage. He cleared his throat a little, and the embarrassed blush returned to my cheeks. I hid my hands behind my back.

"I should escort you," he said.

"But you won't," Marigold said with finality. She motioned for Dahlia and me to get up into the carriage. "I know where to go."

"How?" I asked, getting into the front seat beside her.

Dahlia climbed up on her opposite side.

She smiled. "I've been learning about magic."

I arched my brow. "You know how to use magic?"

Marigold's smile fell. "No. But I'm learning about how to identify enchanted objects. I think I might be able to collect some. It's only for fun."

Philip handed me the reins, much to Marigold's chagrin, but he dropped them when he saw my hands. He took an abrupt step back, and my throat tightened as if he'd grabbed it. I snapped the reins, urging the horse forward and away from Philip.

We barely made it around the castle before Marigold snatched them from me. I'd never driven a carriage. I doubted she had either, but she was far more experienced with horses than I was.

"Tell me more about your plan?" Dahlia asked, and I was grateful neither of them said anything about Philip being disgusted by me.

"Wizards have magic. Magic that can change things." She smiled up at me as if she were the most brilliant person in the world.

I gave her a hug because, in that moment, she was the brilliant one.

We arrived and clamored off the carriage. Luckily Jarrett wasn't busy and allowed us into his humble wooden home splattered in once-green paint and half overgrown with vines. His beard nearly reached the floor, and his back hunched over, but his eyes sparkled with youth.

"What can I do ya fer?" he asked, smacking his lips.

"We need you to change Elisa's dress," Marigold said.

"What kinda wizard are ya thinkin' I am?" He filled his cheeks with air and furrowed his bushy brows.

Marigold put her hands behind her back and sweetly moved her shoulders left and right. "A very wise one. You've shown me how powerful you are."

He blew the air out and turned his full attention to me. "I can give 'er a try. What'n ya wantin'?"

I described what I wanted—a flowing gown with sparkles and color. Without warning, he jabbed his crooked thumb into my forehead.

"Owe! What was that for?" I rubbed the sore spot hastily. "That better not leave a mark for tonight!"

"Relax, Princess." He held his hand up, and I realized there was a small orb of light between his thumb and index finger. He hobbled to the rickety table and dropped the orb into a bowl.

I leaned on my toes to try and see what he was doing, but his shoulder was in the way. Dahlia, Marigold, and I exchanged silent looks and shrugs while we heard the man whisper something.

He turned and threw the orb at me. It struck my dress and the material began to glow. "Naw think what yer wantin'."

"Make sure it's got blue!" Marigold said.

"And pink, just a little." Dahlia chimed in.

I tried to envision what I wanted while the fabric shifted and took on new shapes.

"It would look cool with blue *and* pink," Marigold said to Dahlia, though loud enough for me to hear.

"Oh and a splash of green!"

"All of our favorite colors!"

They both giggled. And then they gasped.

I looked down at myself, and my eyes widened in horror.

"Well …" the wizard Jarrett rubbed his chin. "You like?"

The dress looked like I had gone into an art studio and allowed Marigold to throw paint at me. Pink, green, and blue splotches were everywhere, and where the colors overlapped there were even purple hues. The bottom of the dress had taken on various layers of these same colors, but it was broken up by a hem of white flowers that reached upward on my right side.

"That's the prettiest dress I've ever seen," Dahlia gasped.

I looked at my sisters and saw both of them were mesmerized.

Marigold clasped her hands in front of her and squealed as she jumped up and down. "Oh, you look perfect, Elisa!"

"Everyone is going to stare," Dahlia insisted.

"I suppose we should get to the ball," I said, running my hand over the light fabric.

Marigold giggled. "Mother is going to be so mad."

My heart leapt with giddy excitement. I'd defied my mother. And I didn't care.

FIVE

y the time we arrived back at the castle, the sun had begun to set, and I knew guests were already gathered in the Great Hall waiting for us to be announced. Likely, Mother was running around, frantically trying to find us. The entire ride back, I hadn't been able to keep from running my hands over the gown. Even under the fading light of the sun, it was miraculous. Instead of rhinestones, it somehow glistened like tiny stars trapped in the fabric.

We dropped the carriage off with Philip, who gave me a once-over like I might bite him, and Marigold led the way as we slipped through the kitchen doors. The smell of seasoned potatoes, sweet chicken, vegetables fried in oil, and all sorts of other foods and desserts washed over us. The cacophony of smells made my stomach rumble.

Abby, the head cook, pushed past servants, her face red from the exertion of the task of preparing such a large feast. Everyone, even extra hands, were furiously at work. "Your mother has been searching for you three for the past hour! Where have you been?" Her tone wasn't scolding but worried. She grabbed the towel on her belt and wiped her forehead.

"Don't worry, we're here now," Dahlia chimed.

"And everything smells wonderful," I added.

Dahlia gave my back a nudge, and we rushed through the kitchen, down the hall, and up a back staircase. After all, we had to be presented at the top of the grand staircase. When we entered the hallway at the top of the grand stairs, three servants stood side by side with pillows in their hands and crowns upon the pillows.

"Where were you?" the first servant gasped. Her eyes darted to her right. "Your mother—"

"We know," Marigold interrupted. She fluffed her hair and faced us. "Is everything in order?" She gestured to herself.

After we checked each other to make sure we were all satisfactory, we faced the servants and stepped forward so they could place our crowns on our heads.

Marigold's crown was a simple golden band that looked like small vines of new leaves entwining all the way around her head. Dahlia's was the same but had beautiful little flower buds on it. My crown had large leaves adorning it with little purple stones in the centers of each flower. The stones were representative of the spring stone, a magical stone once in possession of the faeries.

Mother rushed around the corner. "Where have you three been?" She crouched in front of Marigold and ran her hand down her cheek. "You're safe?" She reached out and took Dahlia's hand. "Not a scratch on you?" She examined them, including their dresses. "No speck of dirt."

"No, Mother." Dahlia pulled away with a dramatic roll of her eyes. "We are fine. All of us are fine."

Mother straightened and looked at me. Her cheeks grew red, and her eyes narrowed. At first, her mouth opened, clearly to scold me, but eyes widened when she saw my dress. "What happened to your dress?"

"Isn't she lovely?" Marigold grabbed part of my skirts and held them out so Mother could see all of the colors. "That's where we were, you know. We had to go and meet with Jarrett, the wizard. Her other dress was just too boring for her birthday celebration, so we had him fix it!"

I might have been the only one who saw Mother's expression sour. But I smiled and acted like I hadn't seen it. "It is rather unique. Just like I wanted."

"You could say that," Mother replied blandly. She then tugged off her gloves and held them out. "Put these on. Everyone is waiting. Your father is already out there in the crowd keeping everyone calm." She sauntered past us, though the doorway, and to the top of the grand staircase. She leaned over the railing to tell the herald to begin announcing us.

41

Dahlia rolled her eyes yet again. "We're only fifteen minutes late. I doubt Father had to do any amount of calming."

"Welcome guests to the birthday celebration of Crown Princess Elisa!" The herald's voice carried over the idle chatter, silencing the crowd, while I stared at the white gloves in my hands.

"Princess Marigold." He gestured his hand and Marigold stepped out, skirts gathered in her hands as she skipped, then twirled at the top of the steps and earned a laugh from the crowd. She scampered down the steps to join my mother and father at the bottom.

You don't have to wear them. You could let everyone see what you are becoming.

"Princess Dahlia."

She winked at me. "You look amazing. Everyone's going to love it." She walked out, smiling, and with a little bit of a saunter in her step. She waved to the crowd below as they clapped politely, then walked down the steps.

I bit my lip and slipped the glove on my right hand, covering the scales. *You don't have to wear them. You've always been afraid of who you are, Elisa.* I shook my head and put on the other glove. No one could know.

"And finally, the crown princess of Griswil! Elisa Laika Erikkson."

I stepped out, my stomach gnawing at me to put on a smile. I waved my hand and looked over the sea of faces. Most of them were very familiar, like Princess Ismae, who was jumping up and down with a huge smile on her face. She was the closest thing I had to a friend. I waved back at her.

I stopped at the top of the stairs, held my skirts out, and gave a proper curtsey. When I straightened, the crowd grew silent expectantly. "Thank you, everyone, for making it to my seventeenth birthday celebration. I am pleased to see so many familiar faces." I looked right at Ismae, and she beamed back. "I hope you all enjoy your time with us. Let us dine and dance!" I threw my arms out.

The crowd burst into applause and excited calls and began to disperse.

Spine straight, shoulders back, hands lightly clasped. I went over the checklist as I made my way down the stairs in my multicolored gown.

Ismae slipped through the last of the crowd and caught my hands. "You look positively radiant, Elisa!" She continued to hold my hands as she stepped back. "That dress is stunning. How in the world did you get those colors?"

"A little bit of magic," I answered.

"You cheat." She laughed and stepped forward to wrap me up in a hug. "I wish we saw each other more. It's simply horrible you're ill all the time."

I blanched. "Ill?"

She leaned back and tilted her head. "Why, yes. I write every month. Your mother has to write back during your bouts of sickness."

"Oh … yes." I resisted the urge to look at my mother. "What is it you write about?"

Ismae's smile slowly dropped, but she pulled the corners of her lips back up. "You … don't receive my letters?"

My stomach sank. I tried to recover with a smile and tugged gently on her hand. "Of course I do. Your penmanship is rather impressive." I slipped my arm in hers and guided her away.

"Elisa, I have someone I need you to meet," Mother called from behind me.

"In a moment," I called back without even looking at her.

Once we were a safe enough distance away, Ismae turned to me. "Your mother doesn't give you my letters. And you truly aren't ill?"

I swallowed hard, my mouth suddenly parched. "I … I do get some letters. Clearly, not all of them, and I didn't understand what you meant by the illnesses."

"I invite you to join me for little things. I asked if you could stay over in a few weeks, but your mother wrote back and said I shouldn't plan on you because you were in quite a sorry state." She looked me over again. "I simply don't see what she means."

"Ismae …" I started.

"Yes?"

I looked down at my hands. At the gloves hiding my secret. "I think I understand what my mother meant by illness."

Silence.

"It's nothing. I'm not contagious," I quickly insisted.

Ismae took my hand. "You can tell me anything, Elisa. We're best friends." She smiled.

"I'm cursed." It sort of slipped out on its own. I put my free hand to my lips.

"What do you mean?" I thought Ismae would have an expression of horror, but instead, her eyes sparkled in excitement. "What kind of curse?"

"Oh, it's … that—"

"Are you never allowed to leave Griswil?"

"Ismae, I go to all of the seasonal balls."

She pursed her lips. "True. Then it must be cursed to …" She tapped her chin. "Become furniture? No. It must be cursed with beauty. Still no?" She gasped. "Are you a creature at night?"

"No!" I laughed. "Where do you get these ideas?"

"From reading, of course." Ismae laughed.

"Elisa, please," Mother called again.

I looked over my shoulder this time and saw my family lingering while the last of the crowd made their way into the dining hall, and I briefly caught a glance of a handsome young man and a woman before I looked back at Ismae.

"You can't say a word," I said softly.

She nodded, biting her fingertips in anticipation.

I slipped the glove off my hand, revealing to her the dragon scales.

She clamped her hand over her mouth, eyes wide, and this time I was certain it was out of fear. She did manage to stifle her gasp well enough.

I slipped the glove back on, cheeks turning red with embarrassment. *You never should have shown her. What will she think of you now?*

Ismae grabbed my arm before I could run away. "Elisa, I had no idea. Does anyone else know?" Her expression had softened again.

I shook my head. "Very few know. My family, the scouts trying to find a cure, and servants." I bit my lip, trying to figure out how to read Ismae's face. "The scales appeared this morning."

"We shall have to talk more about this later. Your mother is becoming angry." She gave me a gentle nudge. "You're still my best friend, just so you know." She grinned.

Relieved, I let out a breath of tension and hurried to my mother and the guests.

"Thank you for joining us," Mother snarked. "This is Prince Gerard."

"*Prince* Gerard?" I asked. I gave Mother a glance, but she warned me by tightening the corners of her lips. I flashed a smile at the young man and gave him a proper greeting. "Forgive me. I know Prince Mathias and Prince Keltin. I didn't know—"

"I'm from a kingdom further north called Ashwrya." He smiled back at me. His lips were alluring enough, but the curve of them with his perfect teeth and coy grin made my heart flutter and my words stumble.

"Oh. Yes. Ashwrya. I … I don't believe we have that on one of our maps. Do we, Mother?" I tugged nervously on my right glove.

Gerard smiled and held his hand out to me. "Shall we join the other guests?"

I stared, dumbfounded, for what felt like an eternity.

Boys dancing with me always got my heart racing, but the idea that he wanted to personally escort me to my own birthday dinner was unfathomable. Men didn't escort me anywhere except the dance floor. I'd always imagined Keltin being brave enough to do so, but he liked to linger behind with the other princes.

Gerard coaxed me by raising his eyebrow.

"Of course." I slipped my hand into his and could have sworn my heart was racing so loudly he could hear it. I glanced at my mother for an explanation, but she turned her attention to the older woman.

I took the opportunity to look at Gerard, while simultaneously trying not to stare.

His jaw was defined and came to a light point at his chin, which had a soft dimple in the middle. His nose was thin, thinner than most people's I'd seen, confirming he wasn't from this part of the country. His eyes were set back further as well, but their shade of green was the most stunning color I'd ever seen. Like summer grass hidden under the shade of a tree, but brightened by the light of the sun escaping through the canopy. His brown hair was short on the sides, but the top was braided back into a small bun at the back of his head.

Gerard pulled my seat away from the table, and as I sat, he pushed it in behind me. The table was the large table made for celebrations, with flowers and leaves carved into it and rows of trees. I still hadn't seen if they'd replaced the smaller table and chairs my family used for our meals.

Gerard slipped into the seat at my side, and my sisters took their seats across from me, beside my mother, their eyes darting as they tried to catch glimpses of him without being obvious, and failing miserably.

Ismae sat a few people down the row, and she leaned past them to look at me, then Gerard, then back. She twitched her eyebrows, a smile hesitating on the corner of her lips as if to ask me if he were with me.

I shrugged just enough to let her know I had no idea who he was, and she turned her attention to Keltin, who had struck up a conversation I couldn't hear.

"I didn't get to meet your mother," I said, glancing at Gerard.

"Grandmother," he corrected. "My parents are both gone from this world."

"Oh, I'm sorry."

He smiled reassuringly and put his hand on my knee. Instantly, heat rushed across my skin like the summer breeze on Prince Ulrich's ship. "You didn't know," he said. "Besides, I haven't known either of them at any point in my life. Mother passed when I was only a child, so I don't remember her, and I never knew my father."

The heat of his hand lingered and sent rippling waves of tingling up my arms and down my spine, sending with it a little tremble. "Sh-She was kind to let you in. I mean, not that you were homeless, but that she let you stay. Family is important."

Gerard arched his brow; this time it had a curious curl to it. He leaned closer, and I could smell a hint of sage wood, and my heart hammered against my ribs so loudly I was certain he could hear it. "Not to be too forward, but your mother doesn't come across as one who really cares."

I tried to balance the heat he made me feel, and concentrate on what he said. I reached up and rubbed the inside of my wrist across my cheek in an attempt to wipe away the blush. "She's tolerable," I admitted.

He chuckled and finally sat back in his chair.

A servant leaned between us to place Gerard's appetizer in front of him, giving me a moment to catch my breath and let reality sink in that a handsome prince was at my side and seemed genuinely interested in me. I focused on the new dinnerware. It was vibrant, clean, new white with gold filigree along the edges. The worry Mother had warned Gerard about my temper clawed at the back of my mind. Then again, if Mother had told him about the high probability I would be turning into a dragon by this time next year, he likely wouldn't be giving me that half grin as he looked at me from the corner of his eye.

"Princess Elisa, tell me about you," Gerard said as he picked up his fork and poked the lingonberry sauce-covered potato.

"What do you want to know?" I asked, eyes down on my own plate.

"Interests. Do you paint? Sew? Ride horses?"

I tucked my hair behind my ear. "I'm afraid I don't get out of the castle much," I explained. "I spend most of my days studying to step into the role of the queen when the time comes. Though, I do enjoy studying other things."

From the corner of my eyes I saw him shift in his seat. "What do you study?"

I drew a breath, my stomach suddenly churning. What if he found me boring? After all, Ulrich went on grand adventures on the sea and among his people. Mathias and his sister Tavia of Zelig were actively involved with trade in their kingdoms, from what I overheard at the winter celebrations. Compared to practically anyone else, I was boring.

Gerard raised his eyebrows in a prompting motion.

"I've s-studied a lot about dragons. Everything I can find." I braved a glance and he was chewing, but still watching my face. "I also really enjoy languages. I've learned four so far."

His lips tugged down in an impressed frown. "Four? That's rather impressive. What languages?"

I set my fork down. "I've been trying to learn the fae language, but it's rather difficult because there aren't exactly any around I can speak to and make sure I'm pronouncing things correctly. I've also learned some Dolik."

"Ah, Dolik is difficult." He nodded.

I gasped. "You can speak Dolik?"

He chuckled. "A little. Enough to be able to barter with them."

"I would love to meet one someday." I blushed and picked up my fork again. "My father has meetings with them, so I can understand when they speak, but I don't actually get to participate in those meetings. I also really enjoy painting. When I was a child, I painted a wall in my bedroom."

"I bet your mother wasn't too pleased with that." Gerard's lips spread into knowing grin.

I blushed and shook my head. "She was rather upset. I had to paint it one color. But as I grew older, she allowed me to get canvases, and I paint whenever I get the chance."

"I'd love to see them sometime." He set his fork on the table, dabbed the corner of his mouth, and leaned against the chair, his appetizer gone.

"What do you do?" I asked, finally nibbling my food.

"Oh, I enjoy playing with magic," he said casually.

"You can use magic?" I whispered.

He glanced around. "Do your people not use magic?"

"No. Only wizards do, and there are hardly any left in the land. Jarrett is the only wizard I know of in Griswil."

"Hm." Gerard lifted his broad shoulders in a shrug. "Well, I enjoy magic. There are a lot of helpful aspects to it. I also enjoy hunting."

I raised my brows and looked him over again. "What is your country like?"

"There are far more buildings than here. Your towns are small, and your groves of trees separate families. Our cities are more densely populated," he explained. "We also have a lot more structures built from stone, since we have more mountains than you do here in Griswil."

"We have the Drakespine Mountains that run between us and Arington."

He nodded. "I recall seeing them. But we have many mountains. Even cities built into the sides of them."

"That sounds interesting. I would love to see." I set my fork down, letting the servants know I was done. "I've always wanted to travel northward. I've been to the other kingdoms. We visit for the solstices and equinox celebrations."

"I would like to show you." Again, that coy grin.

Again, my cheeks flushed.

The servant reached over to pick up our plates just as I reached. I don't know what I was reaching for, but I managed to flip my fork from the plate. It bounced off Gerard's shoulder, leaving a small white blob of potatoes on his crisp black overcoat, and onto the floor. I clamped a hand over my mouth in horror. He only laughed and wiped it off with his napkin.

SIX

inner was a smashing success. In addition to getting potatoes on Gerard, I also managed to spill my glass of water, which almost poured on Gerard's lap, but I did manage to recover and wiped it up with the napkin from my lap before it could spill onto him. I understood my clumsiness was a combination of stupidity induced by Gerard's attractive presence and my gloves meant to hide my scales from everyone in the room.

I heaved a sigh of relief the instant dinner finished. I scooted my chair back so suddenly it teetered and nearly fell. Gerard caught it. His hand was muscled, the blue veins flexing beneath his skin. His hands were big, dirt lingered under the edge of some of his nails, and there was a callus on his fingers from a bow's string. Keltin's hands were small in comparison, pale, and pristine.

I tore my gaze away and sunk into the crowd to get some air.

I had no idea a room crowded with people could give me a break.

"Tell me all about him!" Ismae grabbed on to my arm with both of hers. "He's certainly handsome. What's his name? Is he part of a new noble family?"

"He's from Ashwrya," I explained, glancing around. "His name is Prince Gerard, and he lives with his grandmother."

Ismae looked across the hall. "*That* is his grandmother?"

I hadn't had a chance to really look at the woman until that moment, I'd been far too distracted with the strong stranger flirting with me all dinner. The woman was shorter than Gerard, but had the same thin nose and a more feminine version of his strong jaw, but she looked more youthful than most grandmothers.

Ismae giggled. "Well, he seems really interested in you."

"I don't know why. I don't even understand why he's here in the first place." I fiddled absently with my crown and silently wished I could take the warm gloves off my hands.

"Because you're beautiful." Ismae grabbed my hands. "Stop fidgeting. You're stronger than you admit."

"No, I'm really not."

"Elisa, you've got freaking dragon scales on your hands!" she whispered.

"Yes, and if you put me in the middle of the forest, I would have no idea how to get home! I'm not strong or significant in any way. I'm just a princess cursed to be a dragon, and the only hope is the faeries, who are all now dead." I jerked my hands away. The familiar tingling of anger burned in my chest, and after my experience that morning with my little outburst, I didn't want to get upset and do something else I would regret.

"I think you're afraid," Ismae said. "I can't say I wouldn't be if I had a curse. But you really are strong, Elisa. And you're smart and clever. Of course he would have a reason to be interested in you."

"Keltin isn't," I muttered, grateful Ismae hadn't become upset. My anger was already ebbing.

Ismae laughed. "Elisa, that's because Keltin isn't interested in *any* woman."

"Ladies and gentlemen, if we can have a moment before the dancing begins!" the herald called over the crowd.

I leaned to Ismae. "Is he just not ready to be married yet?"

She shook her head. "It's because he prefers men."

"We have an announcement from the queen," the herald continued.

I faced Ismae. "What?" I'd been trying for years to get Keltin's attention, and all this time, he had no interest in me, but not because he wasn't interested in *me*. I joined Ismae's laughter and stifled it behind my gloved hand. How ridiculous I'd acted trying to get his attention.

"If I can have Princess Elisa join me," Mother said, scanning the crowd.

My stomach dropped into my toes. Mother had never done a formal announcement like this on my birthday. I let go of Ismae to join my mother on the wooden steps. I couldn't stop my mind from racing. *What if she is about to tell everyone all about your curse? But she made you wear gloves tonight to hide it. She certainly won't announce I'll be taking on additional duties as the queen. That isn't supposed to take effect until my eighteenth birthday.*

I reached Mother's side and gave her a quick, nervous grin.

Mother held her hand out the opposite direction. "And Prince Gerard?"

He stood at the front of the crowd, and when beckoned, skipped a step as he climbed to my mother's opposite side.

Confusion pinched my brows.

"This evening, I would like to make a wonderful announcement. Princess Elisa is formally engaged to Prince Gerard of Ashwrya." She smiled proudly, stepped back, and motioned for us to meet in the middle.

Gerard held his hand out to me.

I couldn't move my feet. "Engaged?" I spat. "You arranged my engagement?" I faced my mother. "Without my consent, without even a word to me, you arranged my engagement?" Anger flared my nostrils, and like that morning, I could taste it.

The excited applause of the crowd awkwardly faded.

I didn't know if my eyes were on fire, but I knew if I didn't get some fresh air, I would do something I would later regret.

I grabbed my skirts and ran.

The crowd parted as they murmured.

"Married to a prince from Ashwrya, that's a good move."

"Poor girl, her mother should have told her."

"I don't understand what she's so upset about."

I knew in my heart I couldn't truly escape, but at least I could go outside for a little while. I was the "crown princess," able to be manipulated like a puppet on a string, because I truly had no other choice. My life wasn't my own.

I ran to the gardens, tightened my hands into fists, and gritted my teeth. I wanted to scream. I wanted to throw the stone bench against the nearest tree trunk and demolish it. I wanted to tear all of the flowers from their beds.

Pain seared my palms, but I held my fists tight, concentrating on the feeling of my claws against my palms. I tried to count and take deep breaths. But the corner of my eyesight began to glow, and I whirled around and tore my claws down the trunk of the nearest tree—four long distinct marks from my claws.

I let out a shuddered breath and sunk to my knees, gulping in breaths, counting deliberately. *One ... two ... three ...*

"Elisa!" People called.

I couldn't face them. I didn't dare, not with my new claws protruding from my now-torn white gloves.

Four … five …

I closed my eyes.

Six …

You're brave, Elisa. You're strong and intelligent. Ismae's words echoed in my head, and I felt hot tears on my cheeks.

Her words were immediately overshadowed. *The rage of a dragon shall grow inside, until the truth she can no longer hide.*

I reached up and wiped at my tears.

I didn't feel brave or strong or intelligent. I couldn't even control my anger.

I felt a warm presence behind me and glared over my shoulder to see Gerard standing near. I scrambled to my feet, hid my hands behind my back, and forced myself to take a deep breath to suppress the desire to toss him into the side of the castle.

He stopped a safe distance away. "I'm sorry. I truly didn't know. If I had—"

"Remember what you said about my mother?"

He nodded.

"This is a classic example of what she does." My claws still bit into my hands and I could smell the tang of iron in my blood. "I may be the crown princess, but she doesn't involve me in any of the decisions."

Gerard stepped closer. "Come, we can speak with your mother and my grandmother in private. Sort this out." He held his hand toward me, but I shook my head. His brows shifted. "You don't want to touch me now?"

"It's not you," I said softly. Finally, my claws began to retract.

"Ah." He dropped his hand to his side. "It's you?" he arched a brow with distrust in his eyes as if I wasn't the first person to tell him that.

"Did she even tell you about my curse to become a dragon?"

His brows shot up. "No kidding?"

He looked down my body. The moonlight peeked from behind a cloud, lighting Gerard's green eyes as they settled on my side. I still had my hands hidden behind my back. I slumped my shoulders forward. He deserved to know the truth.

I inhaled through my nose with new resolve and closed the gap between us. I held my arms up and kept my eyes on his as I pulled the remnants of the gloves off. In that short fit of anger, the scales had climbed to my elbows. My heart pounded in my ears as I watched his eyes shift from mine to my black-scaled hands.

Gerard reached out. "May I?" he asked gently.

I allowed him to take my arm so he could get a better look. He held my hand so close to his face his breath caressed the back of my hand like that of a warm afternoon breeze. He turned my hand over, using the light of the moon to take in the details of the scales. I hadn't even looked at them so long. He touched his fingertips to my palms and then stroked the scales down my arm.

I shuddered and pulled away. It felt more like the ghost of a touch when you remove your shirt, light and tingling.

"Curious indeed," Gerard concluded.

"That's all you have to say?" I blurted.

He moved his hands away from his sides, palms exposed. "Is there something you would rather I say?"

"I ... I don't know." I hid my hands behind my back again, trying to put into words the confusion I felt. "Is it normal for people to reveal they're a dragon where you come from?"

Gerard chuckled, a sound almost too deep for his young face. "No, but—" he lifted his broad shoulders "honestly, all I can think about right now is how I can help you. We *are* betrothed now. Certainly there is some riddle or cure?" He inclined his head slightly, sincerity in his gaze.

I hesitated. "If you want to help, I would appreciate it. The scales appeared this morning when I found out ..." I looked down at my hands. "The last of the faeries was killed this morning. You see, according to the story, the faeries vowed to cure my curse." I lifted my gaze up to Gerard. "If they don't cure me, or if I don't find a cure somehow, I am to become a dragon by my eighteenth birthday."

"Next year." He nodded and his gaze traced the movement of a Loper firefly. "Hm. So you need a fae." The glowing blue translucent wings of the Loper firefly left a glittering blue trail that faded as it darted around. Gerard reached up and rubbed his hand over his strong jaw. "There could be some still hidden deep within the forests."

I shook my head. "Mother has had scouts searching my entire life. The only sign we got today was when one of them returned with a note from Selina."

Gerard's gaze snapped to me. "Selina?"

"She's the one who cursed me."

His brow furrowed. "The sorceress?"

"Yes. You know her?"

He nodded slowly. "I've heard stories." He rubbed his lips together as he thought, then reached out and took my fingertips in his hand. "Elisa, we can't solve this problem right now. I need more information, which you can spend all day tomorrow giving. I think we should go back inside and finish out your celebration. You only turn seventeen once." He smiled at me, the little dimple in his left cheek appearing.

I knew Gerard was right. Everyone else had been looking for seventeen years. I couldn't expect him to solve the problem in one night. Reluctantly, I accepted his arm and let him guide me back inside. I wasn't sorry for my outburst. My mother had no right to prepare our engagement without telling me. She had no right announcing it to the kingdom without at least telling me first, it's the least she could have done.

The guests turned when I reentered, and I let go of Gerard to hide my hands.

He gently said, "One moment," and left me beside one of the flowering trees at the entrance, only to return with full-length gloves he must have taken from a party guest.

I moved my hair over my shoulder and accepted the gloves. "Thank you."

Gerard gave me his dimpled grin again. "You're welcome. If there's anything to make you more comfortable, tell me."

I blushed.

He didn't make a scene about my return, nor did he embarrass me by bringing me to my mother for a scolding. Instead, he led me onto the dance floor. "You, dear lady, deserve to celebrate your birthday like any other princess." He took my hand in one of his, set his other behind his back, and bowed to kiss the glove.

"You really don't have to," I tried to insist.

Looking up at me, he quirked his dimpled grin and winked. "Nonsense." He straightened, pulled me close, and began to dance.

As a proper lady and future queen, I knew the dance and moved my feet in time with the song, but he swayed his body with mine in a way no one ever had. He kept our bodies close, and I found my gaze locked on him, entranced by those deep, green, mysterious eyes.

Gerard swept me off my feet.

The music flowed through my soul, calming my residual anger. I relaxed my body into Gerard's arms. He nudged my back with his hand, cueing me to move under his arm into a spin and then back. I wasn't anticipating the dip, however, and found myself laughing at his grace and my lack of elegance as I panicked that I was falling.

He chuckled and righted me. "You're a wonderful dancer."

"You're not so bad yourself," I teased, only to bite my lip and immediately question if it was appropriate to tease a prince.

But Gerard laughed. "Oh, you think that dancing was bad, you should see this." As a more lively song started, he pulled me even closer and grinned. I could feel his muscled body against my chest. His body radiated heat. His eyes scrunched in teasing skepticism. "Can you keep up with me?"

"Of course," I scoffed. "The Haltz is my favorite."

"Let us see." He stepped backward, driving me forward, causing me to take long strides until we were centered on the dance floor.

I let go of him long enough to gather my skirts in one hand and met his excited grin.

The upbeat violin intro took off and the swing increasing with it. I moved my feet delicately and quickly right in step with Gerard. He slid his feet with expertise. He rolled me away from his body, our fingertips remaining locked as our arms were stretched. I swung my hips, looked at him, and shimmied my shoulders.

He let out a little laugh, and I tugged his hand.

Gerard's eyes widened briefly before he spun into me, then nudged me with his hip, and I went around him to untangle. He chuckled, took my hand and drew me close again. We instantly fell into the steps and moved in a circle around the dance floor. I hadn't noticed until that moment that the other dancers had cleared off.

As the tempo began it's reluctant close.

Gerard spun us around one last time before bowing to me. He kissed the back of my hand, his emerald eyes sparkling.

The audience broke out into applause a little louder than just politeness.

My cheeks instantly became hot, and I jerked my hand away.

"You don't need to be embarrassed." He straightened and snagged my hand. Gerard leaned and brushed his lips against my ear. "That was the most fun I've had in a while. Come get a drink with me."

I needed more than a drink. I felt like my head had floated off into the stars and my heart had somehow melted. I vaguely recalled noblemen and women congratulated us on our engagement as we passed. A few children complimented my dress, and then there was a blur of color, torchlight glinting off jewelry, and rushed introductions.

Gerard put a glass in my hand.

I sipped the sweet grape juice, relieved as we had a brief moment alone protected by the edge of the table.

Gerard nudged his head a little. "It appears you made your statue of a mother smile."

I looked over my shoulder to where he'd hinted. My mother sat on the throne, and her smile actually reached her eyes. "I'm sure she's proud she made the right decision in choosing you for my husband." I swallowed another mouthful.

"And how do *you* feel about me?"

I considered Gerard over my glass and slowly lowered it. "I don't know if she's right about it keeping the dragon away."

"But?" His dark brows were slightly raised, but I knew by the look in his eye he wanted me to say it was love at first sight.

"But I …" I peered into the glass in my hand and lifted my shoulders in a little shrug. "I think you're different."

"Good different?"

I ran my finger across the rim of the glass. "I … don't think I've ever met anyone like you." I glanced at him again.

Gerard laughed. "I understand that. Not much of an answer, though." He winked and took another drink from his own glass. "But if I may be so bold to say, perhaps some people are just destined to be together. If they have good chemistry—"

"Chemistry?" I raised my brows, not really asking but more surprised he was so bold.

"What I mean is, we seem to get along well." Again, he flashed his crooked grin.

"Yes. I suppose we do." My heart had settled from the dance, but deep in my chest, it remained slamming against my insides. I finished the glass and set it on the edge of the table.

"Come dance again." Gerard took my hand and guided me once more out on to the floor, where we spent the rest of the evening.

Maybe Mother was right after all.

Maybe Gerard really was the key to keeping the dragon at bay.

At least for now.

SEVEN

I woke with a silly smile on my face and let out a sigh as I rolled over to look at the ceiling. I touched my fingers to my lips and let my mind wander. Gerard had been a complete gentleman and hadn't kissed me on the lips. That didn't mean I couldn't dream. For once, my dreams weren't about my transformation. Gerard had been there, and with his protective arms around me, I never transformed.

I imagined how his lips would feel. Warm, like his hands? Rough like his calluses? Soft like his dancing? And of course I needed to find out what kind of woman I would be in this game of attraction. In my books, girls were a tease, or polite but forward. I should have asked Ismae the best way to flirt. She'd always been a flirt with Prince Mathias and Prince Ulrich.

Then again, I could be overthinking everything. Maybe all I needed was some time alone with Gerard.

The door of the room next to mine closed, and I sat up. That room was empty. Or rather, it should have been. More curious than frightened, I slipped out of bed and grabbed my green silk robe. After I had it on, I carefully opened my bedroom door.

A figure stood in the hallway directly across from my bedroom. It was a room that acted as a study for my sisters and me, where we had our academic lessons. When the figure saw it was empty, he slipped inside.

I knew I should go back to bed. It wasn't any of my business.

But a small voice hissed, *Go look. No one should be snooping about this time of day.*

Before I knew it, I had darted across the hall and turned the handle. The figure already had the drawer to the desk open and was rummaging about.

"Allul," I said.

The wall sconces ignited, snapping light into the room in an instant.

Gerard froze and stared at me, his eyes narrowed with a dangerous glint. He relaxed almost instantly. "Elisa." Those handsome lips I'd just dreamt about spread into an easy smile as he straightened. "You startled me."

At his glare, I was ready to scold him. But with the change in his demeanor, I was almost ready to dismiss the oddity of him being in my study rifling through my things. He wore tan trousers and a crisp white shirt covered by a dark brown vest. He had no boots on, which was probably why I hadn't heard him in the hallway.

I inclined my head. "What are you doing?"

He glanced around. "I am aware this looks odd, my being ... in the dark. In this room. Alone."

I folded my arms over my chest.

His eyes settled on me and then grazed my body, taking in every curve.

The way he looked at me made me feel exposed and I suddenly grasped my robe was open, revealing my low white nightgown. I tugged my robe closed and refolded my arms.

Gerard's eyes snapped back to mine and his dimple appeared. "In honesty, I was looking for the spring stone."

My eyebrows rose. "Why are you looking for the royal stone?"

"I was thinking about what you said last night." Gerard left the drawer and walked over to me. "Your curse. You said the faeries were supposed to save you?"

"That's what my mother says."

He nodded once. "I wonder if maybe the cure has been under your nose the entire time. The spring stone has magic, doesn't it?"

"Well, yes, but we don't have it." I laughed a little.

Gerard's brows dipped in confusion. "Your crown last night had fragments of the stone. Didn't it?"

I shook my head. "We have stones that look like it. But the real stone is with the faeries. Why does it matter?"

Gerard blinked and shook his head. "If it's the cure, then it's rather important." He rested his hands on his hips. "These faeries, they are small woodland creatures?"

I shook my head. "No, those are fairies."

He arched his brow. "The pronunciation is the same."

"A little different, but the fae are who we are looking for. Not a fairy. We don't have those here. A fairy is small. They have wings and cause mischief. Fae are like us, but beautiful, have pointed ears, and I think they even have magic."

Gerard nodded his understanding.

I strolled over to my desk and closed the drawer he had been searching in. "Faeries are like us, though beautiful and magical. Their ears are pointed and they are magical. They have a particular love for nature."

"If these *faeries* have it, and you believe they're gone, someone needs to make sure they aren't in hiding," he replied reasonably.

"My mother has already searched, remember?"

"Then the stone is in their ruins. I'll get my men ready."

"Wait, slow down." I put my hand on his chest when he went to pass me.

Gerard stopped and looked down in a way that made me forget what I was going to say. He was close like he had been the night before. He smelled like autumn woods, brisk and bitter.

He placed his hand over mine. "I will be safe. I will take a couple of my men with me."

"But you don't know my kingdom," I argued.

He raised his brows with a playful smile. "Are you implying you want to join me?"

"What? No, I can't," I blundered and pulled my hand away. "It's not what a crown princess does."

He stepped even closer. With nowhere to go, my back pressed against the wooden frame of the door. I wanted to hold his gaze, but shyly averted my eyes while my heart raced, wondering—and wanting—to know what he was about to do.

Gerard lifted my chin. "You said you wanted to travel. If you are to be my bride, I want to take care of you. If that means I journey around your entire kingdom to find the cure no one else could, I will do it. No matter how long it takes me."

"Why?" I breathed.

"Because you're my responsibility. My duty as a prince is to keep you safe and happy." He leaned forward and kissed my cheek, sending a wave of heat from my head to my toes.

I shuddered.

"You're certain you don't want to join me?"

"I-I don't think ... my mother ..."

"Ah. I understand. I shan't be gone too long. I'll be sure to send a messenger frequently." Gerard ran his fingers through my hair and winked.

"But ..." I started.

"Yes?"

I wanted to beg him to stay, to send someone else. There was still so much I didn't know about him. I wanted to ask him to give me a proper kiss on the lips. I wanted to feel his muscled body. And then I immediately felt embarrassed. That's not how a princess should act.

Again, I averted my eyes. "Be safe. Please."

"I will be. Promise." He stepped into the hallway and walked away.

I reluctantly returned to my room to dress for breakfast. My mind consumed with thoughts of Gerard. I made sure to look perfect for him. I wore another one of my favorite dresses—a pale green dress with pink flowers along the bottom hem and a squared neckline that pinched downward in the middle to accentuate my breasts. I put on a simple golden necklace and spent far too much time perfecting the pinned pearls in my hair. Prince Ulrich had given them to me at the summer celebration last year.

By the time I made it down to breakfast, everyone was already seated. My sisters sat to my mother's right with my father, while Gerard and his grandmother sat to my mother's left with a vacant seat for me.

"Forgive me for being late," I apologized.

Gerard swiftly stood and grinned as he took me in. He had an overcoat on now, a brown sort of orange like dying leaves. "I could wait all day just to see you."

I blushed madly. "Thank you, Gerard."

He pulled my chair out for me, and I took my seat. "I was just telling your parents how we talked last night and you told me about your curse." He took my hand and set it on the table, and gently removed the long gloves I'd put on, revealing that the scales had spread. He then tucked my fingers in the crook of his hand and returned his attention to my mother.

I bit my lip, unable to look at my mother while secretly wanting to see her reaction.

"I also explained," he continued, "that you mentioned the faeries. Your mother was just filling me in on their role in your curse." He gave my fingers a reassuring squeeze.

I finally braved a glance at Mother.

My mother appeared uncomfortable, which surprised me because nothing ever made her uncomfortable. Her gaze darted from Gerard to my hands. "The faeries made a promise all those years ago that they would help break her curse, should the time come. But as I've already said, the last of the faeries was found dead yesterday. We received a letter from Selina stating so."

Gerard set his chin on his fist and turned to his grandmother. "Odd that Selina should involve herself in these matters. What would she hope to gain?"

His grandmother, whom I still hadn't even been introduced to, had a smile on her face I could almost interpret as a smirk. "A dragon on her side would be rather valuable, I suppose."

"But why wait all these years? Why wouldn't she have just taken the child at birth? Raised her as her own?" Gerard pondered aloud as though we weren't there.

Certainly my parents had wondered the same thing. I saw them exchange a glance, and my mother adjusted in her seat. She seemed a little paler than usual.

"These are wonderful questions, and we've worried the same questions for seventeen years," she interjected. "We've come no closer to an answer than you will. I believe we should eat." She clapped her hands, summoning the servants and cutting off the conversation.

Gerard turned back to me and leaned in his seat. He glanced at my mother and ever so slightly rolled his eyes. A grin spread across my face, and I successfully resisted the urge to giggle. I liked him even more.

Gerard only removed his hand from mine so I could eat, and I set my hand on my lap.

"Is it true Griswil doesn't change seasons?" he asked, looking at me sideways as he took a bite of his eggs.

"Yes. I don't know why or how, but Zelig never has a spring or summer or autumn. They always have snow," I answered. "Because of that, we and Arington provide a lot of their food while they provide ice and minerals."

"And the other countries are frozen as well? That is why your kingdom is known as the spring kingdom," he said as though it weren't a question at all.

I confirmed with a nod. "I don't know if you can say *frozen*, exactly. But none of us have changed seasons in … decades? Centuries?" I looked at Mother and Father.

Mother dabbed her lips with a napkin unnecessarily. "Yes, Arington often struggles because their days can scorch their crops and their nights can freeze them. Terricina provides all of our fish and other seafood, so Zelig sends them ice to help with their trades. We've managed to help each other through the years. It's part of the Southern Kingdoms Treaty."

Gerard nodded, taking in the information and assessing it. "I've been thinking about Elisa's cure, and I believe the spring stone might be able to help. Even if the faeries are dead, the stone still has magical properties, and Elisa has already told me the faeries are believed to have it."

Mother nearly dropped her fork.

Father nodded. "But as we've already said, the faeries—"

"Are supposedly dead," Gerard cut in. "I can't be certain until I check for myself. I shall search their ruins for the stone. I will leave after lunch."

I found myself biting my lip, leaning close to him, my hand on his arm. "You're certain you'll be all right?"

He smiled reassuringly. "I promise. I've been a hunter since I was a child. I can protect myself. I know how to survive, and should anything happen along the way with an injury, I'm also trained in medicine." He leaned so only I could hear. "And remember my magic?"

"Can I help you prepare?"

"Of course, darling."

My heart roared in my ears, and my entire body ignited with fire.

Gerard leaned over and kissed my cheek, this time letting his lips linger against my skin.

Even though I bit my lip, I couldn't hold back my grin. I fiddled with the bottom of a curl, wrapping it around my finger and releasing it. I didn't understand why Gerard did this to me. I wasn't embarrassed I was so in love … love? Is this what love felt like?

I liked the feeling Gerard gave me of floating on clouds. My heart racing with excitement instead of dread was new and even enjoyable. For the first time, I felt genuine hope that he would be the solution to my problem. I wouldn't admit to my mother, but she was right. Gerard was just what I needed. Even if he didn't find a cure before next year, I would rather spend my last year with him than alone locked in the castle.

Marigold and Dahlia giggled to each other, and I raised my gaze to stick my tongue out at them and cross my eyes. It was a quick gesture and if my mother saw it, she didn't acknowledge me. But Gerard saw it. I knew because his body shook with a chuckle.

After breakfast, Gerard took my hand and we walked to his room on the western side of the second floor of the castle, opposite the castle from my room. "I need to get my bags and restock our supplies," he explained. "I'll need to get lots of food." He opened the bottom drawer of the dresser and pulled out two large bags. "The horses have their own bags, and I'll stock those with the heavier supplies, like cookware and most of the food." He looked up at me. "I'll put clothes and blankets in these."

"What do you use for shelter?"

"We used tents and inns along the way here. It won't be difficult to use them as we travel. Townspeople are pretty generous when you offer them some money and most people will allow a prince to stay in their cottage. If we're too far away, I'll sleep under the stars."

"And if it rains?" I pressed.

"Then I'll be a little wet." He got back to his feet. "I've traveled a lot, Elisa. You don't need to worry about me."

"At least you won't be alone."

Gerard showed me everything he packed. Guilt prickled at me for slowing him down, but I wanted to be with him as long as absolutely possible. I even entertained the thought of asking my mother if I could go with him. I stayed beside him as he supervised the servants packing the saddlebags. There were lots of vegetables and some fresh meat, but most of it was dry. He explained he would eat the fresh meat that evening or it would spoil.

He also showed me his hunting knife, the bow and arrows he'd had tucked in the corner of his room, and the blankets he rolled and tied to the bottom of his bag.

Before I knew it, lunchtime arrived, and he had everything ready to leave.

"I don't want you to go," I finally expressed. "I've enjoyed spending time with you. Being with you. What if you go and my worry causes the dragon to take over even further?"

"I believe your emotions are indeed tied to your dragon." He put his arm around me and held me to his chest. "But I think you're stronger than you believe you are."

"Ismae said the same thing," I mumbled.

"Who?"

"My best friend, the princess of Arington." I gently rested my head against Gerard's chest and put my arms around him. My heart felt like dandelion seeds blowing in the wind. I put my hand on his back and his muscles shifted as he wrapped his arms around me. He was even stronger than I thought.

"She sounds like a good friend."

"Mm hm."

"Maybe you should change the books you read? Certainly there is a book in your library where a princess vanquishes the dragon and not the knight?" I felt the weight of his head as he rested it on top of mine.

"Do you believe in love at first sight?" I hadn't meant to ask it out loud.

His muscles tensed beneath my head, and I looked up to see him nod. "I thought you said you didn't believe in chemistry."

"Maybe you changed my mind." I let go and stepped back even though I didn't want to.

Gerard chuckled. "When I return, we will cure your curse and be married. You deserve a love story like those in your books."

After lunch, I watched him mount his horse and ride away with his two men flanking him.

"I'm afraid I have matters to attend to as well." Gerard's grandmother turned to me. "You are a beautiful woman, and I'm pleased you get along so well." She turned to my mother. "I will wait for word of Gerard's return, but I will not return until preparations are made for the wedding."

"Of course," Mother replied. "It would be convenient to have it on the spring equinox in March. That is the day of our seasonal celebration."

"Less than three months." She raised her brows. "That's not much time for wedding preparations."

"It will help to keep Elisa busy while her future husband is away."

I drew a deep breath as my stomach rolled.

Gerard's grandmother walked down the stairs and climbed into a carriage. I stood beside my mother as the woman left the castle grounds.

"Come, Elisa. We have much to do," Mother said.

I chewed my bottom lip. Although I couldn't see Gerard any longer, I couldn't help but look down the road in the direction he'd gone. He had promised me he would be all right, and I had to trust him. If I didn't have Gerard, who did I have?

EIGHT

"My dearest Elisa," I read aloud. I sat cross-legged on my bed with Marigold and Dahlia looking over my shoulder at Gerard's slanted script. "We passed through the town of Sloval and should arrive in Andorin soon. I would like to carry on eastward to the border of Griswil and along the Drakespine Mountains. I hope to check every corner. I have also stopped to ask villagers, but no one seems to know anything about faeries. Don't give up hope. The search is still new. With love, Gerard."

Waiting for him to write was worse than waiting for the dragon to take hold.

My sisters squealed, and my cheeks blushed.

I'd begun to notice little changes in myself, changes I hadn't told anyone, like my eyesight becoming more crisp. When I went out to the gardens, the colors were more vibrant. There was a beautiful Sickle Flower I knew to have purple and red, but I never knew it had pink streaks and little flecks of green.

I was also growing more confident. The third day of Gerard's being gone, I headed outside to spend a little bit of time with the horses.

Mother stopped me in the hallway. "Where are you going, Elisa? You should be studying your history."

"Why study about the history of our land if I won't be here in a year to protect it?" I argued back.

She blinked at me. "Elisa!"

I surprised even myself. "It's true, though," I pressed. "You know it, I know it. You're only giving me things to do to keep myself busy while Gerard is out looking for a fae."

"And he won't find one," she said definitively, her nose twitching as she sneered. "We've already sent our best scouts and they've already reported everything to us. He's a foolish boy. That is all."

"Did you ever think maybe Selina put a spell on them?" I snapped. "If she's powerful enough to turn me into a dragon, she's powerful enough to make them believe there are no fae left in our land! For once in my life, let me do what I want to do. All I want to do today is go out and spend time with the horses and learn a little more about them. I want to go down into town and look at the buildings instead of staying locked up in here learning about their architecture from a book!"

"How dare you yell at me?" Mother put her hand on her heart as if I had done something horribly offensive.

Even more to her horror, I didn't care. For once, I didn't apologize or obey. I held my chin high and walked right past her, out the back door, and down the hill to the stables.

And it felt wonderful.

I grinned wider than I ever had while my fingertips tingled with adrenaline. I couldn't believe I had just defied my mother!

I heard Philip talking as I drew nearer the stables and spotted an older man leaning against the side of the building. The smell of hay and manure greeted me, and I wrinkled my nose. Maybe being down with the horses wasn't such a good idea after all.

The man spotted me and straightened immediately. I recognized him as the stable master and Philip's father, Bernard. He yanked his hat from his head and nervously wrung it. "Crown Princess Elisa. To what do we owe the visit?" He glanced beyond me to see if anyone else was coming.

"I decided to come and see the horses. Philip might have told you I'm not the best rider." I peered through the open doors and saw Philip with a shovel and a wheelbarrow.

"Oh, certainly not."

"I really am," I insisted with a little smile. "I guess I just want to get to know the horses a little better. Spend some time outside. Can I see Tao?"

"Of course, Your Highness. He's a great horse." Bernard led the way into the stable and showed me which stall Tao was in.

The horse flicked his head and snorted when he saw me, then reached his head out and started nudging my shoulder.

"You appear to have already met," Bernard said.

"Yes." I laughed and started rubbing Tao's head and cheeks. "Philip let me take him on a picnic for my birthday."

"Ah, yes. I remember now. Well, there's grain in that bucket there if you want to feed him."

"How do horses eat if they aren't in a barn?" I asked.

Bernard's bushy brows furrowed over his blue eyes. "They graze on grass and things."

"So if someone is on a journey with horses, they just let them munch on anything?" I asked. I grabbed a handful of oats and held it up to Tao.

"As long as it isn't poisonous, yes. And make sure to travel on roads that have access to water, like a river or stables, so horses can drink. Why the sudden inquiries, if I might ask?"

I let out a heavy sigh. "Prince Gerard insisted on searching for a fae. He took his horse, and I was just wondering how one travels with a horse. It's not something I've ever thought about or paid attention to when we traveled."

Bernard nodded softly.

"Do they wander off?" I looked over at him.

The old man shrugged. "They can, especially if they get spooked, like during a storm. But most of the time, they're pretty loyal. You can tie them to a tree at night as well so they don't wander. It's keeping them safe from predators you need to worry about."

"Luckily, Gerard says he's a hunter." I rubbed Tao's nose again, and he turned his head to search my hand for some more treats.

"I best be getting back to work." Bernard nodded to me, and I returned the gesture.

"Am I crazy to be worried so much about him, Tao?" I asked softly.

Tao's enormous brown eyes watched me lazily.

"Philip, do you know how to protect the horses?" I asked.

He had just reentered the barn from dumping the pile of manure somewhere. He wiped his arm across his forehead. His eyes darted to my hands, but I'd covered them with long gloves. Even if Gerard wasn't ashamed of them, I still was. And clearly Philip was still nervous about them as well.

"We keep them inside here at night and let them out in the fields during the day unless we're doing something. A few men are fixing part of the fence that got broken when a tree branch collapsed on it. That's why the horses are in today. We have llamas with the horses and they help to protect them." He shrugged. "But wild animals tend to go after easier targets, like sheep or goats."

"Do you enjoy being out here with the horses?" I looked over at him.

"Uh …" He removed his work glove and rubbed the back of his neck. "Yes, but it's not what I want to be doing forever. It's tough work."

I lowered my hands. "People don't just stay where they are? I mean, your father is our stable master. What would you do instead?"

Philip chuckled a little. I didn't know if I'd ever heard him laugh or chuckle. "Yes, and he would like me to follow in his steps. I do enjoy horses, but I would really like my own home on my own land. I've been learning from a couple of arborists too, so I could eventually have some trees. Dreams, really. But to answer your question, no. People don't have to stay where they're put. In fact, you know the noble family, the Collins?"

"Yes … yes! They're relatively new. Have a lovely family with five children," I confirmed.

"He started out as a fisherman, but he learned the value of the money-trading side. He learned how to be smart with investments and made some very valuable purchases, which ended up earning him more money, and now he's nobility. Some people start as blacksmiths and become farmers, or servants in the castle leave and start their own lives as tailors or florists." He shrugged. "The possibilities are endless."

I felt my lips tug in an attempt of a smile, but I looked at Tao. "I suppose for some people there are a lot of possibilities."

"I didn't mean … I …"

"I know." I smiled at him. "You didn't offend me. I just think what life must be like beyond the castle walls and if I'm a fool for staying so confined." I stepped away from Tao, and the horse snorted his disapproval. "Thank you for letting me spend some time out here.

I'll likely return tomorrow. It's nice to be outside now and then."

Philip bowed respectfully as I passed.

I spent time in the main gardens, and Marigold and Dahlia joined me after lunch on a walk into the fields around the castle.

"Has Gerard made you more brave?" Marigold asked.

"I don't know if it's him or … something else. I've just been feeling like something is different." I looked at her and put my hand on her head to ruffle her hair, but her skin was hot to the touch and her skin was pale. "Marigold, are you all right?"

"I haven't been feeling very well today," she confessed.

I gasped. "Why didn't you say something earlier? We should get back to the castle now." I took her hand.

"I didn't want to spoil your day," she objected. But she didn't fight as Dahlia and I guided her back to the castle.

She threw up as soon as we got her inside. The servants stepped in immediately and rushed to get her cleaned up and in bed, and Abby was summoned to make her famous chicken noodle soup.

Dahlia and I stood inside the door as the last servant left. "Of course you would fall ill the one day Elisa decides to be brave," Dahlia teased.

Marigold smiled softly but closed her eyes and rolled on her side.

Mother burst into the room. "The servants told me you were ill. What happened?" She wheeled around to stare at Dahlia and me for an explanation.

"We were out on a walk," I began.

"I heard you went beyond the castle walls," she pointed out.

"Of course outside the castle walls, there's nowhere to walk *inside* them," Dahlia interjected. "And it's not Elisa's fault Marigold fell ill."

Mother tightened her lips and walked to Marigold's side. "Poor thing." She stroked her cheeks.

"Can Elisa tell me a story before everyone leaves?" she mumbled.

"Of course, sweetheart."

"Just her and Dahlia?"

Mother's spine went rigid, but I resisted a triumphant grin. I loved being with Marigold. Even as a child, I took care of her whenever Mother was too busy. We were eight years apart in age, but we still held a special bond.

Mother stood, then told Marigold to send for her when she was ready and she would return. She didn't even look at me as she passed.

"What story do you want?" I asked, walking to her small bookshelf still holding children's picture books.

"This one." Marigold patted the book on her nightstand.

I grinned. "Those are my favorite stories too."

The old book was a collection of stories written years and years ago, told to me as a child, and I loved reading them to Dahlia and Marigold. I took the book while she scooted over to make room so I could sit on the edge of her bed.

Dahlia climbed up on the opposite side and hugged Marigold from behind.

"Which story would you like to start off with?" I asked, loving the little creak in the spine as I opened the pages.

"The princess in the tower," she said with a yawn and rubbed her eye.

I chuckled. "All right. Let me find it … Ah, there it is." I cleared my throat. "Once upon a time, an old watchtower stood in the middle of the woods. Once, it had been part of a grand kingdom, but over time it had been forgotten. It overlooked the blanket of trees below. Constructed of stone and mortar, it was strong and steady in spite of its age. It had four windows looking in the four directions of the compass, a sloped and pointed roof, and by all appearances, appeared to be nothing but an old watchtower. Inside of that tower, however—"

"Does the tower have a door?" Marigold asked.

I paused and lifted my gaze from the words on the page. "I've never thought about that. I don't think so."

"But how would Rapunzel have gotten up there in the first place?" Marigold argued.

I was at a loss for words. "Let's say the tower has a door." I looked back at the page and opened my mouth, but Marigold interrupted again.

"Then why doesn't she just go out and find her own prince?"

Her words struck me harder than she ever intended. Why *didn't* the princess leave the tower? Why did she sit around and wait her whole life?

I stared at the pages but didn't see a word.

My entire life, I had been just like the girls in the stories. I'd looked up to these princesses but hadn't realized just how like them I was. I'd been shut up in the castle, hidden away just in case the dragon took hold. I kept my distance from making any true friends because … what if I ended up eating them? And now Gerard was out searching for my cure while I sat in the castle.

Waiting.

Waiting for "my prince" to save me.

"Elisa?" Marigold asked.

I blinked myself out of my moment and looked at her. "You just got me thinking."

A smile slowly spread across her face. "Are you going to leave?"

I closed the book. I ran my hand over the shapes of the letters pressed into the cover and watched the firelight dance across my ebony scales. "Everyone else has looked. Everyone but me."

"I know Mother has sent scouts, and Gerard is looking now, but isn't it time you wrote your own story?" Dahlia pressed.

"I think … I think I want to find the cure myself." I didn't sound confident, but the wheels in my head had begun to turn.

Marigold and Dahlia gave each other a high five.

I narrowed my gaze and looked between them. "Am I to believe you had this planned?"

"Sort of," Marigold confessed.

"Of course we did. We've been trying to get you to have this moment of realization since your birthday, silly." Dahlia pulled the sleeve of her nightgown back onto her shoulder. "And we're going with you."

"Are you insane?" I gasped. "Mother will kill me."

"You don't think she'd get upset enough when she discovers you're gone?"

Marigold cleared her throat. "And who do you think she is going to ask when you turn up missing?"

"No," I said firmly. "I don't know what it's like out there. I don't know if I'll end up putting you two in danger. After all, what if Selina shows up? She'd capture you both." I got up and handed Dahlia the book. "I'm afraid this is something I need to do on my own."

Dahlia sighed heavily. "Elisa, you're not on your own. You've always got us."

"A thirteen-year-old and a nine-year-old?"

"Well, you're only seventeen," Dahlia retorted.

"And you've never been out in the forests or cities anyway," Marigold added.

I rested my hands on my hips. Three sisters gone on an adventure? *That* would be a story. But I had to think rationally. I was the eldest after all. If Mother found us all gone at once, she would likely believe we'd been taken and send every soldier out to search every corner of the land. If they found us, they'd make us return home. I would only get a couple of days to search.

But if I went alone, if Dahlia and Marigold were both safe, Mother might only send a few soldiers out, or even only the scouts. She would know I went off to find a cure. Or I could leave a note explaining I was too afraid to face them as a dragon and secluded myself just in case.

Finally, I shook my head. "I believe it's safer for us all if you stay here."

Both of my sisters scowled at me.

"Mother will send everyone after us if we all go," I explained. "We wouldn't be able to search anywhere for long."

Dahlia relented. "I suppose that's a good point." She rolled her eyes.

Marigold pouted and looked away.

I gave them both a smile. "Just imagine. If I find this cure, everything will be normal. No more dragon. No more curse. No more sorceress looming over us."

Dahlia stood and gave me a hug. "We'll help you get ready. After all, you don't know a single thing about surviving outside of the castle."

She was right.

But I'd already resolved to find my cure and couldn't let a hurdle like surviving stand in my way.

Had I been brave enough, I would have believed it and left that night.

NINE

Gerard had only been gone a few days, but the story—and my decision to leave—sat on my chest like a bag of stones. I knew what I needed to bring on my journey, having spent time watching Gerard pack, but he knew what to do *and* he had two men going with him. As much as I would have loved to have my sisters tag along, I knew in my heart it would be a bad decision.

I rolled out of bed, took one of the candlesticks, and whispered, "Allul," to summon its light. A wizard long ago had brought enchanted objects to us, and the lights and candlesticks were just a few.

First, I needed a bag, and then I would need the horse and saddlebags. Which meant I also needed to get Philip awake. As I walked down the hallway, I paused at a tapestry of Griswil. It had little detail, just the shape of the country, fancy lettering, and a few things we were known to sell—nuts, fruits, and other things trees produced. I'd seen it so frequently but had never stopped to actually look at it. I recognized one thing from it—I needed to know where I was going, which meant I had to find a map.

I tiptoed to the library knowing the table under the window had a map on it. The map had been there for as long as I could remember. So, I took that, rolled it up, and continued on my way.

Unfortunately, I had no idea where to find a travel bag. I had never packed my own things when traveling to the other kingdoms for their seasonal celebrations. Not once had I questioned where my things were kept or the bags that held them.

All this preparation made me understand why Gerard had been snooping about so early in the morning. He didn't want anyone to interrupt him while he searched. Perhaps explaining things would have been worse for him, like they would be for me. Luckily, when I reached the kitchen, I found a large hemp bag on the floor with potatoes in it. The cook would be upset with me for dumping them all over the pantry, but I needed the bag. And, come to think of it, several potatoes.

Gerard had mentioned taking dry meat instead of raw because it wouldn't go bad. I found dry beef, lamb, and even deer bundled up on a shelf by the back door. They had just come back from the smoker's, judging by the red stamp on the wrappings.

As I looked for vegetables I came to the realization I would have to cook all of my own meals. I'd only ever tried my hand at cooking once and failed. Doubt began to creep into my mind. I wasn't confident in my ability to take care of Tao, or traveling, or navigating.

Things were already off to a horrible start.

Maybe if I asked Mother if I could go, she would send someone with me, like Philip. Then again, if I asked Mother, she could very well keep me locked in my room until Gerard returned, and I didn't want that.

I started throwing random pieces of food in the hemp bag.

Footsteps sounded a warning, and I whispered, "*Lulla*," and the candle went out, leaving me in the pantry in complete darkness.

The glow from the nearing candlelight grew brighter the closer it came, and it didn't take long for the familiar face of Abby to appear as she stepped in front of the doorway. She wore a scowl on her face, which quickly changed to surprise. "Princess!"

I sighed. "Allul." My candle lit once more.

"I was about to scold one of the children for getting into the food. What are you doing awake so early in the morning? And—" Her eyes stopped on the bag in my hands and then drifted to the spilled potatoes.

"Please don't say anything!" I blurted. "If Mother knows I'm leaving, she'll stop me."

"Leaving? And where are you going?"

I licked my lips. I needed to stick with the lie we'd come up with last night. "With Gerard gone and the dragon starting to take control over me"—I looked down at my hands for emphasis—"I'm afraid things are going to keep changing. If I'm here and I fully transform, who knows what will happen? I'm going to go find somewhere to stay where I can't hurt anyone."

"Princess Elisa, this is your home."

"I know. Which is why I can't stay." I swallowed hard and looked pleadingly at the woman. "Please. Please don't tell my mother."

"Of course not. I just worry you won't know what to do. Let me see in that bag of yours."

I held it out.

Abby took it and carried it to the spotless counter and rummaged inside. She mumbled under her breath, then shook her head. "This isn't a bad start, but you'll need spices so you can cook something tasty. You really should have someone go with you." She looked at me sideways.

I rubbed my arm. "I thought about asking Philip."

She nodded. "He would be good to bring."

Sunrise glowed through the window over the sink, and I knew I wasn't going to make it out of the castle anytime soon. I still needed a bag for my clothing.

"I would imagine you need cooking supplies as well?"

I grimaced. "Yes, please?"

"I've got some old pots here, let me see …" She rummaged through the bottom cupboard and produced three pots she deemed too big until she came to a small pot and pan just barely bigger than the size of my hand. "These would do wonderfully for you. You aren't cooking for an army." She put them in the bag as well. "Do you have a travel bag?" she asked.

"I was going to search ..." My ears grew hot. "No."

The cook patted my arm. "Let me see what I can dig out of my closet. You stay here. And if anyone asks what you're doing here, just say you're watching the sunrise or something." She shuffled back down the hall.

With Abby's help, I was able to pack for my journey. She brought me a good-sized travel bag and instructed me to pack only clothing that was necessary, a couple of blankets, and she insisted on medicine and a few other items. She even helped me carry everything to the stable.

I was surprised to see Philip already up and feeding the horses, and he looked just as surprised to see me carrying a heavy pouch with the cook trailing behind, her arms burdened with the cooking materials and bag of food.

"Are you going somewhere?" he asked, rushing over to take the bag from me and then Abby.

"It doesn't matter," I replied. "I need Tao saddled and these things loaded in his saddlebags." I walked past Philip to greet the old horse I'd grown fond of.

He leaned out so I could pet him.

"Hello, Tao." I smiled, excitement bubbling in my stomach.

"I recommend you eat breakfast with your family," Abby suggested. "Speaking of which, I must get back and get cooking." She gave a little curtsey and hurried off.

Philip went to a saddle resting on some sort of bench with other saddles and began loading the supplies into the two pouches. "Are you running away?"

"Sort of," I confessed. I turned my head to look at him. "Unless you would like to join me."

Phillip blanched. "You want me to go with you?" He searched me with his eyes. "Are you insane?"

"I would appreciate someone going with me. Besides, you know your way around better than I do. And I trust you." I didn't know Phillip all that well, but he was kind.

He filled his cheeks with air and slowly let it out. "I don't think that's such a great idea. If something happens to you, I don't want to be responsible. It's my life on the line."

I couldn't fully blame him, but the rejection still stung. "Fine. Then I order you to stay quiet about my departure." I left him to load everything onto Tao and returned to the castle for breakfast. I still needed to write the letter to my mother, detailing the lie.

Breakfast was … odd. I acted like it was a normal day while I knew it wasn't. Marigold was already feeling better, and Dahlia was chatting with her excitedly about a dream she had that night about the flowers entering the castle and dancing. My heart already ached for the company of my sisters and I hadn't even left yet.

"Gerard sent another letter," Mother said.

I tore my gaze away from my sisters. He'd just barely sent one the day before, so I was skeptical at first he'd written it, but the envelope was sealed with the same crest Gerard had used before, so it must have come from him. I broke the seal and read the uneventful letter that explained he had reached Andorin and still no sign of the fairies. It had been only four days. I hadn't expected that much luck to be on my side anyway. My heart fluttered, though, when he closed the letter with, "I miss you, my love."

I softly bit my lip and closed the letter.

"Where is he?" Mother asked casually.

"They reached Andorin." I tucked the paper under the edge of my plate and took the last few bites of my eggs.

"And?"

I glanced over. "And still no faeries." I finished my orange juice and got to my feet. "I need to use the restroom, and then I will go to my study." I nodded to my mother and father, and it took every ounce of self-control not to give my sisters a tight squeeze.

Who knew when I would see them again?

I did, however, give them a wink before exiting the dining hall. In fact, I made it all the way to the stables, where Philip had Tao ready for me, before Dahlia and Marigold caught up.

"You're really leaving?" Dahlia asked the instant she was close enough.

"It was your idea." I looked from one to the other. "I will be fine."

"We're coming!" Marigold ordered. "Philip, get—"

"No," I said firmly. "You could still be ill, and I can't turn around to bring you home."

Marigold pouted and folded her arms across her chest.

Dahlia jumped forward and hugged me tightly. "I love you. You'll find a way to break this. You will. And then you'll come back and everything will be perfect. The way it should be."

Marigold took Dahlia's place when she stepped away.

"Good heavens, you two." I wiped at my eyes before either of them saw tears. "I'll be quite all right. I'll be safe. You two be safe as well. Okay?" I put my hand on Marigold's cheek.

She nodded. "Mother won't know until dinner."

Dahlia straightened. "I'll keep an eye on Marigold."

I almost stayed.

I almost gave up, and would have had the little voice in my head not insisted I leave that moment. I got on Tao's back and began my journey, giving one last look over my home and my sisters.

The castle had been built from dark maple wood, while the roof and accents were from a lighter walnut. The line along the top of the roof had curls, almost like the waves of the ocean, and the walnut shutters had also been carved into intricate designs, not to mention the beautiful eagles that sat at each corner of the roof.

It would be days, possibly even weeks, before I saw my home again, but leaving it behind also filled me with excitement. I was on my way on an adventure of my own.

The temperature was perfect, the sun glowing in bright patches between branches or through long stretches between trees. I unrolled the map, which I'd made sure was easily accessible, and held it in front of me. I knew where the castle was and pointed to the road I was on. Gerard had gone eastward, so I would head westward. Perhaps, eventually, we would meet up when I turned to the north, and then I would travel with someone.

It had taken Gerard four days to get from the capital city of Fonland to the town of Andorin. Using that small space on the map as a reference, I looked at the town of Handlin, where I was headed, and estimated it would take a day to get there. I rolled the map back up and tucked it away.

I chose to enjoy the time I had. Birds sang, a gentle breeze began to blow, and I watched in amusement as a squirrel scampered along a branch and disappeared up the tree. I'd chosen to take a back path instead of the main road, mostly so the soldiers wouldn't find me right away if Mother sent them after me.

After a few hours, however, my excitement died and anxiety sat heavy in the pit of my stomach like a rock. I tried to take in every detail of the foliage. The flowers lining the trail changed little—tiny bright white and yellow flowers with a shocking orange streak down the center of each petal, large purple flowers with huge black centers, and now and then a bluebell or hyacinth.

Stories made adventures feel so grand.

I had no idea how boring a journey could be.

With no one to talk to, and the same trees and flowers for hours, there wasn't much else to do but think. Think about Gerard in Andorin, a city northeast of Fonland. I'd never personally been there, but according to the pictures in the books Mother made me read, it was rather large and sat upon a hill among the peach and apple orchards. I also thought about the letter I left behind detailing to my mother I was going into hiding until Gerard returned. She would know it to be a foolish idea on my part, because how were they to tell me Gerard was back? How would they know where I went? I wasn't *that* resourceful.

My stomach growled, and I lifted my gaze to the sky. I couldn't really tell, even with the gaps between trees, what time of day it was. Judging by the second growl, I estimated it must be around lunchtime. I didn't want to stop to eat, even though I did want to stop to stretch. My legs and back already ached due to my years of inexperience.

I turned in the saddle and rummaged through the top of the bag and pulled out an apple and the small jar of peanut butter. I bit off a piece of the apple, dipped it in the peanut butter, and ate it. It was a fabulous snack, and then I ate a small sandwich Abby had put in as well. I would miss her cooking and dreaded what would happen with dinner that night.

I dusted off my lap, licked the last bit of peanut butter from my index finger, and heaved a bored sigh. "Well, Tao, it's just you and me. I didn't realize how long this journey was going to feel. Any ideas on how to find a fae?"

Tao tilted his head side to side as if to say "no," and I giggled.

I leaned down and patted his neck.

More hours passed.

When the path widened and I spotted a village at the bottom of the hill, I smiled, grateful to have finally reached somewhere. According to the map, this should have been Handlin. These arborists focused mostly on limes and lemons. At least, that's what I had learned from my geography classes. Clearly I'd misjudged the distance on the map. I didn't expect to reach there so soon. I had gauged it to take me until the end of the day. I had hoped to stop and rest there for the night, but there were still plenty of hours in the daylight for me to travel. I didn't want to lose on travel just for a place close enough to sleep.

I couldn't resist a grin as I entered the town and heard children laughing. A group of them ran down the street with a dog running alongside, barking with excitement. I'd always wanted a dog. A mother called out, "Be careful!" as they passed.

I had no idea how the people of my land truly lived. This was my opportunity to see firsthand. The houses were tiny. Each home was perhaps only as large as my bedroom, with wooden roofs and walls. The homes stood in front of orchards of trees I recognized as orange trees, based on the paintings I'd seen, but I frowned. Handlin was supposed to produce lemons and limes, unless this particular orchard happened to harvest oranges.

A woman carrying a basket of clothing froze when she saw me.

I waved. "Good morning!"

"Y-Your Highness." She curtsied so low I thought she was going to end up on the ground.

"It's a lovely day," I said.

"Yes, indeed." She hesitated before rising back to her feet.

"I don't believe you've seen any faeries?"

She gave a quick smile when she realized I was only joking. "Afraid not, miss."

I shrugged and waved again. "Carry on."

Her eyes locked on my hand.

I'd completely forgotten about my hands until that moment, and my ears burned as I rushed to hide them. "Good day."

I didn't look back.

I knew I hadn't packed any gloves. The thought hadn't occurred to me once.

The walk through the town was gratefully short, and I carried on down a road, past a few wagons returning from somewhere or on their way to another town. Each time I was greeted with complete surprise, and I realized how much I'd missed by keeping myself shut up in the castle. My people had rarely seen me. I vowed to change that when I returned.

Until then, I needed to find a fae.

TEN

The sun began to set behind us, and I knew it was time to stop, get Tao some water, and I needed to figure out how I was going to sleep, not to mention how on earth I was going to cook my first meal.

I pulled the map out again. I had chosen to travel westward past Handlin. A river was supposed to run along the road, but I had failed to pay attention to that as we traveled. According to the map, the river started at the south end of the Drakespine Mountains, curved up around behind the castle, around the north side of Handlin, and then crossed the road and went northward to Tiswil. If I was where we were supposed to be, we should have seen the river cross the road at some point that day.

Then again, the arborists had to divert the river using canals and ditches to create their irrigation systems, but this map didn't have any of those marked. Even if I could only find an irrigation ditch for Tao, at least it would be water.

"Think you can find some water?" I asked. "Apparently I'm terrible at this. I have no idea exactly where we are." I pushed my lips to the side of my face and tilted the map, getting a look around. I *had* to be somewhere west in the gap between Handlin and Tiswil. Yet, I couldn't see a river anywhere.

Tao turned off the path to our left.

I ducked my head, but then the branches became too low for me to stay on his back. To make it easier, I swung my right leg off to get down, but dropped, hit the uneven ground, and landed on my bum hard.

I winced. "Ow."

At least no one was around to see that *lovely attempt,* I thought.

I got up, rubbing the tender spot on my behind, and took Tao's reins to continue deeper into the trees until he led me to the shallow, but wide, river. I exhaled a breath of relief. "Good job, Tao." I patted him on the neck and let go of his reigns.

Tao didn't hesitate to take a few steps into the water and lean down to get a drink.

I dropped my pack on the shore, grateful to get its weight off me, and groaned as I stretched. "This is going to be a long journey," I said to the horse. "I've got to figure out how to cook a meal and set up the camp. You'll stay close, won't you?"

Tao lifted his eyes, acknowledging me, then dipped his face back in the water.

I leaned precariously across the mud to open the saddlebag still on Tao's back, and barely managed to get my finger on the edge of the pot. Carefully, I removed it from the bag and got it away from the river without dropping it. After gathering a few dried logs and twigs, I opened the pack and removed one of the enchanted candles I'd brought with me.

"Allul," I said.

The candle lit, and I set it under the sticks until they finally caught and I had myself a little fire. I grinned at how clever I was and said, "Lulla," to put the light out. However, when I did that the fire also went out. I scowled. Apparently lighting a fire from an enchanted candle also made the fire enchanted.

The second time I lit the fire, I blew the candle out, then set it on a stone for the wax to cool before I put it back in my pack. I untied the bedroll from the bottom of the bag and laid it close to the fire, filled the pot with water, and set it on the logs of the fire.

I hadn't realized how rapidly the sun set when you had a lot to do.

Tao finished drinking and returned to shore, and I opened the saddlebags to try and pull out some food to cook. To my amazement, Abby had written down a series of recipes for me. My heart swelled with gratitude.

The first recipe was for the cured deer Abby had wrapped for me that morning. I removed the vial of oil, dribbled a bit in the pot, then unwrapped the meat and used the cloth to drop it in the pot, then set the pot on the fire. I tossed the rag aside and rummaged

106

through the saddlebag for the fork, knife, and spoon I'd watched Abby pack.

I followed the instructions to the best of my ability, and before the sun set completely, I had a meal of almost uncooked potatoes and delicious deer meat. I rinsed the dishes off in the river and laid them on the nearest stone to dry.

As soon as the last of the light was gone and night blanketed the sky, the temperature dropped. Even though I sat in front of a crackling fire, my back was cold. If I turned to warm my back, my front got cold. I pulled the two blankets from my pack, wrapped them around me, and lay down on my meager bed.

I looked over at Tao as he lay down with a whinny.

"I know, it's not the barn. I bet you were much warmer there."

He itched at his back with his teeth, and I grimaced.

"Sorry, I don't know how to take the saddle off. And even if I got it off, I don't know how I would put it back on. Hopefully, when we get to the next town, someone will be willing to give you a proper bath and then you can have a break from the saddle and bags.

He didn't seem happy about it, but he relaxed.

I looked up at the stars. I'd seen them hundreds of times, but there was something inspiring about seeing them in the middle of the forest with a crackling fire beside me. I closed my eyes and tried to get some sleep.

In spite of having the mat, there was a rock in my ribs. I scooted the mat a little, only to find a tree root under my legs. No matter where I moved, or how I lay, something poked at me through the thin mat, and it was barely more comfortable than just lying in the dirt.

When I finally got into a comfortable spot, I surveyed the clearing one last time and gasped when I saw a pair of eyes staring at me from the brush. I froze in horror. The eyes drew nearer, pausing now and then to assess and see if I was dangerous. When it got close enough to the fire, I realized it was just a small raccoon. It scurried past the fire toward the river.

I blew a raspberry through my lips, relief washing over me, and closed my eyes again. I tried to convince myself I wasn't vulnerable, that no wolf was going to show up and eat me.

Eventually I fell asleep.

When I woke, however, I had never felt so sore in my entire life. Every part of my body ached as I sat up, including my stomach with hunger. The air was cold enough I could see my breath, and the fire had gone out during the night.

I managed to find the candle again and got the fire started, only to realize I hadn't considered what I would do for the bathroom. That was an adventure in and of itself, and I would be wise to leave that out when I wrote the book about this.

I managed to scramble an egg and nibbled on a couple of pieces of jerky, then packed up the camp, smothered the fire, and got back in Tao's saddle to continue my journey.

The second day wasn't any more adventurous or exciting than the first day. I spent a lot of time daydreaming. I imagined what it would be like to have a little home by the river, living as commoners did, and doing housework while my husband worked in the orchards or on the farm.

That led me to wonder more about Gerard. Where would we live after we were married? Would I go to his kingdom? I paused mid-chew on my chunk of dried and seasoned deer meat I'd grabbed to snack on. He'd never been introduced as *Crown* Prince, which meant someone else was before him in line to the throne. Because of that, he would live with me. Perhaps he and I could get to know the kingdom a little better together.

At lunch, I retrieved a small satchel of cheese, some crackers, and a little handful of dried berries. I hoped Tao was eating enough, and that thought alone caused me to stop and climb off his back.

"You need to eat, Tao," I said. "And this is the perfect time for me to stretch my legs." I put my hands on my hips and leaned from one side to the other.

He didn't object, though he continued walking down the path.

"Wait, where are you going?" I hurried after him. "You need to eat."

We turned down a bend in the road, and the ambiance of the forest suddenly changed. My fingertips prickled. The breeze changed directions. A meadowlark gently warbled somewhere in the distance, but there was something ... special about this place.

Tao's ears shifted backward, and he slowed to a stop without my prompting. I didn't understand what had prompted Tao to stop here, of all places, until I walked a few steps to see around the thick trunk of a tree. Although the road bent eastward, just beyond the trunk was a small pathway. Tao had stopped there and looked at me as though telling me to go that direction.

It looked like no more than a game trail. Yet it beckoned to me.

The instant my foot touched the trail, a rush of peace washed over me. *Yes, this is the way*, the voice in my head told me. I walked a few paces and looked over my shoulder at the horse. In the rays of the sunlight, he seemed to glow. And then I blinked and the mirage was gone.

"Are you coming?" I asked.

Tao shook his head with a snort and began to nibble on some pink flowers.

I carried on alone. The worn stones on the path were organized in rows and each was the beginning of a long, leveled section. These created a natural staircase that had been covered after years of neglect. One section was ruined from obvious signs of mountain runoff.

All around me, the tall trees gently swayed, their leaves shifting overhead. I was beginning to grow accustomed to the peace of the forest. I tilted my face up to the sun and let out a heavy breath, releasing stress with it.

As I watched the trees move, I inclined my head. I felt no breeze. It wasn't uncommon to see the trees ripple before a breeze touched my skin, but I didn't feel a thing.

A chill ran down my spine, and I stopped walking.

My shoulders tightened and my gaze darted from the trees on one side of the path to the other. Only then did I hear their whispers. The human side of me wanted to turn around and flee, but the dragon side of me was instantly curious.

The dragon side won out.

Carefully, I began walking again. This time, I was more alert than before.

I'd been raised on tales of trees that could talk, back in the days of faeries and dragons. I'd also heard faeries had once been able to speak to the trees. Perhaps the trees were excited about my presence. Somehow the lack of birds tweeting and other forest noises told me otherwise.

In spite of their warning movements, I relished in the sounds of the trees.

At the top of the small staircase, I turned to look the way I'd come. The path had curved around the front of a hill. I hadn't noticed the path from below. Tao chewed on a mouthful of thick green grass, and lifted his gaze to me as if he'd felt it.

I took the last step and faced the open space before me. The knee-high grass was being over taken with spindly weeds, and flowers poked up here and there. Everything was still, once again confirming there was no breeze.

Beyond the open meadow stood a large, beautiful ivory building.

I didn't need to be a fae to see this building must have been significant.

The alabaster wood had aged and had nearly been reclaimed by the vines engulfing half the building, but it still stood out from the dark trunks of the spruce and pine trees. I couldn't recall having ever seen a building more beautiful. Like the castle I'd grown up in, the windows were tall and narrow, closing to a point at the top. Most of the panes were missing or broken. The frames of the windows had been carved to look like a spiraled rope. No, vines, and now and then leaves poked out. The edges of the roof were also carved, and the roof itself curved into a low dome with a spire at the top.

The building had clearly been abandoned.

From the carvings of leaves on the askew doors, knots of wooden symbols between the windowpanes, and mere architecture, I knew this had once been a fairy cathedral. I tentatively approached, mesmerized by the vines guiding their way along the gaps in the wood like the veins of a hand.

The door sat ajar, beckoning me to enter.

I halted at the threshold. My heart clenched. My throat tightened.

The faeries had run away from their homes, their lands, their places of worship.

I was the cause of their fleeing to safety.

I was responsible for their deaths.

I couldn't bring myself to step inside. I was unworthy to be there. Tears stung my eyes. I didn't want to be disrespectful or irreverent. If there were any fairies here, would they even show themselves to me?

I wiped at my tears and turned away.

Don't go!

"Oh hush," I told myself.

The faeries could have a magical spell on the place, making it appear as though it's abandoned, to keep it hidden from the world. You've come so close!

It was true. This was the closest sign I had to faeries even existing in the first place, aside from the stories I'd been told my entire life. If the faeries had seen me as I traveled, they likely would have avoided me—if they knew *I* was the cause of their suffering.

The black space in the doorway called to me, like when you stand at the edge of a dark pit and something feral inside you tells you to leap.

I drew a deep breath and followed my feet across the threshold.

The trees went silent.

A huge weight pressed in on me as if my mother's eyes were watching my every movement. I reached out and gripped the frame of the door, feeling the brittle wood break under my fingernails. The sunlight behind me lazily peeled away the darkness, allowing my eyes to adjust to the sudden dimness. To my right, the room was far more narrow than it appeared outside. Rows of broken benches lined the path to the stone altar, and light shone on it from the broken panes. Had it not been for the domed roof and intricate carvings, one might have argued its purpose had once been that of a greenhouse.

I wet my lips, taking in the weeds that had broken through the stone floor and the wooden benches that had been reclaimed by the roots of trees. In my mind's eye, I could see faeries garbed in glittering robes, sitting in the chairs, singing words to songs I didn't know, giving their offerings on the altar before a priest.

Their entire culture had been lost to us.

I turned to my left. A shallow space I assumed had once been a pond was now bone dry. The sunlight glinted off golden frames. I stepped into the darkness and turned to look at the paintings on the walls to my left and across the room. Most paintings were images of people or places.

One painting in particular caught my attention. Hidden beneath the vines, a lavender eye peered out. I walked around the dried pool, branches and leaves snapping and crunching under my feet. I tugged the vines away to reveal the image hidden behind it.

Stunning lavender eyes looked back at me with such intensity I staggered backward. She could have been real. The woman sat straight, but she looked more regal than a queen. Even in the painting, she had an air of grace. Her long blond hair was braided on the left side, her dress was silver and white, and her hands rested on the pommel of a sword with a purple stone set in the hilt.

My heart jumped. *That* had to be the spring stone.

The stories of the faeries didn't do the painting any justice, and I doubted it truly captured the real beauty of the mysterious woman.

The sound of something hitting the ground made me jump, and I wheeled around to survey the room. No dust appeared to be settling from the ceiling, there were no new holes, so the roof hadn't fallen. No trees had broken or benches had collapsed.

I swallowed hard. My insides were screaming at me to run, get out in the sunlight, but my body moved against my will toward the direction the sound had come from—a small alcove to my right. I peered over a tall weed and stopped when I saw a foot.

My eyes widened. The hair on the back of my neck prickled.

This was the one thing I'd wanted my entire life—to find a fae. But the thought this could be that moment, that I could truly have found a cure ... I didn't believe it. It seemed too surreal.

I took one step.

Then two.

With a final step, I saw beyond the wall, to the form of a young man in a heap on the floor. I rushed over immediately and fell to my knees but could only stare.

His skin was pale but, unlike mine, it looked like it had a glow, not that he'd been locked in a castle his entire life. His hair had a soft blue hue, and his clothing was far different than any I'd seen in Griswil. The material reflected the sunlight like the sun glistening off a lake.

My heart raced so hard, my hands trembled. I reached out and brushed the hair from his face to look at the curve of his thin nose, his pointed chin, soft blue brows, and then ... pointed ears. They were pointed.

This was a fae boy.

A real fae.

A living fae.

At least, an unconscious one. The sunlight blinded my eyes, waking me from my stupor. I reached out and shook his shoulder, but his eyes only shifted behind closed lids.

"Hello?" I asked. "Do you need help?"

No answer.

I heard whispering again and lifted my gaze to the window nearby.

The tree just beyond shifted a few of its branches, whispering again.

I shook my head. "I don't understand."

Stop listening with your ears, my inner voice instructed.

I closed my eyes and felt peace wash over me, like when I'd first begun up the trail. As I relaxed, the muscles in my body tingled and my heart calmed. I opened my eyes again. The sunlight spilling through the window focused only on the boy's lips. I looked at the window. The tree's leaves and branches blocked out all other light.

"You want me to touch his lips?" I reached out and touched my fingers to them. "He is still breathing."

The tree trembled as though to say "no" and moved back into the shape it had been in, once again directing the sunlight onto the stranger's lips.

I pursed my lips to one side of my face. "He cannot speak." Again, I glanced at the tree.

I could have sworn its branches were made into lips that puckered.

"You want me to kiss him?" I gaped.

The tree stretched its branches.

I blinked. Kiss the boy? One I'd never met? I felt a blush crawl into my cheeks.

"But I am betrothed," I tried to argue.

He won't know. He's asleep! my inner voice yelled at me.

I touched his cheek and turned his face. This boy was the most handsome being I'd ever seen. I almost dared think he was more handsome than Gerard. If the tree wanted me to kiss him, who was I to argue?

But I'd never been kissed.

Grateful no one else was near, I leaned down. *Oh, for the sake of all the stars in the heavens!* I crushed my lips to his, entirely too hard and not a beautiful moment at all. Our teeth tapped against each other, and I jerked back as suddenly as I'd moved forward. I wiped my mouth. I didn't dare look at the tree. It was probably laughing at me.

The boy's eyes fluttered and languished open. They widened immediately before he bolted upright and pressed his back tightly to the wall. "Ayan din?" he demanded. His eyes darted and locked on my scaled hand.

I hurriedly hid it behind my back. "My name is Elisa," I said carefully.

I had studied the fae language my entire life, but I'd never heard it with my ears before, and I wasn't confident by any means in speaking it. I also didn't feel it necessary to introduce myself as the princess. He was already startled, and if the faeries blamed me for Selina killing them, I wouldn't tell him I was the princess.

"What is your name?" I pressed.

117

He stared at my face with the same beautiful lavender eyes as the woman in the painting. "Your hands ... are black," he said in perfect English.

My heart jumped in panic. "They're only gloves."

"Then why are you hiding them?"

I bit the inside of my lips. If I was honest, he would likely run, and I couldn't risk that. "It's ... only that—"

"You're the princess, aren't you?" He climbed to his feet in such a sudden movement he leaned and nearly fell.

I jumped to my own feet. "Please don't go!" I blurted, reaching out for him.

"Why not?" He looked like a cat ready to dart at any moment.

"Because ... because I need your help."

His lavender eyes narrowed. "Why should I help *you*?" He emphasized each word and his voice dripped with such animosity it stole my breath.

I couldn't swallow, although I tried. "Why are you here?" I asked, trying to change the subject.

"It doesn't matter to *you*. And you avoided my question." He crossed his arms.

"You avoided mine," I said back, mimicking his pose. "I asked your name."

"Why would I give my name to the woman who could get me killed? I've already entertained you too long." He turned with such grace the leaves under his boots didn't even shift, and walked several steps before I came to my senses.

"Please! Please, I'm begging you," I said, rushing after him. "You have to help me with my curse!"

"Not my problem."

I grabbed his arm before he could make it out a side door I hadn't noticed before.

He looked down at my hand, hissed, and pulled away. "Don't touch me."

I expected to freeze and cry. Or worse, snap at him and tear him apart. The conflict between the two emotions forced me to step back and tighten my hands into fists. "Your people promised to break my curse. I would think you have honor."

The boy's jaw flexed, and he glared down his nose at me. "We would never make such a promise."

"You have the spring stone! I know it can save me!" I hated that I was begging. "Please, just ... try. Once the curse is lifted, your people will be safe."

"Is that a threat?" He twitched his blue brow.

"I helped you just moments ago. I don't even have a weapon on me!" I patted my sides to point out I wore no weapon belt and then yanked up my skirts to show him I had no dagger hidden on my ankles.

He stood in the doorway, looking me over like I might tear him to shreds.

I couldn't blame him. But I also couldn't let him walk out.

"I received a letter the day of my birthday. It said the last of the faeries was found dead. I left on my own to search the kingdom myself. I had to know if there were faeries, and I found you. You're my only hope of breaking my curse. Please." I gasped a breath, holding back the tears. "Please help me."

His face softened, and for a moment I believed he would relent. "Like I said, I've never heard of such a thing." He stepped outside.

"It was years ago! When I was born!" I chased after him.

"I don't care."

I stepped in front of him and put my hand on his chest, stopping him. "You *will* help me. I am the crown princess of Griswil, your ruler."

His lip twitched, and again, he moved away from my touch. "Or what?" he sneered. "You'll kill me too?" He stepped around me. "You are *not* my ruler. You don't rule any of the faeries."

I didn't chase him this time, though my feet wanted to. I didn't beg him to save me. But I wasn't about to give up. I watched the direction he went, and he disappeared around a tall bush. I sprinted back to Tao, who'd only moved a few feet, and jumped up onto his back.

"Come on, Tao!" I kicked him in the ribs.

He gave me a confused snort and looked at me as he started in a walk.

"No, you need to run! Come on!" I kicked him a few times, harder.

He skipped into a trot, making his way up the path and around the abandoned building, and I directed him in the same space I'd seen the fae boy disappear. When we broke through the bush, I found a little path and grinned.

"Keep going, Tao. I found a fae."

ELEVEN

We got stuck at a crossroads.

The fae had completely disappeared and left no sign of his passing. If he had, I wouldn't have noticed it anyway. It wasn't exactly my expertise. But there was a path leading left, and one leading to the right, and I had no idea where to go.

Neither direction looked different.

"What do you think, Tao?" I asked.

He only snorted in response.

"I don't know either." My heart sank to the pit of my stomach. "To think I was that close …" I looked down at my dragon arms and gritted my teeth. I promptly turned on the seat and dug into the saddlebag until I found the bandages. I wrapped them around my hands, and then arms, ripping the last piece off with my teeth. Only my fingertips were exposed, but at least the rest of the scales were hidden.

I shoved the remaining bandages in the bag and guided Tao to the right. Unless the road split again, I could turn around and come back this direction knowing all I had to do was continue straight. If I didn't find a fae town this way, there would have to be one the opposite direction.

The path descended, and the further we went, the more the trees seemed to step away from the path, which allowed the hot afternoon sun to shine down on me. At first, I didn't mind, and I even welcomed the warmth. After all, spring mornings were cold, and since Griswil was forever in a perpetual state of springtime, it felt nice to have warmth.

A few hours later, gauging by the sun's angle, the full heat of the sun was on me. My arms and hands were uncomfortably warm in particular. I didn't understand why the black scales felt cooler than having them wrapped up in white cloth. From my studies, dragons were cold-blooded, just like lizards, and soaked up the heat from the sun. Perhaps I'd been so cold the night before because the temperature of my blood had dropped too. Still, there was a lot I didn't know about the way a dragon's body worked. And I didn't want to.

Finally too hot, I had to stop and direct Tao off the path and under the shade of nearby trees. My stomach loudly reminded me it needed sustenance. A break for food and from the sun for a little while sounded wonderful.

I stretched my back the instant I stood on the ground. I couldn't hold back a grimace as I tried to straighten. Sitting on a horse all day caused my hips and lower back to ache in a way they'd never hurt before.

Tao turned his head and scratched at his back under the saddle.

I knew I hadn't taken the saddle off him once, and if he was as hot and sweaty as me, he must have been terribly itchy and uncomfortable. But if I took it off, I would never get it back on.

"Maybe I'll try taking that off tonight," I said, trying to reassure him. I reached out and patted his hot neck. "Hm. You probably need some water. But I haven't heard the sounds of a stream or river ..." I looked around.

Having followed the river the last couple of days, I had become accustomed to seeing certain types of foliage, like the tall weeds with brown fuzzy parts that looked like fat caterpillars, and thin flowers with white stems and pink tips. None of those plants were nearby. Perhaps further in the trees?

"I'm going to try and find some water for you." I took the water pouch and sipped from it as I pushed through the undergrowth and made my way toward the tree line.

Like the trees at the cathedral, these trees began to whisper, and I glanced up at them.

They were taller, the trunks thicker.

I'd been intimidated by the trees before, but one had ended up helping me to wake the fae. I wasn't intimidated now. So I stepped further into their shade and glanced over my shoulder to make sure Tao was staying put. I was lucky to have him for a companion. Philip's father was right about not needing to tie up a horse loyal to me.

"I'll be back!" I called to him.

He lifted his head and swiveled his ears. He lifted his chin, looking at the trees, and snorted with a toss of his head.

I carried on into the forest, stepping over fallen logs and around bushes. Still, there was no sound or sign of water. I thought we had gone in the same direction as the main path we'd been on, but the river must have been farther away than I'd thought.

With a dejected sigh, I turned around and began walking the way I'd come.

The trees seemed to crowd in on me, and their whispering became louder.

I swallowed hard and quickened my pace. Maybe these trees weren't as helpful as the others had been. I finally broke into a run, darting around trunks, and jumped out into the sun.

Tao blinked at me, his left ear swiveling again.

I drew a big breath. "I'm all right. I just got a little frightened." I glanced up at the trees, which had stopped moving. "I didn't find any water, though. Maybe this path will get us closer to the water."

I took a few moments to get some food out— bread, more dried meat, and an apple for both me and Tao, which he loved. And then we carried on our way again.

And nothing happened.

No signs of water, no signs of any fae village, nothing.

I began to wonder if I needed to return to the castle and tell them about my findings, that clearly they had missed something in their searches, and that we needed to amass an army to help find them again and get rid of this curse once and for all.

We rounded a large bend in the road, and the trees' whispering resumed. I rolled my eyes. "I'm not walking through the forest to harm anyone. I'm trying to find the faeries, that's all. And if we could find water, we would be very grateful. Tao is very thirsty." I rubbed the horse's neck for emphasis.

The trees grew silent, and I finally relaxed again.

"Look ahead! A meadow! That will be the perfect spot to rest for the night." I rubbed Tao's neck again. "I'll take the saddle off, too, so you can get some proper rest tonight."

We entered the meadow, and I climbed off, dropped my bag on the ground, and bent over to look at the latch holding the saddle on Tao's belly. It wasn't difficult to unlatch at all, but when I tried to lift the saddle off, I immediately dropped it. It was a lot heavier than I'd anticipated, especially with the saddlebags. I removed the saddlebags, heavy from the food and cookware, and tried to lift the saddle again. With a grunt, I managed to lift the saddle enough to slide it off his back and onto the ground.

"There." I wiped my hands on my dress.

His skin twitched, and he trotted to a nearby tree to get a proper scratch on the bark.

I crouched and laid out the bedroll first, pushed aside weeds to make room for a fire, and then removed all the twigs I'd collected from our previous camping spot. I stacked the sticks on top of each other, grabbed a few pieces of the nearby dry grass, and dug out the candlestick I'd been smart enough to grab. When the fire was lit, I opened the saddlebag to take a look at what to make.

Unfortunately, I didn't have water tonight unless I used what was in my second water pouch, which wasn't ideal. What I wouldn't do for some fresh fish. I knew I could grill some vegetables, so I took the small knife, cut up a pepper, and dropped in some pieces of the dried meat. I cut up a potato and finished it off with some carrots.

It tasted as good as it sounds, meaning not very good at all. The potatoes were burnt on the outside and crunchy in the middle, as were the carrots. The dried meat was even drier than before, but I had to eat. I forced it down and then lay on my back under the open sky to watch the stars peek out as the sun's brightness faded.

"I really miss Dahlia and Marigold," I admitted out loud. "This would be a lot more fun with them here. And I bet Marigold would have some ideas of what to cook." I sighed and rolled over to check on Tao.

He was lying in the cool grass, likely relieved to relax for a few hours.

I pulled the bandages from my hands to allow my arms to breathe and stretched my fingers before I closed my eyes and rested my head on my arms. Going out on an adventure sounded like a wonderful and brave idea. I regretted it now. I wanted a proper bed, a proper meal, and for every muscle in my body to not ache.

I was also lonely.

This was nothing like the books.

I was just drifting off to sleep when an intense pressure took hold of my ankles. I winced in pain before peeling my eyes open to see what was happening. To my shock, tree roots had wrapped around my ankles, pinning them to the ground, and more roots were slowly clawing their way from the soil.

"Tao, run!" I screamed.

I reached for the saddlebag, but roots shot up from the ground and grabbed my left arm. I gasped but managed to snatch the bag with my right arm before the roots could grab it and pulled out the only knife I had. Without hesitation, I drove the blade into the roots. This sent a shockwave through them. They violently trembled, and then even more sprung up around me.

"Someone, help!" I screamed, tearing at the roots.

Tao trotted over, snorting, but as he drew closer, the roots tried to reach for him too. He started stomping his feet, then rose up to his back legs and let out a shrill whinny.

"Leave him alone! Ah!" The roots seized my arm holding the knife and yanked it down to the ground.

"What are you doing? I didn't do anything to you! Stupid trees." I tried to pull away, grappling at the roots, but the harder I struggled, the tighter the roots became. "What do I do?" I asked myself. But the voice that had been guiding me didn't know either.

I tried relaxing. I took slow breaths and stopped moving.

The roots pulled on my arms, forcing me to the ground, where they wrapped around me. I tried fighting again, struggling, gritting my teeth.

You can't let yourself die! What kind of a dragon are you?

"I'm not a dragon!"

Defend yourself, you fool!

I growled, trying to get my hands under me. I managed to lift my shoulder from the ground but couldn't get anything else off. I let out a shout, which strengthened into something much deeper and stronger, and the roots stopped moving.

I yanked against them, pulled upward, and one hand broke free. But when I tried tearing at the roots with the claws of my free hand, more roots came. It was as if the trees had waited for more to join in the fight. The roots continued to wrap around me like rope, pinning my arms down to my sides and legs together.

"No!" I screamed.

The soil grew higher and higher as they dragged me down. A tingling wave washed from my head to my toes as I began to lose sensation in my body. Roots wrapped around my face, and the last thing I saw was a wishing star streak across the night sky.

This was how I was going to die.

TWELVE

The raw voices of the trees whispered around me, and I heard a man's voice reply.

"She is no danger to you. I am aware she was in your forest. You don't get many travelers through here, but do you truly do this to each of them?"

He paused as the trees replied.

He sighed. "I know. I left her at the cathedral. I shall warn her to be careful where she travels. Now, let her up."

The roots began to reluctantly slide from my body.

When my face was freed, I gulped in the chilled air, and once the roots had completely returned to their place in the ground, I jumped to my feet and ran to the center of the road, the farthest I could get from any of the trees.

130

I put my hands on my knees and closed my eyes as I grasped to comprehend what had happened. "They tried to kill me!" I coughed. "The trees tried to kill me!"

The figure stood beyond the light of the fire, but I knew it had to be the stranger I'd met. He'd said he left me at the cathedral. His shoulders rose, and the firelight reflected off his eyes.

"You shouldn't be in this forest," he said, voice flat as if I were a stupid child.

"How was I supposed to know?" I snapped.

"Everyone knows not to enter the Ancient Wood."

"Evidently not me." I took another deep breath. "It's not on the map." I looked around, but couldn't see it. The whole area was a mess of overturned soil, my packs were dumped everywhere, and food lay scattered about.

Tao trotted over and nuzzled me repeatedly.

"I'm fine. I really am okay. Just ... afraid. I don't think I'll get any rest tonight." I wrapped my arms around his neck. "Are you hurt?" I crouched to check his ankles, but aside from some sore marks, they appeared to be fine.

"The dragon princess," the boy muttered.

I looked sideways at him. "What's that supposed to mean?"

"You should gather your things. I'll lead you out of the woods and you can be on your way."

I frowned and straightened. "Were you following me?"

The boy didn't answer.

"You really hate me enough to not talk to me? You don't even know me!"

"I don't need to," he snapped in response. "My people are dying because of you. My being willing to lead you out is the biggest act of kindness you will ever receive from any fae. I recommend you take advantage and then get your little royal-ness back to the castle."

I gritted my teeth and stormed over to my scattered supplies. The roots had completely destroyed my bedroll, I don't know why I even bothered to roll it up and bind it to the bottom of my pack. I got on my knees and started shoveling things into the pockets, ignoring the fact I also shoveled in handfuls of dirt and rocks.

Tears stung my eyes.

Hot and angry.

I had almost been killed by trees for being in the wrong part of the forest, I had found a fae who hated me so much he wouldn't even give me his name, I didn't know where I was or how I would sleep that night, and I would never break my curse.

I held the empty linen that had been for the dried meet on my lap. Most of the apples had survived, and the potatoes and carrots, but everything else was lost somewhere in the upset ground.

I will never break my curse.

Tears trickled down my face, and I smeared them away, not caring that I was smearing mud all over my face.

When I returned to the castle, Mother would be so angry. I would never be allowed from my room again. If Gerard found another fae in his travels, maybe there would be hope, but for me finding it myself? None.

I put the crook of my arm up to my mouth to stifle a sob.

The adrenaline shakes had left my hands, but the harsh reality that I really wasn't brave at all brought even more tears. I sniffled and tried to compose myself. I got to my feet and called for Tao.

He trotted over and waited patiently. I set the blanket on his back, then tried to hoist the saddle from the ground, but I was too exhausted from fighting the roots, still hungry, and too emotional.

With a shout, I threw the saddle down and spun around. "Are you going to just stand there and laugh at me in the dark?" I snapped.

"I wasn't laughing," the boy replied calmly. "I was watching you."

"You could at least help me." I lifted the collar of my dress to wipe at my face. "Please," I added softly.

He walked over and scooped up the saddle, easily lifted it, and set it on Tao's back. "Yes."

"Yes, what?"

"I followed you." He turned and faced me. "I was curious to see what you really were."

I sniffled. "Then why didn't you warn me about the forest before I entered it?" I replied, gesturing to the trees. "None of the trees look any different!"

He inclined his head. "You don't get out much, do you?"

I tightened my lips.

"I ask because anyone could see that these trees are much bigger than the new forest. The trunks are dark, the leaves are dark, the branches stretch much higher."

"Again, why didn't you stop me?"

He opened his mouth.

"Because you wanted the trees to take care of me?" I rolled my eyes and grabbed the saddlebags. I struggled with them, but when the fae stepped over to help, I pulled away. "I wouldn't want to touch you and poison you with my dragon scales," I said sharply.

His lips tightened, and he stepped back.

I set the bags on Tao's back, then grabbed my pack and put it on my bruised shoulders. "Lead the way, fae." I gestured down the road.

"It's this way." He gestured in the opposite direction I'd pointed.

I muttered under my breath. I stayed close to Tao's side and started walking, trying my hardest not to limp, but my left leg ached terribly.

The fae boy easily caught up and walked just a little ahead of me down the path. Suddenly, he said, "My name is Dormir." He looked over his shoulder at me.

I nodded softly.

"You truly came out here on your own to try and find a fae?"

I nodded again, my voice feeling raw. "My whole life my mother has sent scouts to try and find a fae who can help, but none have been successful. The faeries hide, and … I can't blame them." I glanced down at my hands. "I *know* your people are dying because of me. My curse." The lump in my throat tightened. "All I want is to be rid of this curse. I want to turn eighteen and become the queen I was raised to become. And then ... and then your people won't have to die. Selina wouldn't kill you."

Dormir scoffed. "Selina? Forgive me for not believing your story, Princess, but you pretend you're innocent."

"You believe I had a choice in whether or not to become a dragon?"

"I believe you have a choice in how you treat my people. You could provide shelter and protection. We are, after all, still part of this land."

I blinked. "We haven't known where your people lived. I can ask my mother."

Dormir shook his head. "Don't bother."

I was too tired to try and make sense of him. "Do you know about the spring stone?"

"I'm surprised *you* do." He looked over.

"Do you think ... maybe ..." I resisted the urge to look away from the road. "If you took me to your queen, perhaps she could use the spring stone to release me from this curse."

"You truly have no idea, do you?" he said, stopping in the road.

I shook my head. "I stayed in the castle because I was afraid I would hurt someone. Mother hired teachers for us—me and my sisters—but ... " I paused and bit my lip. "This is the longest I've been away from the castle. And I've never gone anywhere on my own."

His blue eyebrows lifted in evident surprise. "Why would you hurt someone?"

I held up my hands. "Remember?" I muttered. I started walking again, pulling Tao with me. "I know how to get back from here. You don't have to lead me. At the crossroads, I go left, past the cathedral, and then ... and then it's another day's journey to the castle."

"I would think you would be happy to be back in your bed."

"Bed, yes. I will be thrilled to see my sisters as well." I said nothing else.

"But?" Dormir pressed.

I stopped. "Would you want to go back to the castle knowing you'll turn into a dragon by the end of the year?" I scowled at him. "Would you want to go back to a life locked up like you're glass ready to break at any moment?"

He shrugged. "You have a home, good food, a family who loves you—what else could you want?"

"Freedom." My mouth blurted before I could stop it.

Dormir lifted a single brow this time.

I walked past him. "Goodnight, Dormir!" I stopped only long enough to get on Tao's back and then nudged him forward.

"Where will you rest?" Dormir called after me. "Your horse needs water."

"Well, I don't see a river nearby," I called back.

"That's because you don't know how to look." He caught up easily and walked at a brisk pace alongside.

"I thought you didn't care."

"I don't. I worry about your horse."

I rolled my eyes. "Tao is fine."

"How would you like to go all day without water?"

I frowned, knowing Dormir was right and hating it. "All right, lead me to water and then you'll never have to see me ever again."

We continued down the path a ways further, but then Dormir turned toward the trees.

"This way."

"Trees," I pointed out.

"Yes. But you're out of the Ancient Wood, so these trees won't harm you." He motioned to me with his hand. "See how they are smaller?"

For all I knew, he could be leading me to my death, and I wouldn't know any better.

Without any other choice, I followed. Luckily Dormir really did lead us to a river, and Tao was excited to walk in the water and get a drink. I stood on the shore with the only blanket around my shoulders, watching the stars overhead.

"Did you have those when we first met?" Dormir said, breaking my dreamy state.

"What?" I looked over at him.

"Your horns. They're new?"

I dropped the blanket and reached up to touch my head. Indeed, two horns jutted from the sides of my head and extended backward. They were short, as if they hadn't fully grown yet, but I didn't care. I searched the rest of my head, but no change seemed to have happened anywhere else. I hurried to the shoreline and tried to look at my reflection in the water but couldn't get a good look.

"No," I breathed in dread.

"You really are upset about this, aren't you?" Dormir stepped up to my side.

"Selina cursed me. I can't … can't be a dragon. If I turn into a dragon, she will take me. She will make me kill my family and destroy my kingdom, and then she will take over. I can't—I *won't* let that happen." I didn't care that I sounded desperate, but I needed to convince myself more than Dormir.

"For what it's worth, I am sorry," he said.

"No, you're not," I whispered. "You don't care." I snatched the blanket from the ground and sat down against a tree, refusing to look at the fae. "If you cared, you would help me."

"It isn't my fault—"

"No, but it's your problem," I snapped. "You think life is hard for you now? What, because you have to hide? Some of you have been killed? Imagine if Selina gets her hands on me! Imagine what damage I will do as a filthy, fire-breathing dragon!"

Dormir blinked, stunned to silence.

"Point me which way to go, and I'll go as soon as Tao is ready. Go on home. Who knows if it will still be there in a year." I looked away. My body trembled. "Your people will be wiped out. Extinct. Gone forever for good."

"You have got to be the most pathetic person I've ever met."

"Excuse me?" I stared at him, mouth agape.

He shook his head. "You heard me. Your whole life, you stayed hidden in a castle? Did you bother to even learn about dragons?"

"Yes. I studied everything I could about them in our books," I snapped.

"Then you would know that dragons aren't filthy, fire-breathing monsters."

"All they want is treasure, and they kill anyone to get it!"

Dormir sighed. "No, they don't. And they aren't brainless lizards either. Do you know how to calm yourself when you're angry?" Dormir's voice was becoming more upset.

I glared. "My father taught me."

He shook his head and looked at the stars. "You're so naïve. You don't even know the truth about fae."

"Then enlighten me."

Dormir took a breath, but suddenly his body relaxed, his eyes rolled, and he collapsed.

I gasped and jumped to my feet. "Dormir!" I fell beside him and shook him like I had in the cathedral. "Dormir, what happened? Dormir?"

He didn't move.

I groaned. "I really don't want to have to kiss you again."

THIRTEEN

He didn't wake on his own.

I dragged Dormir's unconscious body to a more level area and then covered him with my torn bedroll. Reluctantly, I curled up beside him for warmth, even after starting a fire. When I woke the next morning, he was still there, unmoved from where I'd put him.

More than a little confused, I reached out and shook him again. "Dormir?" I asked. I looked up at Tao. "What do you think?"

Behind me, the trees whispered.

"I don't *want* to kiss him again," I argued, looking at them.

I grumbled more to myself as I got to my feet. As if everything didn't hurt enough before from riding a horse and sleeping on the ground, my body now had the additional pain from being attacked by tree roots. Marigold and Dahlia would probably laugh when I told them that part of the story.

As I moved, the smell of horse, sweat, and dirt wafted off my body. I was positively filthy and suddenly grateful Dormir had been asleep and unable to smell me. Nothing about my appearance showed my royal heritage. Luckily I had a spare dress with me, and I dug it out of my pack. Unluckily it had been in the same pack with my blankets, which had been thrown by the roots. I shook the dress off and held it up. Other than the dirt smudge on one side, it was still mostly folded and clean.

I gave Dormir one last look before I shed my clothing and reluctantly stepped into the cold river. My shrill gasp was so loud I thought for sure I had woken Dormir. Swimming in a river was chilly, but nothing compared to the frigid temperatures of this water. It must have been the water hadn't had time to warm up from the sun. It was too late to go back, though, so I rinsed off my body and hair the best I could.

When I felt clean enough, I ran out of the water and wrapped myself up in the only towel I had. Yet, as I dried my body, little leaves or debris still clung to my skin and there was still dirt that wiped off from the towel. I grumbled to myself before wrapping the towel back around and starting the fire again. It didn't take long for the warmth to penetrate the towel.

Dormir was still asleep. He hadn't budged from where I'd left him.

Pursing my lips to one side, I finished drying off and then pulled the clean dress on. It wouldn't be so bad to be home and have a proper night's sleep and proper bath. There wasn't much to do with my sopping wet hair either, and I couldn't find my brush, so I had to wrap it up in a towel and bundled up in a blanket.

Tao snorted, drawing my attention to him. He stepped forward and touched his nose to Dormir's cheek.

"I don't want to kiss him again," I argued.

Tao's chestnut eye moved to me.

"Fine." I leaned down and kissed his cheek.

Nothing.

"What an unusual state he's in." I got a good look at Dormir's face, but not even his eyes moved. "What could cause someone to do this?" I looked to the horse, as if he could answer my questions.

Tao nibbled at Dormir's hair, snorted, then meandered back to the river.

"Here goes nothing." With no other choice, I pecked him on the lips.

This time, the kiss was more graceful. I took the time to register how he felt—soft and warm—and how he smelled. Dormir smelled like spring soil and orange groves.

He let out a sigh, and his eyes fluttered before opening. I bolted upright and pretended to busy myself with the pot, though I didn't even have water in it. I watched him from the corner of my eyes. Dormir blinked a few times, focusing on my trees overhead, and then closed and rubbed his eyes with the base of his hands.

"It happened again, didn't it?" He groaned and sat up.

"Is it common for you to just fall asleep on a whim?"

"When I become too emotional, yes." He rested his arms on his knees and sighed. And then he gave me a curious look. "How did you wake me up?"

I shrugged. "You just did," I lied, well aware of my cheeks growing pink. "I can rummage through the saddlebags and find something to eat." I limped to Tao.

"We were arguing," Dormir muttered to himself. "What were we arguing about?"

I shrugged, uncertain if he was really asking me or just thinking out loud.

"Oh, yes. You being ignorant to our plight."

This time, I looked at him, and a playful smirk played on his thin lips.

"You led us to water and were going to drop me off on the path back to the castle. That hardly seems like a plight."

"I don't mean us, as in you and me. I mean me and my people." He shook his head.

I opened my mouth, but he held up his hand, silencing me.

"I don't know anything about Selina, other than I hear she is a powerful sorceress. As far as your curse and our supposed promise? No. Your mother passed a law forcing us from our lands to a very specific area to

143

the far eastern border of Griswil." His eyes remained locked on me, his lips tight. "If she had it her way, she would banish us completely from our own lands.

The color drained from my face. "That doesn't make sense. Why would she push you all away when she knows you can cure my curse?"

Dormir inclined his head. "You're not listening. We don't know anything about your curse. To be entirely honest, I'm not sure I really care either. We've had to retreat to the mountains and try and make a life for ourselves there."

"But that means ... Mother knew all along where the faeries were. Which means ..." I still couldn't comprehend it. I didn't want to. "I don't believe you," I said with finality, looking at Dormir with confidence. "You're only saying this to make me upset. You're trying to play a hand and gain what, exactly?" In reality, I didn't want to accept that my mother, my own *mother,* had hidden this from me while at the same time knowing this was just like her.

My biggest question was why? Why would she pretend like this?

If the faeries really couldn't help cure me ... could it be possible I wasn't cursed at all?

Dormir got to his feet and reached his hands out. "Can I help you with breakfast?"

"No. I can do it." I pushed past him and set down two apples, the twine-wrapped muffins—one of the only items untouched from the tree incident—and the pouch of water. When I sat down, I landed harder than intended and grimaced.

Dormir watched me as I ate my pathetic breakfast. He finally rubbed the back of his neck and exhaled through his nose. "What if I take you to them?"

I glanced in his direction. "Take me to the faeries? Why would you choose to do that now? What changed your mind?"

"You've come on your own all this way. Clearly, you've been lied to. Maybe one of the elders can give you a better answer than me?" He shrugged. "What do you have to lose?"

The dry muffin in my mouth was barely edible, and I chewed slowly.

Dormir took that as a silent "yes" and said, "We shall leave when you're ready, then." He nodded once and walked over to Tao.

I swallowed. "Do you really think they'll help?" I asked hesitantly.

Dormir looked over his shoulder at me. "In the least, they could answer your questions about your supposed curse." He held his hand out to Tao. "Where did you get this horse?"

"He's been around for as long as I can remember. He's the only horse I can ride. I think it's because the other horses sense the dragon within me." I took the last bite of the muffin and dusted the crumbs from my lap.

"Curious," he said softly.

"Why is that? Because a horse can like something as disgusting as me?"

Dormir rolled his eyes at me. "No, because I think he may be a unicorn."

I laughed.

The edges of Dormir's lips pinched.

I pointed to Tao. "A unicorn? Unicorns have horns. I'm not *that* naïve."

"They're almost extinct, Elisa. If they hide, they could disguise themselves as a regular horse."

"All right, fae boy. Show me to your people. I think my unicorn could use some proper rest, and I could use a bed for a night." I gestured with a dramatic flourish.

Dormir rolled his eyes and muttered something in his native language.

Tao answered by nodding his head up and down.

Dormir smirked and patted his nose. "All right, Elisa. This way." He directed us back through the trees and onto the main path.

When we made it to a bridge, Dormir motioned me to stop and walked to the edge. "I am Dormir, son of Tayvin. I return from my visit to find peace."

I wanted to ask what on earth he was doing, but Dormir seemed to sense my unease and lifted a finger telling me to wait longer.

He leaned to his right, peering over the edge. "I would like to pass and return home."

Finally, there was a knock from under the bridge.

"I take a horse with me as well."

A frantic series of knocks and Dormir smiled over his shoulder at me. He put his finger to his lips and motioned with his hand for me to follow.

Tao moved before I could nudge him, and I wondered for the first time if Tao was more than an ordinary horse.

146

We reached the other side, and Dormir said, "Sorry to be so sudden. There's a troll under the bridge. They say he doesn't usually cause trouble, but where I'm fae and off my land, I really didn't want him upset for trespassing."

"A troll?"

His words sunk in.

I shook my head. "I understand magic is real. I know you are a fae. But unicorns and trolls? Aren't those creatures supposed to be gone?"

"Supposed to? Yes." I didn't like the look of animosity Dormir threw in my direction.

I looked over my shoulder to see if I could catch a peek of the underside of the bridge. "You're telling me … all of these creatures live in our land?"

Dormir nodded. "And more, which you clearly haven't seen either."

"Clearly," I muttered.

For the next hour or so, all I could do was think of everything I'd missed being locked away in the castle. I wished I had been more brave so I could have seen these magical creatures and protected them from whatever hunting or laws were passed.

Eventually, Dormir asked about my family. I told him all about my sisters, how they'd even begged to come with me but I refused to let them. He didn't ask, but I told him about my studies, what I did every day, what things I liked. Things I really should have told Gerard. Once I started talking, I had a difficult time restraining myself. Evidently being alone for two days makes one desperate for conversation.

I finally stopped when I realized he wasn't saying much. I cleared my throat. "How many days is it going to take us to get to your city?"

Dormir raised a brow. "If you allowed me to ride Tao with you, we could save time. If not, by the end of the day tomorrow for certain."

"I thought you said your land was to the east?"

"It is. Which is the direction we're heading."

"That's preposterous," I frowned. "This is the direction I've traveled since I left the castle. I passed Handlin only a few days ago."

"Handlin? No. That's to the west of the castle. The sun rises from the east and sets to the west. See?" He pointed to the sky. "We are about two hours away from midday."

I felt more a fool. I continued to show Dormir why I shouldn't have been out on my own. I'd read the map wrong. No wonder the river wasn't where I thought it to be. Dejected, I didn't dare ask another thing.

"Did I upset you?" he asked.

"No. I … I thought I knew so much." I wrapped the leather strap of the rein around my hand, feeling insignificant. "What kind of queen will I be if I can't even hold a map in the right direction?"

Dormir's hand touched my leg.

I shifted my gaze to him.

"You're still alive? Aren't you?" His smile hesitated. "That accounts for something."

"You had to save me from trees, Dormir." I dropped my head and raised my brows.

"In your defense, if no one tells you things, you don't know what to expect."

I let out a heavy sigh. "Which will also cause me to fail as a queen. Look, if you riding with me will get us there faster, then come on." I patted the saddle behind me.

"Are you in a hurry?" he teased.

I moved my foot from the stirrup. "I would like to not turn completely into a dragon." I reached up and touched the horns on the sides of my head. "I just hope these aren't permanent. I can hide the scales."

"I think they're neat if you ask me." The saddle leaned as Dormir climbed on. He sat directly behind me, his body pressed up against mine, and a rush of heat shot through my body, just like when Gerard had danced with me. "This is much more comfortable than walking."

"Is this how you impress all of the girls?" I asked over my shoulder.

"No one is vying for my hand if that's what you're aiming at." Unlike Gerard, when Dormir gave me a half-grin, he didn't have a dimple. But his grin lit up his lavender eyes.

Tao started to walk a bit faster than he had been previously.

I turned in my seat to study Dormir's face. He barely looked older than me. "Why not? Hasn't the time of age come for you to find a wife?"

"How do you know I don't want a husband?" he challenged.

My cheeks flushed pink, and I averted my gaze. I hadn't even considered that. "I'm sorry. I didn't mean anything by it. I was just thinking, you're … oh, never mind."

Dormir chuckled. "I'm not, by the way. Not looking for a wife or a husband. People avoid me just as much as they avoid you."

"Why is that? You're handsome enough."

He laughed out loud. "Just enough, hm? It's the narcolepsy. In case you missed it, my name actually means sleep. No one finds it attractive when you're talking and suddenly the person you're talking with collapses in a heap of sleep. No one knows how to wake me up, either."

I knew how to wake him up, and the thought brought a mix of butterflies in my stomach and a sinking sense of dread. "What's the longest you've ever slept?" I asked, successfully changing subjects.

"Hmm, I believe it was ten days."

"Ten days?" I gasped and turned to look at him again. "You were asleep for ten days?"

He nodded.

"But … how do you wake up?"

Dormir shrugged. "I wake up on my own. My mother said, as a child, she could kiss my forehead and wake me. Now, that doesn't work." He tilted his head and his eyes narrowed with suspicion. "Your face is as red as a rose. What is it?"

I shook my head. "That must be hard for you."

As we rode in silence, I had no choice than to focus on Dormir's body. I'd taken in his enchanted beauty while he slept, but hadn't *really* noticed his body until it was pressed to my back on the saddle. We rocked with each movement of the horse, and Dormir's body rubbed against mine.

Dormir was muscled, but lean—unlike Gerard. Comparing the two, Dormir was a little shorter, elegant, and mysterious. Gerard was bulky, dashing, and inexplicable. Complete opposites. Still, Dormir's eyes lit up when he smiled, and there was something about Gerard that made me wonder if I'd fallen too quickly for him. After all, Dormir wasn't afraid to speak his mind and disagree with me.

"What you said about roses," I finally said. "I've always wanted to see them."

"Another thing we no longer have in this kingdom," Dormir sighed. "There used to be all kinds of rose bushes everywhere, in pink and red and white. Some even a beautiful shade of blue."

The wheels in my head began to turn. "Remember how I told you about my birthday? There was a note that morning, and at the bottom, it had an additional line about my curse. It said that if I pricked my finger on a rose, something would happen." I shook my head. "I wish I could remember the wording. When I get back to the castle, I'm going to sit with my father and mother and have them tell me the truth," I insisted, looking back at him.

Dormir nodded. "You can try." He didn't sound convinced.

I pursed my lips. *But if she her finger pricks, then her and the dragon will no longer mix? No, that isn't it. If a rose shall her finger … that doesn't sound right either.* I blew air out through my nose.

If only I could remember.

FOURTEEN

We didn't make it to Dormir's land by nightfall.

We stopped beside a roaring river, which Dormir explained led the way to his land.

"You don't want to get in this water," he warned. "Notice how loud it is? This river is running high." He gestured to the shoreline. The water looked like it had carved out the edges of the dirt sides. "And it's fast. See those white tips? You can stay on the shore, but I wouldn't go any further in."

"You hear that, Tao?" I said.

The horse was already headed for the water's edge and didn't acknowledge me.

I pulled on the reins, stopping him.

"When we get to my land, I'll have to show you the waterfall. It casts a double rainbow." Dormir got off Tao's back first.

I grinned. "I've never seen a double rainbow before. I can't wait to see what that looks like!"

"I have a feeling it is something you will absolutely love." He put his hands on my waist. "May I help you down?"

I hesitated. When had he tied his hair back into a ponytail? Had his eyes always been so big? The color reminded me of pale purple lilac. "I can manage," I finally replied. "I'm trying to learn independence, remember?" I patted one of his hands.

He let go and stepped back to give me space to climb off. "Can I help you with dinner tonight, at least?"

"You went from hating that I touched you to being willing to cook?" I leaned close. "I'm beginning to wonder if you have ulterior motives." I raised my eyebrows as high as I could.

Dormir blinked and his face paled. "N-No! Of course not! I—"

"I was joking!" I laughed and playfully patted his shoulder. "I would love some help. It turns out I'm not so good at cooking."

"It so happens I know my way around a campfire," he winked and nudged me with his elbow.

I tucked my hair behind my ear and looked up at his beautiful face.

His smile softened and the left edge pulled up higher until it spread into a bigger smile.

The trees around us whispered.

He glanced at the sky. "They say it feels like we will get rain tonight. We might need shelter. Did you bring anything with you?"

I shook my head. "I don't know, to be honest. I would think we had a tent. Not that I would know how to set it up …" I looked up at the still-blue sky with white fluffy clouds. They hardly looked threatening, even as they grew pink with the setting of the sun.

"How about we get the stew cooking, and then we can set up the tent?" He started putting potatoes from the saddlebag into the pot. "That will give the potatoes and carrots time to cook up perfectly."

"Will you teach me?" I walked to his side and held my arms out.

"Of course." He handed over the pot, then walked to the other side of Tao and rummaged in that pack while I set the pot on the ground and searched the nearby underbrush for some twigs.

"Whoa, stop!"

I jumped back when Dormir shouted. "What?" I said in a panic.

He took my wrist and guided me to the side. "This here is called poison oak. See how the leaves are waxy?" He pointed to the plant I had nearly come in contact with. "If you brush up against that, even just touch your clothes to it and then touch the wax off your clothes, it will give a nasty rash."

I stared. "How do you tell the difference from these plants?" I gestured with my free hand.

"Have you ever heard the saying, *leaves of three, let them be*?" He looked down at me.

"Yes, now that you remind me. My parents told me when I was a child, but it was so long ago, I forgot."

He nodded and pointed to the leaves again. "Clusters of three leaves. Poison ivy also has three leaves. Both plants are really dangerous to touch and can be hard to identify, so just be careful."

Dormir's fingers held on to me gently, tenderly. He was truly concerned.

Again, we were caught staring at each other.

He looked down at our hands as if he just realized he was holding on to me, then dropped his grip. My heart dropped with it, and I bit my lip. Dormir rubbed the back of his neck as he walked to where he'd dropped the carrots.

I swallowed hard and retrieved the sticks.

Once I had a fire going, Dormir took me down to the riverbank and instructed me to wash the dirt from the potatoes and carrots. He showed me how to use the knife to cut off bad pieces and peel them.

"I noticed you still had some flour left untouched, and salt. We can make some biscuits." He glanced to his right and then left. "Ah ha. There are mushrooms on that tree. Do you like mushrooms?" He looked back at me as he walked to the plump white mushrooms growing on the base of a tree.

I shrugged. "I don't mind them."

"Good. There are some other things here we can throw in." He plucked them off and returned to my side.

Dormir explained step-by-step without doing anything else for me, and I paid every bit of attention. When the stew was finally on the fire, he returned to Tao's saddle.

156

He patted a rolled-up piece of material on the back of the saddle. "This is a tent."

"I thought that was part of the saddle," I admitted sheepishly.

Dormir gave me another warm smile, then shook his head and released the two latches. "I'll need your help, though. Fae don't use tents the same way you humans do. Or ... part humans." His eyes darted to my hands.

I knew he meant it in jest, but that didn't mean it didn't sting. I curled my fingers and got to my feet to help him, not that I was much help. Princesses didn't put up tents.

"I think these go inside each other," Dormir said. He held up two pieces of wood and showed me a hollowed space on one end, and a small tip on the other. He wiggled the poles together.

"Oh neat!"

He gave me a triumphant grin.

I had unrolled the canvas, and luckily it wasn't one of the enormous tents I'd seen on the competition grounds. This one was much smaller. "It looks like poles go on these two tips. I think the small sticks go along the bottom."

"Those are stakes." He carried the sticks over.

I held the poles while Dormir nailed in the stakes, and the canvas pulled taught as he did so. Hesitantly, I let go, only to give a victorious grin when it stayed upright. Together, we successfully got the tent up.

"We did it!" I ducked out of the open flap. "See? Princesses aren't completely useless."

"I suppose not," he agreed. "Now, let's eat. I'm famished."

Luckily Abby had packed two bowls, and Dormir served us both. There was just enough stew for two servings. Once he'd poured the soup in the bowls, he flipped the pot open-side down and set it on the fire.

"Don't do that, you'll smother it!" I exclaimed.

"No, look." He pointed around the bottom. "It's resting on the bigger logs. We're going to make the biscuits. Where is the mixture?"

I reached over and retrieved the larger bowl. He'd had me mix flour, salt, water, and the last of the honey. He showed me how to flatten the mixture in between his hands, then he set the dough on the underside of the pot.

"Won't the ash make them dirty?" I frowned.

"No, it adds a nice flavor. Besides, you can wipe it off when it's done cooking." He winked and took a bite of his stew.

"How did you learn to cook?" I blew on my spoonful before putting it in my mouth. My eyes widened, and I looked down at the bowl of food. "This is really yummy." I took another bite.

"All fae learn how to cook from young ages. We live off the world around us. Our homes used to be part of the forest, so we needed to know how to use everything. I suppose teaching changed as we began to be pushed further from our homes and became more out of necessity than tradition." Dormir didn't look up as he took another bite.

"If what you say is actually true—"

That earned a sharp look my way.

"About the fae being pushed off their lands," I continued. "Where do you live now?"

"I told you. The mountains. Which is not ideal for forest-dwellers. We have to have farms in the valley, and we are in constant fear that the queen will send her army to destroy them. It would kill us if she chose to do so."

I frowned.

"It really would," he said more firmly.

"That's not what upsets me," I retorted. "It's all of this. Your being forced from your homes at all, my mother lying to me, this stupid curse, and the thought I might not ever find a cure."

"I can understand your frustration," he replied.

I didn't know exactly *how* I would convince my mother to change her foolish laws, but I did concoct an idea as I ate. "I have an idea," I finally expressed while Dormir licked a bit of soup from his bottom lip. "When you're done breaking my curse, you could come with me to speak to my mother."

Dormir slid his large biscuit off the pot and flipped it over to bake on the other side. "You really think it will be that simple? Just go in and tell her to change the law?"

"I don't know what else would work," I confessed. "You could act as an ambassador. I don't start making laws on my own until I'm officially eighteen, and even then, my mother has to approve of them until I'm married and take my position on the throne. That won't be until she dies or hands over her power."

"Ah. I see." He tilted his head toward the nearest tree, and moments later the hushed rush of wind began to grow.

"The storm?" I asked, setting down my empty bowl.

"No. Someone is coming." He moved fast, releasing his hair from his ponytail so it fell over his ears. "Do you have a cloak to hide your horns?"

"No," I said, sensing his panic. I dug in my pack regardless, hoping to grab a blanket, at least.

Dormir moved faster. He pulled the cloak from his shoulders, wrapped it around mine, and tugged the hood up so only my face showed. "Don't act too surprised, and whatever you do don't let them know about my being a fae and you being the princess. We don't know who they are," he said to me.

He settled back down and light glittered around him, muting his blue hair to yellow like mine, hiding the glow of his skin, and making his eyes change to blue. He handed me the cooked biscuit and plopped the last bit of dough on the pot to cook. His eyes darted toward the road.

I wasn't much in the mood to eat the warm bread. My stomach knotting with anticipation

Dormir's eyes were narrowed on whoever was approaching, and I feared he would run at the first sign of danger.

Thunder rumbled overhead, and a flash of lightning lit up the sky just in time to illuminate three riders on the road headed straight for us. My heart jumped into my throat, and I seized Dormir's hand.

He gave me a gentle squeeze and looked at me from the corner of his eye. He nodded his head slightly, offering me silent comfort. "How is the biscuit?"

"Fine," I answered back.

"Ho there!" one of the riders called.

Dormir let go of my hand and climbed to his feet. "You're aware there is a storm nearing?" he answered.

"Yes. We spotted your fire and thought we might join you for shelter."

I couldn't see around Dormir's body, but I heard the creak of leather saddles as the three riders dismounted. Their boots hit the ground, breaking twigs or crunching rocks.

"I'm afraid we don't have much room in our tent," Dormir replied.

"We have our own. Men, set up the tent. And who is this lovely lady with you?" The man leaned around Dormir's side.

I gasped. "Gerard?" I leapt to my feet and sprinted to him. I threw my arms around him and held on tight. "What are you doing here? I thought you had reached Andorin and continued beyond!"

His body was rigid when I first wrapped my arms around his torso, but he relaxed and patted my back. "We had, but we received word that the fae had moved to the mountains, so that is where we are heading. What are you doing out of the castle?" He pushed me away, hands on my shoulders, and gave me a stern look. His eyes shifted to Dormir.

"I wanted to find the fae on my own. I didn't want to wait for you to save me."

161

Gerard gave me his perfect smile, but it didn't reach his eyes. Not like Dormir's smiles. "You're very bold to be out here alone. Who is your companion?" He slid one hand down to my back and extended the other toward Dormir.

"This is Dormir. He …"

Dormir's jaw flexed just enough in warning, so I said nothing about him being a fae. He took Gerard's hand, offering a smile of his own. "I am—"

"A servant," I interrupted. "He works out in the stables."

"Ah." Gerard shook Dormir's hand and let go. His eyes moved to the tent, then down to my face. "And you've been sharing the tent with him?" His brows lifted in an accusatory gesture.

I pursed my lips and stepped back. "Are you accusing me of something? The only reason we were to share tonight is because of the storm moving in."

Gerard shook his head. "I meant no offense. You are my *betrothed*, and I want to protect you." I hated how he emphasized the word, like I was something he'd won in battle, and I knew he only said it because Dormir stood close by.

I also didn't miss Dormir's body go rigid at the word.

I inhaled through my nose. "I know you do."

"Which is why, tonight, I will share the tent with you," Gerard continued. "Dormir here can sleep with my men." He looked at the fae. "You're fine with that, I trust?"

"Of course," Dormir answered stiffly.

"Good. Clean up your meal. Princess Elisa looks positively exhausted." Using the hand on my back, he directed me toward the tent, shouldering one of the bags from his saddle. "I truly can't believe your mother let you do this," he chided.

"She didn't," I said firmly.

He glanced down at me and held the flap of the tent open. "You left on your own? Did you tell her you were leaving?"

"I left her a note." I glanced over my shoulder at Dormir. Something about Gerard's sudden appearance made me uneasy, but I stepped into the tent and crouched beside my shredded bedroll.

"What happened there?"

"We were attacked by trees in the Ancient Wood." I waved my hand dismissively. "It's not an issue. Dormir saved me."

"That was kind of him." Gerard unrolled his own bedroll and motioned. "Take mine."

I didn't even try to object. With the changes occurring with my body at an alarming rate, the hope with Dormir, and sudden anxiety of Gerard's presence, I just wanted to sleep. I untied Dormir's cloak from my neck, suddenly feeling guilty. I hoped he would be warm enough that night without it. I lay down and pulled the blanket up just as the clouds parted. Rain slapped against the tent and pounded the ground outside.

"Will we get wet?" I asked, looking through the darkness the best I could, nervously spreading Dormir's cloak across the blanket for added warmth and protection. All I could see was Gerard rearranging the bedroll and finally lying down.

"It appears your *manservant* was intelligent enough to set your tent up on the higher ground, so no, we shouldn't."

I frowned at the word "manservant," knowing he implied more than a stable boy. "Gerard," I said firmly.

Gerard rolled to his side to face me.

"He *isn't* my manservant," I said.

He exhaled through his nose. "I understand. Forgive me for such sharp words." He reached across the short space between us and touched my cheek. "I worry for your safety. You left the protection of your castle to, what? Prove something?"

"No, to search myself for a fae. I've never done that. Not once. I don't want to become a full-fledged dragon knowing I sat in the castle my entire life and did nothing. Now, at least I can say I tried." I shrugged. "Besides, you did invite me, remember?"

Gerard moved his thumb down my lips, pulling them apart.

We were so close, his breath danced across my face. This was the closest we'd been since the night on the dance floor. And I couldn't deny I wanted to be a little closer. The air had gone chilly, and he would be the perfect source of warmth, but that thought was replaced with the image of Dormir's arms around me.

Gerard shifted closer. "When did the horns come?"

I absently reached up and ran my hand over the hard curve. "Yesterday," I answered.

"How?"

164

I shrugged. He didn't know, but I was catching on that my bursts of anger were becoming more frequent, and with each of those uncontrolled bursts, a new dragon feature was being added to my body.

"You're so beautiful."

"Horns and everything?" I asked, rolling my eyes.

He chuckled and closed the little space there was between us. "Yes. And when we do find a fae, they will help. And then you'll be back to yourself. Though, I should really take you home in the morning …"

"No!" I blurted. "We're too close."

Gerard tilted his head. "How *did* you know the fae were this direction?" he asked, suddenly curious. His thumb stopped on my chin.

My heart started to beat a little faster. "My mother, of course."

"Ah. Yes, she would know." He leaned down and kissed me on the forehead.

I closed my eyes as a rush of heat trickled from my head to my toes and everywhere in between. "We shouldn't," I whispered.

"I know." He kissed each of my cheeks, and then my lips.

My chest began to burn like when I held my breath too long, but I was breathing. My fingertips ached as if I held them over a fire, but all I could feel was Gerard's muscled arms. His kisses became more intense, fierce. His hand slid to the back of my head, holding our lips tighter together, so tight it almost hurt. But I also didn't want it to stop. I wanted him in a way I'd never felt before. He rose up onto his elbow and hovered over me, pressing so tightly to my body he almost stole my breath. His free arm slid down my arm, my side, and curve of my hips.

Warning bells went off in my head.

I should stop him.

This was too much. Too fast. Regardless of his status as my betrothed, I knew this was too much. But I couldn't break my lips away to tell him. When I tried to move back, he moved his head so I was pressed into the bedroll.

The heat in my chest started to burn.

Gerard's hand slid up my thigh, under my dress, and to my backside.

I finally tore my lips away. "Gerard!" I gasped.

"Sh …" he whispered against my lips.

I put my hands on his chest and tried to push him away. "No. We need to stop."

"Not yet." His hand squeezed.

The burning in my chest exploded, and I shoved Gerard in the chest with both hands so hard he flew off and hit the side of the tent. I blinked. Stunned.

"You … want to stop?" he asked stupidly.

"Yes." The heat in my body immediately started to lessen, though it tingled across my scales like a warning. I rolled away from him, adjusting my dress and blankets. If I hadn't been a dragon … would I have been able to stop him?

FIFTEEN

Things between Gerard and I the next day were ... strained. After pushing him off me, he had moved up behind me to hold me during the night. I didn't mind, because it was freezing, but my heart told me what he'd tried was selfish. He wasn't going to stop. He'd almost gone too far.

When I looked at him the next morning, hot bile stung the back of my tongue.

In spite of it being so cold I could see my breath, I was the first out of the tent. I kept the blankets wrapped around me and promptly walked over to Dormir's side at the fire. I wanted him. His comfort. His warmth. I dropped his cloak in his lap before I leaned against his side and a tremble ran through my body. I should have wanted to be with Gerard, the man I was engaged to, but his stunt from the night before caused me to have doubts about his kindness and motivation.

Dormir straightened when my shoulder touched his, and he glanced around.

Gerard walked out of the tent and stretched with a loud groan. He still had his hair braided across the top and pulled up in a small bun, like when we'd first met, and he walked around the tent and into the trees.

Dormir put his hand on my back. "Come with me." He snagged his pack from his side as he stood.

I didn't refuse and followed him back to my tent.

"I have a spare set of clothing. You will be much more comfortable in pants than your dress." He reached into his pack and pulled out his bundle of clothing. "You should fit." His eyes watched me, his brows soft with concern.

Did he know?

I accepted the clothing from him. "Are you worried about something?" I asked.

He glanced over his shoulder.

Gerard and his men were getting breakfast started.

Dormir cleared his throat softly. "I … The trees told me you were afraid last night. I came to your tent and—" He shook his head and turned away. "It's none of my business."

I reached out and grabbed his arm. "I was."

He raised a brow.

My cheeks flushed, and it was my turn to look away in shame. "I was afraid," I answered softly. "I couldn't … He wouldn't stop." I picked at lint on the clothing that wasn't there. "He and I are to be married.

But, still. What he … what he wanted to do? What he *tried* to do?"

"I had actually opened the tent flap in time to see you shove him off." Dormir reached out and took my hand. "I am impressed you were able to stop him on your own."

I looked at the fae, and he smiled back at me. "Would you have stepped in?"

His smile fell. "I was about to. I'm only sorry I hesitated."

I shook my head. "Please don't feel bad. Like you said, it wasn't your place. You didn't know if I had … asked for it."

"You told him to stop."

I took his other hand. "You would have been right there. Thank you." I gave him a reassuring smile and kissed his cheek as a rush of relief washed through me. Knowing Dormir had been right there was enough to bring me comfort.

"Hey, Doorman!" one of Gerard's friends called.

Dormir rolled his eyes. "I think it's intentional," he muttered. He sighed and smiled. "I best help them with that fire or we'll never get on the road."

He was right about the clothes being far warmer and much more comfortable, especially when riding on the horse. His pants were a little long, but he was also several inches taller than me. Nothing a little rolling of the pant leg couldn't fix.

I helped clean up after breakfast, ignoring Gerard's objections, and finally we were on our way. Dormir was at the front, on Gerard's horse, and Gerard sat behind me on Tao. I wondered how it was possible Gerard and his friends hadn't realized Dormir was a fae. His eyes were purple and his hair blue. Perhaps Dormir had some sort of magic he could use to disguise himself. Maybe it didn't work on me because I'd already seen him as a fae.

Gerard tried asking me about my journey, but there wasn't much to tell, and we soon fell into silence. I wished it was just Dormir and me, so I could ask him more questions about the fae lands, about his life, his family. I'd spoken so much the day before, and he'd patiently listened but didn't offer any information about himself. I wished I'd asked more questions. Now we were stuck together in tense silence.

"Do you need to rest?" Gerard asked the third time in the hour. The sun hadn't even reached its highest peak yet.

I snapped him a glare. "If you ask me again, I'm going to take an apple and throw it at you. I am quite comfortable and have traveled all day the last few days. If we stop, that's less time traveling toward our destination."

Gerard blinked at me. "My apologies."

I looked down the path just in time to see Dormir stifling a giggle with a grin. He gave me a quick wink and returned his attention forward.

A few hours later, Dormir held his hand up, halting us. He turned in his saddle. "We're about to cross the border. I recommend we keep a walking pace. Do not draw your weapons for any reason." He looked past me at the men.

They nodded their understanding.

At first, the forest didn't look any different from where we had been traveling. Then I realized tall quaking aspen trees lined the path and the evergreen trees seemed to have climbed down from the mountains. The path also took on a sharper incline.

Around us, the wind rustled the leaves and branches. I wondered if they were whispering to Dormir, but he wasn't saying anything.

One of the men cleared his throat softly. "How is it you know the location of the faeries?"

"I've traveled this way before," Dormir answered simply.

"And you happen to remember? After one time?"

"It's not uncommon if you have a good sense of direction," I threw in. Then, I quickly added, "Ask Gerard. He knows his way around. I bet he could even find his way back to the castle from here." I gave Gerard an added smile—the nicest thing I'd done that day.

Gerard smiled in return. "Yes, I imagine I could." He gave the man a look.

The pathway disappeared behind a thicket of trees, but as we came around, Dormir stopped his horse, and I followed after. Two women and two men stood on the path, side by side. Judging by Dormir's expression, he knew they would be there.

The two women had pink hair so light it could have nearly been mistaken for blond. The two men had dark-purple hair, like the color of chateau wine— so dark it was almost black.

"The border guard," Dormir introduced.

I resisted the urge to point out they didn't look too happy to see us there.

"Why have you crossed the border?" the woman on the left asked.

"I've come—" I started.

Gerard interrupted. "We seek a meeting with your council of elders."

Her eyes darted to Gerard. "Our *queen* doesn't meet with outsiders." The corner of her lip tugged in a little sneer as her nose wrinkled. "Especially humans," he spat in evident disgust.

"Please. It's urgent." Gerard took my hand.

I knew the faeries would have seen the horns on my head. They weren't fools.

"It's about my curse," I added. I pulled my hand away from Gerard and held it up for them to see.

The border guards turned to Dormir.

He nodded his head once. "She believes we can help," he said, answering their unasked question.

The faeries asked a question in their language, to which Dormir replied.

I glanced from one to the other. They'd asked a question about us being either safe or trustworthy, and Dormir had used my name, which meant he at least trusted me, but I don't think he trusted Gerard or his men.

Gerard leaned down to my ear. "So he's a fae? You kept that hidden from me?"

"I don't trust your men," I whispered back.

The woman returned her attention to us. "We shall take your weapons while you are on our land. I trust you understand why?"

"I'm aware of my ... queen's orders," I said. "That faeries have been forced into this part of the country." I wasn't sure if Gerard knew, so it was the easiest way to give him information if he didn't.

Gerard's men grumbled as the faeries stepped forward and took their bows, arrows, swords, and daggers. The faeries then motioned for us to follow them and began walking down the path.

"This is a good sign," Gerard said, giving me a reassuring smile.

A glance from Dormir told me he wasn't so certain. At some point, Dormir's glamor disappeared, revealing his blue hair and purple eyes again. He did offer me a comforting nod.

The path wound through the forest, and the sun began to set.

When we reached the base of a cliff, we stopped.

"The horses will need to stay here," one of the fae men explained in a deep voice. He held his arm out toward stables carved into the side of the cliff. "We shall take care of them while you are visiting."

"I need to stretch my legs anyway," I said and slid off Tao's back.

He turned and nudged me, so I gave him a hug. "I will come back for you. Just get some rest and eat lots of apples. He does enjoy oats as well, but he's getting along in years," I said to the fae.

The man's lips softened into a smile, and he nodded softly. "Did Dormir speak to you about his heritage?"

I grinned. "I didn't believe him. Is it true?"

The man nodded.

I gave Dormir a casual wink. "You were right."

The man laughed lightly and said something to Dormir.

He blushed and spat back a retort.

"This way!" the woman said.

"What are your names?" I asked.

"We should hold introductions until after the queen has met with you," the woman replied.

"Our people have very little trust with outsiders," Dormir explained to everyone. "You will have to be careful with how you address others. Please show the utmost respect."

I nodded. "Of course. We don't want to start off on the wrong foot."

The path hugged the cliff's side so narrowly we had to follow each other. One man and woman led us. I followed Dormir, Gerard followed me, his men behind, and the other two faeries followed at the rear. I glanced once down at the mist-covered forest and valley below. It was one of the most beautiful sights I'd ever seen.

"This view is beautiful," I said aloud. My heart reached out over the view. I wondered what it would be like to fall from that height, to feel the wind on my face even for just a moment. If I fell, could I fly?

Dormir grabbed my arm, and I realized I'd taken a step toward the edge. "Yes, it's beautiful. But use caution. If you fall from this height, you won't survive."

"Of course not." I stepped back, and as soon as I looked down, my stomach lurched. I held tightly to Dormir's hand and pressed my face into his back. "I'm afraid of heights."

"A little ironic, considering." Dormir chuckled.

"I can carry you," Gerard offered, placing his hand on my back.

As I straightened, Dormir looked from Gerard to me, then shrugged me off. Dormir didn't like Gerard, I saw that much, but at least he was being respectful.

"I can manage on my own," I insisted.

The sky darkened, and a soft glow began to wind its way along the cliff face as if the stone itself was glowing.

"What is this?" I asked, reaching out to gently touch the light.

"The earth is alive," Dormir explained. "Even the stone. With a little bit of coaxing and a hint of magic, we can manipulate the earth, like having the stone glow to guide our path."

"It's magnificent," I said.

"We've reached the city," the woman at the front called back. "Please stay right with us. Do not attempt to wander away."

I stepped around the rock edge and gasped. Built against the cliff were dozens of wooden homes, precariously connected by bridges or ropes. The homes were lit with white lights, illuminating forms of people in the windows or out on their porches.

The path led up to a large building with spires like the cathedral back in the forest. In fact, it looked similarly constructed as the castle, only clearly built with more haste and with less detail.

Those faeries near enough to observe stared at us. More faeries appeared.

Dormir nodded to them as we passed.

We were led up the path, lit by glowing orbs overhead as we entered the shallow cave.

"Anything we should know about the queen?" I asked softly.

"I recommend you be honest," Dormir replied.

I nodded, but I suddenly felt my heart starting to race. What would she say about me? Would I be considered more of an outcast because of my curse?

The sentries at the entrance pushed the doors open, then fell into step alongside us as we entered.

Gerard stepped up to my side and put his hand on my back. "Everything will be fine," he reassured. "Let me do all of the talking."

"Excuse me?" I blinked.

"I think it would be best if I spoke. I'm more experienced in these sorts of discussions." He flashed a smile. "You can stand at my side and be your beautiful self." He returned his attention forward.

Speak for me? Control the discussion?

Maybe it really was better for him to talk. He knew I didn't have experience, not when it came to discussions such as this. I'd *learned* about it, but what good was I if I'd never done it before?

We entered the throne room, and I instantly felt out of place.

The queen sat upon her throne, regal and beautiful. Her long blond hair reached down to her waist, and she held the jeweled sword I'd seen in the painting at the cathedral. She held the sword across her lap in a nonthreatening way and studied each of us. "To what do we owe this visitation?"

"My name is Prince Gerard. I am the crown prince of Ashwrya. The—"

"Northern country," the queen interrupted. "What brings you this far south? And with this party of misfits?"

I didn't miss her gaze freezing on Dormir before moving to me.

I wanted to speak. I wanted to explain my position. I opened my mouth, but Gerard spoke first.

"I traveled to Griswil to meet my betrothed, the crown princess Elisa." He put his hand on my back.

"May I explain?" I asked.

Gerard shook his head. "We're in the middle of a discussion, darling." He looked at the queen. "When I arrived, I learned my beloved had been cursed."

"Gerard, please let me talk," I requested.

"Elisa, you don't know how to barter." He patted my hand as if I were an invalid or old lady who had lost her mind, and the hair on the back of my neck prickled.

"With all due respect, this is not your curse," I said sharply. "This is not your kingdom, and I am not yet your wife. These negotiations are my responsibility and mine alone."

He flashed a smile but ran his hand over his mouth. "This is my expertise. I thought we agreed I would guide the discussion."

"No. *You* wanted to. This is my responsibility."

Gerard lowered his hand and his lips tightened ever so slightly. He glanced around at the eyes staring at us. Finally he stepped back, gesturing toward the queen with a swoop of his arm.

Confidence surged through me, and I straightened my spine. I faced the queen and stepped forward. "I am Princess Elisa."

The queen's eyes darkened.

I hesitated. "I … am the daughter of Queen Rachel." I licked my lips. "At birth, the sorceress Selina cursed me that I would become a dragon by my eighteenth birthday. At the same time, the faeries vowed to help break the curse. Since then, Selina has been killing your kind, and … Dormir explained your people were exiled as well. I have come to ask for you to uphold your vow. And to please help me."

The weight of the queen's gaze made me glance at Dormir.

"Did I say something wrong?" I asked.

He shook his head and stepped forward. "I found her at A'Luvien."

"And you felt it was wise to bring her and these men to our home? The princess? Daughter of the woman responsible for doing this to us?" the queen spat.

Dormir's jaw flexed. "Queen Misla—"

She held up her hand, cutting him off. She looked at me. "You and your friends will leave at first light."

My breath caught. The guards moved to guide us out, but I didn't budge. "No."

Misla's brow shot up. "Did you just tell me no?"

"I have come all this way." I stepped forward, but Dormir's hand shot out, stopping me from getting much closer to the queen.

The guards had also taken steps forward, hands on the hilts of their swords.

"If you don't help me, I will be a dragon before I'm eighteen!" I held up my hands to show her the black scales. "I already have these *and* horns."

"And why should I help *you*?" she asked in a hiss.

My heart started to race. I needed to keep calm. This was the most important discussion of my life. "Maybe you and I can help each other. You help me with my curse, and I will speak with my mother. We can meet, faeries and humans, and discuss our future together in this country."

Misla shook her head and leaned back on her throne.

My fingertips tingled, and I lowered my hands.

At least she was contemplating my suggestion. She got to her feet, lowering the sword to her side. "I do think an arrangement can be made. Arrest them. Put them all in prison."

"What?" I squeaked.

Dormir flinched and rushed across the stone floor to kneel before the queen. He spoke in their native language as the guards moved forward and took me by the arm.

Gerard put his hand on my hip and leaned to my ear. "I told you to let me speak. Now we have a bigger problem."

I tried to find words, but my tongue felt fat in my mouth, and the guards were pulling me away. Dormir slumped to the ground in one of his episodes, and my heart pounded faster and harder.

"Did he just faint? How pathetic," Gerard mumbled.

"He's … got a condition," I said breathlessly. My heart raced so fast I feared I might faint as well.

Imprisoned by a fae queen—this hadn't been part of the plans at all.

The guards directed us toward stone steps at the front of the cave. A group of men in front of me, Gerard and the others behind me. Gerard was right. I had failed. If I had let him speak, would the queen have had mercy? Would Gerard have convinced her to help? Would he have been able to avoid us being locked up in prison?

"Stop him!" one of the guards shouted.

I spun around in time to see Gerard leap over the edge of the steps and land surprisingly gracefully on the roof below. He then slid and disappeared into the darkness below.

My gut wrenched. "He left …" I choked.

Gerard had left me.

Dormir was unconscious.

And now I was a prisoner with faeries my mother had exiled.

The guard in front of me seized my arm roughly, likely to prevent me from following Gerard, and the other fae guards did the same with Gerard's men. I didn't even resist. My stomach churned as the guard dragged me up the stone steps, then across a wooden bridge to four shallow caves with metal bars on the outside.

The guard stepped in front of the closest and said, "Unpar."

The bars lifted, and he shoved me in with such force I stumbled and fell to my hands and knees. I whipped my head around and watched in dismay as the bars sunk back to the stone floor. Gerard's men complained as they were put in the cells nearby.

I backed up the few feet to the back of the cave and pulled my knees up to my chest. I was desperately trying not to panic. I had to breathe and not allow my emotions to create even more dragon features.

But tears stung my eyes.

My heart wrenched in my chest. I buried my face in my arms and broke into sobs. The faeries were supposed to help. That was part of the promise from my curse. Gerard was supposed to save me because, clearly, I was like every girl in the stories. I couldn't save myself. What a fool I was to have thought otherwise.

SIXTEEN

My eyes hurt.

My throat was dry.

I was freezing.

I rubbed my arms as I sat against the cave wall. I didn't know if I'd actually slept that night. I'd been too worried about Gerard leaving me. I worried about Tao being locked up in a stable without someone he knew. I worried about Dormir.

I got to my feet and walked to the front of the cave. I was too afraid to touch the bars. Who knew if there was fae magic? I looked down over the valley, knowing somewhere in the distance was my home.

"Elisa, you're awake."

Relief washed over me as Dormir stepped into my view. He had changed his clothing into a deep royal blue with silver accents.

My brows pinched.

Royal and regal.

Like the queen.

I met his gaze again. "Did you lie to me?" I asked, gesturing to him. "You are royalty as well?"

"I didn't lie to you," he said quickly. "Fae can't lie."

"I can't believe you! You made me believe ..." I clenched my teeth and turned away. I couldn't get angry. I couldn't risk sprouting a dragon tail or something else right now.

"I didn't trust you enough to let you know I'm a prince."

I wheeled around. "I told you I was a princess! How is that any different?"

Dormir shook his head. "My people aren't trying to kill yours."

I scoffed. "So what is the plan now, *Your Highness*?"

He frowned, but I didn't care that I'd offended him.

"Just answer me *one* question." I tightened my hands into fists. "Did you bring me here intentionally? So your *mother* could imprison us and you could get justice for everything?"

"Elisa, your anger," he warned.

"You speak to me of anger?" I shouted. "You passed out because of yours."

Dormir's brows shot up. "I won't sprout more scales."

I snorted and retreated to the back of my cell. "Am I allowed a blanket, at least?"

Dormir stared at me, then finally rubbed the back of his neck. "I will see if they will allow that. They are talking right now about using you as a bargaining chip."

"You mean, holding me for ransom."

He lowered his hand.

I rolled my eyes. "I don't know *why* I put so much trust in you." I turned away.

"So you're just like your mother."

"I'm *not* the one who imprisoned you, Dormir!" I snapped. "I trusted you! I relied on you to get me here and—"

"And I did!" he yelled back. "Not only did I get you here safely, I saved you in the Ancient Wood *and* got you council with my mother. It's not my fault you didn't articulate your needs well enough to convince her to help you."

"Well"—I faced him—"perhaps we should give you an award. Or better, why don't you just take me back to the Ancient Wood and allow the trees to kill me? It's better than being kept here for who knows how long. And what will you and your sweet mother do? Watch me slowly turn into a monster?" I scoffed. "And to think I was afraid of Selina." I turned away again, furious I had nowhere I could run and hide from him. My nails bit into my biceps. "You should have left me to die in the trees," I choked.

Dormir didn't answer.

My stomach clenched and I took a deep breath to steady my anger. Even if I was furious with him,

I needed someone there. The silence stretched, and I was afraid he'd left, so I glanced over my shoulder.

"I'm sorry," he said. He looked at me with disgusting pity.

I wiped a tear from my cheek and sniffled.

Dormir looked at the bars. "You seem like a really nice girl. I'm sorry this happened to you."

"But I deserve this because I was born." I don't know why his words stung so much. I thought we had built a friendship. He looked at me in a way Gerard didn't, and we were engaged. But what would I know of friends? I walked back to my corner and sat down. "You sound just like my mother," I whispered.

"Elisa …"

"You can go." I refused to meet his gaze.

"Maybe I can talk to my mother again. Get you another—"

"I said go!" I yelled. My black claws extended, and I felt like I could breathe fire.

Dormir actually took a step back.

Tears of anger, frustration, and self-hatred burned through me. I hated what I was. I hated I was so naïve to not know what my mother had done to the faeries. The faeries didn't have a cure, they didn't even know about my curse. This entire journey had been for nothing.

And now I was stuck in prison.

Because I was too gullible.

Sometime later, I looked up when I heard footsteps. I scoffed at myself when my heart sunk because it wasn't Dormir. To think I'd hoped to see his lying face.

The woman opened a single bar and slid in a tray of food. "Your breakfast. Lord Dormir also requested I bring blankets."

I walked over. "Thank you," I said softly. "Will—" I took a big breath. "Will he get in trouble for being mixed up in this?"

The fae woman with long red hair didn't answer.

"His mother didn't appear too pleased last night. He shouldn't be punished for my foolishness." I took the blanket and hugged it to my chest. "Can you please tell him I'm sorry?"

She smiled briskly. "I can deliver your message."

"And thank you for the food." I set the blanket on the floor and sat on it as I pulled the tray onto my lap. I didn't feel like a princess at all. I didn't want to think what my mother would do when the fae queen told her of my stupidity.

What if Mother left me here? What better way to get rid of her transforming daughter?

With nothing to do, my mind ran wild with worry. I paced. I studied the landscape. I wondered what, if anything, would have changed in our world if I had died in the Ancient Wood, if anyone would even miss me. Marigold and Dahlia would.

The woman returned to bring me lunch, and I couldn't bring myself to ask about Dormir.

She returned at dinner.

I didn't see Dormir.

I wrapped the blanket around myself and stood near the bars.

I was so unaware I didn't hear someone approaching until I felt the shadow fall over me. I turned and gasped. "Gerard! You came back!"

He grinned at me. But there was something sinister in his eyes. He dug into his pocket and produced a beautiful purple stone.

"You found it! Can it cure me?" I reached through the bar, but he pulled away.

"No, it can't." He smirked. "This was quite a fortunate circumstance—for me." He eyed the bars as he stepped back. "I mean, breaking your heart was going to devastate you anyway, but now I don't have to worry about any repercussions from your family. The faeries will have killed you, your family will mourn, and I will take the throne."

"What ... are you saying?" I asked, my words strained.

His gorgeous green eyes met mine. "The faeries have already sent a message to your mother, detailing how they would like a trade. They will return you if she gives them more land. Of course"—he looked to his right the same instant I heard screaming—"They won't live that long. It was foolish of them to have only one way up to their cliff city and to build it completely out of wood." He chuckled so darkly I couldn't believe he was the man I had once fallen so in love with. "Now they will die, and you will perish with them. I couldn't have planned this better." He held his arms out to his side. "And with you gone, who will take the throne?"

"My sisters!" I shouted.

"Hm, I will have to get them out of the way, then." He rubbed his chin. "Of course, I will have to be very calculated. It might take me a week or so. We have to have a funeral for you, and I have to work my way into your poor, sad mother's heart."

"Gerard, you can't possibly leave me here!" I gripped the bars to my cell. "You need to save me!"

"No. I really don't." He pocketed the gemstone and winked. "Farewell, Elisa. I hope you don't suffer too much." He disappeared out of my line of sight.

"Gerard!" I pressed my face against the bars. "Gerard!"

I couldn't see what was going on, but I heard the screaming. And I realized the sound hidden behind was the sound of fire. With their wooden structures, I knew the city would burn like kindling. Someone needed to do something! I hoped the faeries would have some sort of contingency plan. Surely, they would have prepared some method to get water on the wooden structures should something like this happened.

But the screams weren't stopping.

If only there was a way to help them …

I hadn't heard my inner voice for a little while. I seemed more comfortable with Dormir around, and now with the chaos, the voice seemed to know I needed something.

I took a breath. "No one can help them."

You weren't born to die in a fire! You are a dragon!

I drew a shaky breath. "No. I can't …"

If you don't accept who you are, they will die.

The words echoed in my mind. The fae city was being destroyed, and I knew no one was trying to save them. They'd already gone through exile, and now this. But if I accepted myself as a dragon ...

"What's the worst that could happen?" I wondered aloud. "Mother will lock me away the instant I get home, regardless. Gerard has already left me and took the stone. Dormir ... he could have been trying to get help like he promised. But how could he worry about me, a prisoner, when his city is going up in flames?"

I had to take a hard look at myself.

If I came to terms with who I was, I could save the faeries. If I didn't, I could die with them. Yet if I transformed into a dragon and the faeries put their fire out, then I would be a dragon without a home.

The wind carried the smoke in front of my cage, and I knew I had no choice.

If I didn't help them, no one would.

Even if they had locked me away, the right thing was to save them.

I looked down at my black, scale-covered hands, then reached up and touched my horns. One last time, I studied every inch of myself as a human girl. Crown princess of Griswil. I knew after this I would never be the same.

And I understood I was okay with it.

I drew a deep breath and closed my eyes. "Here we are, dragon. I've feared you my entire life. I'm tired of hiding. If you really are my destiny, then so be it."

I held my arms out and inhaled. A tingling sensation overtook my fingertips, then coursed down my arms. I opened my eyes and watched in stunned silence as my scales rippled like a bird's feathers. The black melted away and changed to a beautiful green with yellow hues like the leaves of trees in springtime. My clothing seemed to melt into my body as the scales covered it, and the bones in my fingers began to pop and twist—yet it felt completely painless.

My claws extended, taking place of my fingers on my hand, which became much larger than it had been. I expected to be afraid, but opening my heart to the dragon had also opened my wonder. I turned and watched as a tail reached out across the ground, and my stance changed to my hands and feet.

The small prison couldn't contain my size, and as I grew into my dragon form, I pressed against the bars at the front. They groaned in protest and, with a coaxing push, broke. I placed my clawed feet on the edge of the opening and leaned out to survey the damage.

The faeries had gathered at the entrance to their cave city, but for some reason there wasn't a way down. I didn't have time to look over myself now the transformation was complete. The fires were spreading, and several faeries were trapped, screaming for help.

No better time to learn than the present.

The voice in my head … was me. The side of me I'd never been willing to face.

I spread my wings as I pushed out from the cave. However, panic stopped my heart as I dropped. I had misjudged the weight of my dragon body, and with great effort flapped my wings. At first, they felt heavy, foreign, and slow, but with each push against gravity, I lifted into the air. Now was not the best time for flying lessons, but I had to figure it out at some point. I rolled from one side to the other, testing the turn of my wings against the wind.

"A dragon!" a woman cried. "Please, help!"

She stood on the porch of her small home with a young child in her arms and two clinging to her legs, coughing. Their home wasn't on fire yet, but they were trapped by the smoke. I flew over, the wind from my wings pushing the smoke aside, and reached out my hand to them. The children began to wail, and they clung behind their mother.

"It is safe, I promise," I reassured, but it was difficult to hold my hand steady while beating my wings so I didn't fall from the sky.

The mother set the youngest on the ground, picked up her oldest, and tossed him into my hand. I caught him easily. She did the same with the daughter, and then picked up her infant, took a breath, and jumped herself. I managed to keep them all in my hand, my claws curled to allow some kind of barrier, and tried to hold them as steady as possible as I lowered down to the ground.

I landed rather hard, and the little girl tumbled from my hand with a scream. I managed to reach my other hand out and catch her before she hit the ground and heaved a sigh of relief.

The mother ran over and hugged her children as soon as they were safe and looked up to me. "Thank you."

I nodded to her and flew back into the sky. There were still a lot of faeries trapped, and I had to move much faster than I was. Luckily, the longer I flew, the more natural my body began to feel. Soon, I had cleared those faeries who were trapped and turned my attention to the large group trapped in front of the palace.

I descended from the sky, trying to push the smoke away and give them fresh air to breathe. "I am here to help," I explained as I touched the ground and lowered my body to the earth. "Climb onto my back. I believe I can carry all of you at once if you are careful."

The people turned to their queen for permission.

The queen motioned without hesitation. "She has saved many of our people already. Go!"

Some people clamored, climbing up, grabbing on to whatever scales or horns were down my spine, and others allowed me to open my hands and pick them up. It took me several trips before I returned at last to recover the queen, her guards, and Dormir.

The queen stood with her soldiers, and one of them had Dormir's slumped form over his shoulder. The guards struggled trying to get him up until I offered to carry him in my hand. He looked so small and fragile.

Once they were on, I carried them down to the ground with the rest of the people, who watched as their only sanctuary burned down in flames.

"Why would you do this?" someone asked, looking at me.

"Yes. I saw you come with those men. You came to burn us down?"

People began shouting at me, and my heart sank. "I didn't do this," I insisted. "I was locked away in your prison."

Queen Misla stepped in front of me. "It wasn't she but her companions who started this." She turned to me. "Though we don't know why."

"I don't know either. Gerard was my betrothed. He wanted the spring stone so he could help cure me. Or so I thought. I can't answer for him. He betrayed me as well as you. I can, however, promise that he isn't done. He left with a threat to take my throne, so I must stop him before he hurts my family."

Gerard would regret leaving me to burn.

I had accepted the dragon within and would use it to bring him down.

SEVENTEEN

"Where will we go?" someone asked.

I looked over the small crowd. "What about that cathedral? A'Luvien," I asked. "There's an entire forest there, young and waiting. I think the trees would be happy to see you return."

"We need somewhere safe. If soldiers come for us there, we would be exposed and vulnerable," Misla explained. She looked up at the burning buildings with a look of dismay.

I turned and followed her gaze.

The city was gone, lost to the fire. The stables where the horses had been kept was also destroyed, but none of the horses were there. It was likely Gerard had taken at least one of them when he fled, so all I could pray for was that Tao had fled to safety.

194

I didn't know what else to suggest. I didn't know where they could go and be safe—I couldn't even tell west from east. Gerard had destroyed their only home, the only place they were legally allowed to live. They could stay near the mountains, but the night was settling in, and the cries of the children reached out to my heart. I couldn't carry all of them at once either. I wasn't big enough or trained enough.

"I could scout for a location," I offered. "But I'm afraid I still wouldn't know the best place. Perhaps I could take Dormir with me?" I hinted with my head toward Dormir's form.

Misla walked over to Dormir and knelt at his side. She reached out and smoothed his hair. "He tried to argue on your behalf. He said you were kind and only trying to look out for your people. He also explained you didn't know about us and that there is much you don't know." She turned her gaze to me.

"It is true," I admitted. "My mother kept me hidden away so I wouldn't turn into a dragon. She never told me about your exile." I sat down on my hindquarters. "What, exactly, is wrong with him?"

"Dormir had an accident as a child. A few days ago, he went to A'Luvien to plead with the gods so he might find relief. It is rather unfortunate. He is fine unless his heart begins to race too much, such as when he is angry, frightened, or stressed." She leaned back on her feet. "I believe it is also why he won't try and find a wife."

"It seems a little odd to me that the way to wake him is through a kiss."

195

Misla gave me a startled look. "How did you know?"

I was suddenly grateful to be a dragon so she couldn't see my blush of embarrassment. "The trees told me." I was about to explain the entire story, but a sound on the wind caught my attention. I got to my feet immediately and inclined my head as if that would help me hone in on the origin.

Giant wings.

As the sound drew closer, the faeries began to mutter to each other.

I looked at Misla.

"It sounds like ... like another dragon," she said in disbelief. She stood close by, searching the skies like everyone else.

A massive black form appeared overhead. I heard a rumble through the sky and understood the words. "Don't be frightened. I am coming to speak with you." The dragon landed a moment later.

He was at least twice my size, much bigger than any home I'd seen along my journeys. His scales glinted in the dim light, but I couldn't quite make out the colors. Brown, possibly with a bit of red? Then again, it could have been the reflection of the flames.

"You're a dragon!" he stated excitedly.

"Yes, I am," I replied.

"A new dragon ... You must be ... But how?" He looked at Misla, then back at me. "I need you to come with me."

I blinked. "I'm sorry, but I don't know you."

"Of course not." He shook his massive head. He had six horns on the back. "But I need you to come with me now."

"I can't. I am in the middle of helping the faeries. In case you missed their burning city?" I flicked my tail.

The dragon looked up and suddenly transformed into a tall man with broad shoulders and clothing unlike anything I'd seen. He wore robes like a wizard, but they were elegant and made of flowing material I could only compare to silk. He also had a beard braided into two sections at his chin, like the horns he had there in his dragon form.

He lowered his head to Misla. "It has been long, Your Highness." He bowed to her.

Misla stepped forward, her eyes wide and pupils dilated. "Nicholia. It has been long, dear friend." She bowed, then straightened. Suddenly she ran forward and wrapped her arms around him. "It has been so long."

"Forgive me for not recognizing your plight with the fire. I saw the dragon and had to come." He looked at me again. "You don't understand how important you are, young woman."

I laughed. "I already know I was cursed, though I'm beginning to wonder the validity of that, considering part of that story also details that the faeries will save me, and they've never heard that before. My name is Princess Elisa."

He shook his head. "You're so much more than a princess. You're the favored."

"Stop." I shook my head. "I just barely accepted that I'm a dragon at all. Besides, I have other pressing matters. The man who started this fire is on his way to take the throne. I don't have time to go speak with dragons."

Nicholia nodded once. "I see. You know nothing of the truth? That you were taken?"

"No. I was cursed," I insisted. I repeated my memorized curse. "*A curse upon her head, I place, that all will see her truest face. The rage of a dragon shall grow inside until, the truth, she can no longer hide. When she reaches her eighteenth year, her destiny will be made clear. She will hear the dragon's call, then she will come and destroy you all.* I've just turned into a dragon, so the last part of that curse is destruction."

Misla stepped away. "They changed the prophecy," she muttered.

Nicholia rubbed his chin. "The only recommendation I can make is that you trust me and allow me to take you to the other dragons. We can help teach you how to be a dragon, and your real parents can explain what happened."

I started to pace. "You tell me that, not only are there other dragons, but I have birth parents and there's actually a prophecy, not a curse? And where have they been all this time? Why didn't they come save me?"

"There's so much you don't know," he said delicately.

"He's telling the truth," Misla added. "Nicholia is one of the elder dragons. He wouldn't lie."

198

Nicholia looked to Misla. "Perhaps the roses can help."

"Roses?" I looked at Nicholia. "There was something about a rose bush in a letter on my birthday …"

He gave me a little smile. "I know it's hard right now, but can you please trust me? You can carry some faeries, and I will carry the rest. We will take them to where the dragons have been hiding all these years. They will be safe, and you will get the truth. You can choose what to do after that."

My head was reeling. As if transforming into a dragon wasn't enough!

I felt a hand on my foot and looked down to see Misla.

"I know this is overwhelming for you, child. Everything will make more sense when we get to the dragon lands."

Overwhelming didn't seem to cover it. Numb, yes. I nodded and leaned forward onto my belly so she and her men could climb onto my back. As they went to lift Dormir, he grumbled and began to wake.

Misla climbed back off and over to him. She placed her hand on his cheek with tenderness. "Take your time."

His eyes rolled and he tried to lift his head.

"Focus on me. There you go."

He looked dazed, but had come back from whatever place his mind stole him off to. "What happened?" He rubbed his head and winced at a tender spot.

"I will catch you up as we fly to the dragons' nest." Misla kissed his forehead and returned to my side.

The two soldiers helped Dormir to his feet, but as soon as he set eyes on me, he scrambled backward, just like he had the first time we met. One of the soldiers caught Dormir when his boot caught a rock and he fell backward.

"This is Princess Elisa," his mother explained. She hurriedly explained how Gerard had stolen the stone, set the town aflame, and how I'd saved them.

Dormir looked up at their home, now in ashes, and his shoulders slumped. "At least Elisa was able to save us. That couldn't have been an easy decision for you," he said, looking up at me. "I know how afraid you were to become a dragon."

I nodded softly. "It is done. I guess we get to go to the dragons and get some more answers, and then I've got to stop Gerard from whatever he's got planned."

Dormir rose to his feet. "Thank you."

Most of the people climbed onto Nicholia's back since his dragon form was so much bigger than mine. He guided me into the night sky. It wasn't until I truly got in the air that I realized my vision had changed with the dragon. I could see through the darkness as if the sky were lit by a bright summer moon and saw orange-red details in the forest below.

"What are those?" I asked. "The orange marks below."

"Those are animals. You're able to see with what's known as infrared vision. Your dragon senses can pick up on creatures, movements, and differences in the landscape that no one else can. You've got hunter's eyes now."

We flew along the Drakespine Mountains, heading northward. I knew that only because the mountains ended at the south, toward Terricina, and we hadn't reached the end. Nicholia turned to the right when the mountains gaped into a deep pass. We flew through it, then over an open expanse until he reached a cluster of tall white-capped mountains.

"Where are we?" I asked.

"We flew over the Weeping Woods, and we're on the border between Arington and Ashwrya."

"We flew across the entire country?"

He rumbled a chuckle. "You fly much faster than you could ever run. Travel is cut significantly. You'll never want to travel any other way."

Dawn appeared on the horizon.

"Earlier ... you transformed out of your dragon form. I didn't think dragons could do that?"

Nicholia looked over at me. "Very few can. It's an adaptation to try and keep us safe and hidden. I'm a scout, and it's my responsibility to gain information. I can't do that in this world as a dragon."

"Why *have* you all been hiding?"

He smiled. "You ask a lot of questions. We're nearly there. Unfortunately, if you are pressed for time, we won't be able to answer all of your questions tonight. You will need to return when you are done handling your situation with the gem snatcher."

I nodded.

The mountains had a ring of thick fog encompassing their base. Nicholia guided us through the valleys and toward the mountaintops until he descended into a beautiful meadow. The waking sun spread light down across the valley, slowly revealing every beautiful crevice. In spite of it being high in the mountains, the valley was covered in lush green foliage. A magnificent waterfall with a constant and comforting roar pooled on one side and then traveled down a thin stream and carried on into the valley.

Simply put, it was magical.

The trees were much smaller and had much bigger tops. The leaves were also tiny, like flower petals, and drooped with hanging flowers. The trees seemed almost blue in the light, and the flowers all around us glowed in the remaining darkness in vibrant purples, pinks, greens, blues, and white.

We landed in the open space between the waterfall and the mouth of a cave.

The faeries climbed off our backs. Many children rubbed their eyes as they were helped down and then picked up.

"The cave still has rooms inside and should be fully stocked except for food. Go on and I'll send some people in to help." He turned to me. "You and I are going to go talk with the dragons. This way." Nicholia led the way to the waterfall and then stepped through. The water splashed across his back, and he disappeared.

I stared in momentary surprise and looked over my shoulder.

Dormir stood watching me. He smiled and waved.

I smiled back.

He followed his people into their cave, and I followed Nicholia into the dragons'.

It was time to learn the truth.

EIGHTEEN

I stepped inside a massive cave at Nicholia's side, my heart pounding in my ears, and then I wondered if dragons even had ears. I glanced at Nicholia and didn't see any exterior ears but spotted a small notch under one of his horns, protected by a curve in his skin.

He let out a low rumble in his chest, some sort of signal to other dragons nearby.

We entered a massive cave with stalactites hanging high overhead and glowing with the same kind of glow the faeries had summoned into the stones along the path to their mountain kingdom. Four stalagmites rose from the floor, and it was only then I recognized the stalactites and stalagmites weren't made of stone at all but enormous crystals.

The center of the cave was open, save the four stalagmites, and along the back curve of the wall were

204

two large eroded steps, as if the gods had built this cave for the dragons at the time of the mountains' creation, as if they knew dragons would hold council in this room. Beautiful purple and blue flowers grew from tiny pools of water, also offering a soft glow to the room and making it even more magical than it was.

Heavy footsteps came from my left, and dragons walked out from the tall mouth of a side cave. To my right, even more dragons, and they spoke to each other as they took their places on the platforms above me. Only two dragons looked identical. The rest were different colors, sizes, had different horns or none at all, spikes or ridges down their backs, smooth tails or tails with spikes or knobs. Two dragons were even bigger than Nicholia, and a small handful were as small as birds.

My heart swelled as if I was looking at my sisters, as if I were at home with my family.

Still, I felt very small and insignificant in this grand hall of dragons.

Two dragons approached from my right and I held my breath. They both glanced eagerly at Nicholia, who nodded in reply.

"I have brought the faeries with me," Nicholia said loudly, for all to hear. "Their home was burned down, and they have nowhere to go for now. I am allowing them to stay in the old caves, but they will need food and we need to check on any injured."

Dragons trotted down from where they stood without hesitation. They bowed their heads to me as they passed and left the cave. I couldn't help but think there was merit to Nicholia's statements. They all looked at me as if they'd never seen a dragon before.

"What name did they give you, child?" the woman before me asked. Her scales were brown, and she had a long narrow nose that came to a tip like a bird's beak. Her horns curved like mine, and she stood with the elegance and poise of royalty, but her eyes were warm—much different than the mother who had raised me.

"My name is Elisa," I answered.

"That's a beautiful name." She looked over at the man at her side.

The male dragon was green with what appeared to be tree branches for horns coming out from his head to look like a withered forest. He watched me with kind eyes. "This must be very shocking for you," he added carefully. "My name is Rowen, and this is my wife, Isaline. We believe …" He drew a breath. "We are your parents."

The lump in my throat tightened. I desperately wanted to believe it was a lie and the truth at the same time. I'd longed my whole life to be noticed by my mother, to make her proud, yet she was still my mother. She had been there through every significant moment, such as when I'd completed my first big mural of a dragon—even though she didn't like that it was a dragon, and seeing real dragons in the flesh, I realized just how horrible of painting that was. Still, Mother had stayed at my side when I was sick. She'd taught me about politics. She'd made most of my birthday celebrations delightful.

I wasn't sure I was ready for a set of new parents. I didn't know what to say to them either. Here stood a man and a woman—both dragons—claiming they were my real family. If I was truly a dragon, which clearly I was at least part, it would only make sense that my parents were dragons. But if my mother had an affair with a dragon that could shift, like Nicholia, I could be part dragon because of that. Or she could have told the truth and I really was cursed by a sorceress. Or there was the simple reality that these were my parents and somehow I ended up with humans to raise me.

My head ached as I tried to make sense of everything.

Nicholia turned to address the other dragons. "I know this is rather shocking to all of you. This is Crown Princess Elisa of Griswil. Until today, she didn't know she was born a dragon. The parents who raised her are the king and queen of Griswil and raised her to believe that not only was she their daughter but that she was cursed to become a dragon."

"Despicable," someone nearby spat.

The dragons were none too pleased. Several others voiced their outrage.

Nicholia nodded. "I know. She feels the same way. Elisa is overwhelmed right now, and we ask you to please not demand too much. The next few days we will …"

Nicholia's voice faded from my attention when Isaline gave me a soft smile. "Why don't you come with Rowen and myself, and we'll talk, just the three of us?"

I nodded. "That would be nice." I surprised myself with how small my voice sounded.

She smiled a little wider and led the way down a nearby hall and turned into another cave, though it could only fit about ten full-sized dragons. "Perhaps you can tell us a little bit about this curse you were told as a child?" She sat on one of the large pillows along the outside of the room.

Rowen sat at her side.

I found myself longing for Dormir so I could hold his hand and feel his reassurance, but I sat across from them as confidently as I could. I didn't know how I would hold his hand as a dragon, but his presence alone would be enough. I cleared my throat and repeated the curse I had known my whole life. "But the dawn of my seventeenth birthday, a week ago, there was a letter that came. It said something about a rose and then me having a decision or the kingdom would be at risk."

Isaline glanced at Rowen.

"Roses?" Rowen muttered.

"It would make sense. The human queen banished them shortly after ... *Elisa* was taken. Perhaps the garden of roses is the answer?"

Rowen turned to me. "Did you ever see roses in Griswil?"

I shook my head. "Mother said they were a cursed plant, regardless of what stories said. They were poisonous and a single prick could make you sleep forever."

"I would like to take you to the garden of the roses," Isaline said. "I don't wish to overwhelm you more than necessary, but I believe the queen took your prophecy and twisted it to fulfill her desires."

"Prophecy?" I looked at each dragon. "Not a curse?"

Rowen shook his head. "As Isaline said, you are dear to us for more than the reason you are our daughter. You are the first dragon born in many, many years. A prophecy was given about your arrival. The prophecy says this: *A blessing upon her head I place, for she will save the dragon race. When she faces her greatest fear, her destiny will be made clear. She will hear the prophecy's call, and the reign of humans will finally fall.*"

On one hand, a curse.

On the other, a prophecy.

"I don't understand," I finally admitted out loud. "There's so much conflicting with how I was raised. What if I'm not your daughter? What if I'm not this ... special dragon who was supposed to save the dragons? I'm just a girl." I looked down at myself.

"And what if you are more than you ever dreamed?" Isaline asked.

"A prophecy," I repeated. I wasn't just a girl. I wasn't just a princess either. Deep in my heart, I knew their words rang true.

Isaline rose to her feet and walked to me. "Come with me." She offered me a reassuring smile and left the room.

If I wanted answers, I had to try and find them.

Rowen smiled and nudged his head. "Go on."

I followed her farther down the hallway, which wound and sloped upward toward the top of the mountain.

"I can't imagine how confused you must be," she said over her shoulder.

"I am," I confirmed. "May I ask some questions?"

"Absolutely."

I didn't know where to start. All the answers I wanted to know came at me with no sensible order. "How old was I when I was taken?"

"Just a child. Only two years of age." Elisa, what you must understand is, we desperately tried to keep you safe. We tried to keep you hidden and protected because our world was in chaos. The dragons and faeries were at war with humans, who had come in and were taking over the land." Pain was etched between the scales on Isaline's face, but before I could dwell on it, she looked away. "We failed," she whispered. "They came in the night when I was on patrol. Rowen had worked all day, building fortifications with the faeries and was exhausted. They slipped in and took you right from his arms. He fought for you. He killed half of them, but he was in his human form, and they nearly killed him." When I didn't answer, she looked back at me.

210

"I have no recollection of any of that," I explained. "I should remember. But I don't—"

"It is possible they had a wizard remove those memories from your mind," she offered.

"It's very likely," I answered, thinking of Jarrett, the friendly old wizard Mother always went to for everything.

Had he been the one to remove my memories?

I wondered what he thought every time he looked at me, knowing my true heritage and knowing he had used magic to suppress it all. Did it make him happy? Terrified? Proud? I would have to ask if I ever got the chance.

"You mentioned human form. I saw Nicholia transform too," I said. "Are all dragons able to do that?"

"In the past, dragons were unable to transform. Nicholia was one of the first to do so. Quist was one of our mighty kings, the wisest dragon known. He was gifted with a rare magic and bright mind. In fact, he is the one who gave us the prophecy about you." She smiled at me. "Quist explained that learning to transform would be the next phase of our existence, our evolution. For a while, many frowned upon those who chose to be a shifter, but Nicholia saw the advantages long ago. In the battle against the humans for Griswil, he convinced many others to accept it as well. Rowen and I happily followed him."

Isaline stopped at the mouth of the cave. Starlight and moonlight spilled through the opening, reflecting off her scales and giving her a glow.

I'd trusted Gerard, and he'd left me to die. I'd trusted Dormir, and he left me locked in a cell. If I trusted Isaline ... would she do the same? Then again, I felt in my heart that she was telling the truth. The sincerity in her eyes told me she was trying to give me answers. And if I had to follow her to a garden of thorns, I would risk it to know the truth.

I followed her through the opening and found myself in a garden with cliffs on one side. A hedge of fat yellow roses and small pink roses protected us from the dangerous edge. In fact, the entire garden was filled with roses of varying colors. To my right was a row of snow-white roses, and clustered with them, gorgeous beige roses. I'd seen roses in paintings before, but never in real life, and they were breathtaking. Some had large wide petals, others had tightly wrapped tiny petals.

"To transform back into a human form, all you need to do is recall who you were before," Isaline explained. "I imagine it will be rather easy for you since you were raised a human."

Glittering light grabbed my attention, and I turned to watch Isaline transform into an elegant woman with blond hair, bright blue eyes, and my chin. I knew I didn't look anything like the mother who had raised me, but I never imagined I could ever look so much like someone.

Isaline looked just like me. Or rather, I looked just like her.

I imagined myself as I had been, and in little time I was a young woman again.

"Elisa—" Isaline's breath caught, and tears glistened on her lashes. Her fingertips brushed her throat.

"I look just like you," I finished for her. Based on looks alone, Isaline had to be my mother. She just had to be.

We stood feet away from one another, both too hesitant to move any closer. And then I did one of the bravest things I'd ever done.

I stepped forward and wrapped my arms around my mother.

NINETEEN

Isaline sniffled, and I leaned back to find her wiping tears from her eyes. "Go on. You need to find out the truth." She gestured toward the roses.

Reluctantly, I stepped away and turned to the nearest roses. They were pink and reminded me of Dahlia. The sharp thorns under their heads looked dangerous but lured me closer. If I wanted to know the truth, according to that letter, I needed to prick my finger on a thorn.

I licked my lips and grabbed the stem of the rose. A thorn dug deep into my thumb, and I hissed and pulled back. A single drop of blood landed on the petal and sunk into the center of the flower.

A blessing upon her head, I place, for she will save the dragon race.

A curse upon her head, I place, that all will see her truest face.

Whispered words rushed around me, a mix of the curse I'd grown with and the prophecy just revealed. Dizzying white light flashed behind my closed eyelids.

Everything stopped.

I peeled my eyes open and found myself on the shores of a lake I'd never seen before. The gentle waves lapped at my bare feet. I wiggled them deeper into the sand, squishing it between my toes. I'd been to the ocean's shore at Terricina last summer. Prince Ulrich had snuck me on one of his ships for a day excursion with Ismae. She pretended not to be interested in him, but I knew then that she was madly in love.

Mighty dragon wings beat overhead, and I raised my eyes to catch the sunlight glint off a golden dragon as he flew by. His shadow stretched across me. I turned to watch him land in an open space behind me, so gently he didn't make a sound.

"Quist!" a woman greeted.

"What news do you bring?" a man asked.

The golden dragon tucked his mighty wings against his back. "I bring a prophecy," Quist answered.

I ran to the side of the mighty dragon to get a proper look at him. The others had mentioned his name, Quist. Mother said he had been one of their kings, and I could see why. His golden scales shone as bright as the rays of the sun. Two ridges came to a tip at his nose, but stretched upward over his eyebrows, then curved out on each side of his head and into two large, translucent white horns. Smaller white horns protruded beneath those, acting as a shield to his neck. His claws were the same shade of white. He had a short face, but his smile spread all the way up to his ears.

A woman I recognized as Isaline stood hand in hand with a young man who must have been Rowen.

"Are you here to help us with this war?" Rowen asked.

He shook his head. "You can do this without me. But I do have a promise. You will be blessed with a child."

Isaline and Rowen gasped simultaneously, and Isaline put her hand on her husband's chest.

"I must also give you her prophecy," Quist continued.

"Her?" the man asked.

Quist nodded. "I saw her." He looked to his right and locked his eyes on me.

He couldn't possibly see me. Everything was in a blur like a memory. This was from the past. He couldn't see me, could he?

"The sun god showed her to me. She is brave and strong, and will be one of the keys to saving us all." He looked back at the two, and the glint off his scales blinded me.

The blinding sunlight dimmed, and I found myself standing on a burning battlefield. Tall and mighty trees stood around me, groaning as their trunks swayed, and their words whispered in a ripple: "Tell the faeries. More danger. Humans coming!"

I looked to my right. A mighty army was climbing the hill led by a general on an armor-clad horse whose face was hidden behind a helmet. Following the voices of the trees, I turned and ran away. I stumbled and fell to my hands and knees, my heart racing and fear choking me.

"Evacuate!" a voice shouted.

I lifted my head and saw the beautiful architecture of the faeries—grand carvings, tall windows, and statues. More than that, everything was familiar from the carved railings of the staircase to the wooden doors. It was the castle where I'd grown. My home.

A fae woman held a child against her chest and wore a crown upon her head. The child clung to his mother, his purple eyes wide in fear, but he didn't cry.

"Misla, the humans are near," a man said as he ran to her. "We've evacuated the city below and—"

"Now the castle." She shoved the child into his arms. "Take Dormir to safety. If he dies, the royal line will be lost forever."

The man snatched her hand. "Where are you going?"

She reached up and touched his cheek. "I have to ensure everyone is out of the castle."

"Let me do that," he insisted.

"It is my duty as queen." She ruffled Dormir's hair before kissing his forehead. "Stay with Papa, little light. Hold this tightly." She placed a purple stone into his tiny hand. "Don't lose this. It's magic and will keep you safe." She winked and then ran.

"They lived in the castle," I whispered, watching Dormir's father carry him down the hall toward the stairs.

A low whistle sounded before the wall exploded. Shrapnel flew at me. I flinched and ducked, but nothing struck me. I looked through the hazy dust and saw a shadow looming before me. I ran through it and out onto an open meadow.

Dazed, I slowly turned in a circle until I saw a mighty golden dragon, Quist, standing before me.

I took a deep breath. "Can you hear me?"

"Yes," he answered. "Elisa, you were chosen long ago before you came to his earth. You were powerful even then, and confidence radiated from you. You are that same woman if you choose to be. You've heard the prophecy. You've seen the short history of your land. You feel in your heart the truth."

"But I don't understand," I interrupted. "If I was so important, how is it the humans got me? And why did no one save me?"

He shook his head. "The humans heard of the prophecy and wanted to prevent it from coming true. During the dark times, they launched a war against faeries and dragons alike. You were so young. They took you and fabricated a lie to keep you human. As you heard, they twisted your prophecy and made you believe it was a curse."

I pondered a moment before asking, "When my scales first appeared, they were black. Now they are green. Why is that?"

"Because you've been suppressing your dragon side," he explained. "You were raised to believe dragons were bad, that you were human. When your dragon side fought to come forward, you forced it down. You hated yourself so much, your scales came in black. Had you maintained that hatred, you would have been a black dragon with a much darker future. If they could have kept your dragon side at bay long enough, you never would have transformed at all."

I blanched. "Never?"

Quist nodded. "Had you been raised a dragon and never transformed into a human, you would never be able to. They nearly succeeded and would have if you hadn't been brave enough to find the solution."

I closed my eyes. "It is my destiny, then, to destroy them?"

"I cannot answer that, for that part of the prophecy has not yet occurred. It only says you will end their reign. Your choices and decisions determine the fate of your sisters and the people you knew as family."

"What of the faeries?" I asked. "I want to help them. I want them to have a home. I noticed ... as I traveled ... the abandoned cathedral looked very much like the castle. And I saw the vision with Dormir and his family in the castle."

Quist smiled solemnly. "It is true. The humans also took the kingdom from the faeries, which is why they were exiled. When the humans obtained you, they pushed the faeries further away under the guise of Selina killing them."

"Selina is real?"

Again, he nodded. "She's a powerful sorceress. But she did not curse you."

I flexed my jaw. "But if I was so important, why didn't the dragons save me? I'm supposed to accept that I'm a dragon, fine. But you want me to accept that I'm some important person you have a prophecy about? And they just left me to be raised by humans?"

"They couldn't." He sighed heavily. "With the war and dangers in the world, they most likely would have been killed. Your father was gravely wounded trying to prevent you from being taken. He nearly lost his life. When the war turned in favor of the humans, many dragons fled. Many hid. Dragons are mighty but not invincible, and even with the powers of the dragons and faeries combined, they still lost." He tilted his head. "Not to mention the humans had you. The dragons didn't know whether or not they would kill you if they caught wind of an attack."

Tears came to my eyes. My head felt like it would explode. "What do I do?" I asked helplessly. "There's so much I still don't know."

He began to fade into the sunlight. "You have to make the decision yourself. Trust in who you are."

"But I have more questions! What about Gerard? Who is he?"

"Like you, he was raised by darkness. He has another destiny to fulfill."

"That doesn't answer my question."

Quist only smiled and disappeared.

I blinked and found myself in the garden again. Exhaustion sat heavily on my slumped shoulders. I turned and faced Isaline, and when I saw her worried expression, my frustrations immediately melted away.

"What did you see?" she asked.

I ran to her and threw my arms around her again. "You really are my mother."

She let out a laugh and hugged me tightly. Her tears dripped onto my head. My own tears ran down my cheeks. I didn't know what our relationship would mean or how we could build it. I'd been raised in an entirely different life, and I longed for nothing more than a relationship with my mother. Now I would have the chance to have one.

"You must be positively exhausted." She cupped my face as I stepped back. "You need a proper bath, warm pajamas, and a bed."

I laughed. "I haven't slept in a bed in days."

She went to pull away, but I stepped forward and caught her hand. She stopped and smiled at me. "Yes?"

"What about the faeries?" I pressed. "Are they safe here?"

She nodded. "Many faeries fled here with the dragons during the war, so we are used to having them near. We used to be allies after all."

I let go and exhaled all the tightness in my chest.

Isaline, my mother, led me back down to the main level and past the waterfall entrance to another side of the caves. I was surprised to see doors instead of openings, just like a castle would look were it built into a mountain. She stopped at one particular door carved with trees and guided me into the home.

"The shifters live on this side of the mountain, and the dragons live in the bigger caves," she explained as she stepped in. "I imagine Rowen is helping situate the faeries but will return before you sleep."

The room was decorated just like a home would be, with couches and a rug in the center. The stone at the back rose into a natural platform, and a large bed rested upon it. Above the bed was a tapestry depicting two dragons with their tails entwined, and I knew it was Isaline and Rowen. Other paintings lined the cave walls, depicting trees and magic.

"We have a bed over here, should you like to stay with us." She pulled a curtain back, revealing a small alcove with a bed and a single painting above it of a small green and yellow dragon.

"Who painted all of these?"

"Your father. Rowen," she corrected. "He's always been an artist. He painted that the day you hatched …" Her brows pinched and lips twisted in pain at the memory. "He painted a lot as he was trying to heal from the physical and mental wounds when the humans took you."

I reached out and took her hand again. "I do want memories with you. A relationship. The woman who raised me never treated me as one of her children. I think in my heart I always knew something wasn't right. I just didn't know anything else."

"Whatever your decision, I will accept." Isaline put her hand on my cheek. "But know Rowen and I welcome you with open arms."

"Did you have a different name for me?" I asked.

"We called you Aura because you were our light." She tucked her hair behind her ear. "The bath is on this side."

The room opposite the alcove was fit with a deep pool of warm water. My mother explained it was a natural spring, and they had used magic to divert the spring into the apartments for each of the dragons.

I didn't take too much time to soak in the bath in spite of the comfort the warm water offered me and my sore muscles. I wanted to sleep away the headache clawing at my mind. I climbed out of the bath and pulled on the nightgown my true mother had given me.

My mother.

My real family.

My true home.

I would face Gerard, save my sisters, and help get the throne back for the faeries.

I felt lips kiss my forehead and peeled my eyes open, not realizing I'd fallen asleep on the couch. Mother had given me some tea and a warm blanket while I waited for my father to return.

Rowen gave me an apologetic smile. "I didn't mean to wake you."

I stretched and sat up. "I wanted to speak with you before we turned in for the night. So thank you for waking me." I smiled back.

He was incredibly handsome. His long brown and green hair was tied up in a ponytail, and his brown eyes reminded me of chocolate. He had a square jaw and a terrible scar on his left jawbone and down his forehead above his right eye. I realized that eye was a little foggy.

"The scars ... are they from when you tried to protect me?" I asked.

His brow pinched, and he nodded. "I did try," he sighed.

I hastily got to my feet and took his hand. "I know. I saw. Quist showed me when I pricked my finger. He showed me when he told you and ... Mother that I would come. And the faeries being forced from the castle. He answered questions."

"Quist did?" Rowen's brows lifted in surprise. "No one has seen him since the day he spoke with us about you. What did he tell you?"

"Not much, I'm afraid." I sighed and let go. "Only that he had the prophecy, but it's my decision how I fulfill it." I looked around at their home. "Nothing will be the same no matter what I choose. Is everyone actually ready for that?"

"Elisa, we will follow you into death, if that is what it will take to protect our people."

I wasn't so sure.

TWENTY

W e've waited seventeen years for her return. I
could watch her all day."

"But she can't, darling. You know she has pressing
matters."

The grogginess in my mind didn't want to subside.
I wanted to stay in the peacefulness of sleep without
any responsibilities or "pressing matters." I just wanted
this all to be done. But I forced myself out of bed,
reluctantly dressed, and met my parents at the table
behind the couch for a hearty breakfast.

"Dormir has been asking about you," my father
said with a little chuckle. "I can't help but think the
boy likes you." He twitched his brows, though there
was stiffness to his right one due to the scar.

"Rowen! Don't tease her about that," Mother
scolded.

225

I giggled, my cheeks immediately burning pink in spite of myself. The parents who had raised me never would have teased like this. "I will have to find him after breakfast. Does he know I'm okay?"

Father gave me a knowing grin. "I made sure to tell him."

I would have been content pretending all was right with the world, and I even considered proposing it to my father and mother at breakfast. We'd talked about little things, like how Mother was part of the border guard and Father helped maintain the structures of the mountain passages. When he wasn't doing that, he took his own turn patrolling. They insisted they didn't want to bore me, but I wasn't sure I could have a boring conversation with them. Everything was so new.

When I'd had my fill, my mother ushered me away. "I'll clean up here, you go meet with Dormir. I'm sure he has a lot to ask you."

I stepped out into the sunlit meadow beyond the waterfall and took a deep breath of wet earth and nearby flowers.

"I don't think I've seen that big of a smile on your face since I've met you," Dormir said as he approached. His purple eyes glittered bright. He was garbed in the royal blue of his people. "Is everything …" He shifted his weight.

"It's fine," I replied. "I've already forgiven you."

His smile stiffened. "Elisa—"

"I feel right at home here," I continued before he could add anything. I began walking without

226

direction. Dormir rushed to stay at my side. "It's … perfect. I could stay forever. My real mother, Isaline, she took me to the garden of roses."

Dormir's brows shot up. "Isaline and Rowen are your parents?"

"You know them?" I asked.

He nodded. "Those that hide behind the waterfall are all the dragons who remained after the war. Isaline and Rowen have always been two of my favorites. They're fearless and completely devoted to each other and their people."

"Are they royalty as well?"

He leaned his head to the side. "Dragon hierarchy doesn't work the same way as it does with us. They don't have just one leader, but a small group."

"Nicholia is also one of them," I added.

"You're catching on fast." He grinned. "Quist was the greatest of them, but … no one has seen him in many years."

"I saw him last night," I said proudly.

Dormir leaned forward. "Actually saw him? Or just a memory?"

I shook my head. "He spoke to me. He confirmed that Isaline and Rowen are my true parents, didn't offer any help about Gerard other than he was raised in darkness, or something dramatic like that, and told me whatever I choose from now on is my decision to make." I rubbed my arm, feeling the weight of those words. "I'm not even eighteen yet and it's up to me to make a decision that will affect three different races."

Dormir stepped closer and nudged me with his arm. "If anyone is to do it, I'm glad it's you."

"And not the prince of the faeries?" I teased with a grin.

He stopped and took my hand. "Elisa, I do feel horrible for what happened with Gerard. I didn't leave you to abandon you either. You were alone in prison in a place you didn't know with people you trusted. Me."

"Dormir," I tried.

"Please let me finish." He looked into my eyes. "I didn't leave you to cry alone. I was speaking with my mother, begging her to listen to you. I told her I trusted you, that you could help us. I was trying to convince her to use you as a partner. I even volunteered to do what you suggested, be an ambassador. That's why I left you." Dormir's eyes searched my face and worry lined his brow.

My heart jumped. "I had hoped that's why you left. I was so afraid—"

"I know." He grimaced and tucked my hair behind my ear. "I should have told the guards to put you in the guest room." He dropped my hands and ran his fingers through his hair.

I reached out and took Dormir's fingers. "We can't change what happened. I believe that you were trying. All we can do now is move forward. Will you come with me when I go to the castle? I need—I mean, I don't need *you*"—I let go of him—"I just mean I need someone I know. There. With me. To, um, to make sure I don't do something stupid." I nervously played with my fingers. My excitement overtook my brain and I suddenly felt foolish. "Because I tend to do a lot of stupid things. If you haven't noticed."

The corner of Dormir's mouth pulled in a crooked grin. Gerard used to do that, and it always made my heart flutter. Dormir's grin made my heart melt. "You aren't worried that a narcoleptic fae will ruin everything?"

"Of course not. I saw—" I bit my lip.

He arched a blue eyebrow. "Saw what?"

"I saw the day the faeries left the castle. Your mother put you in your father's arms and gave you the spring stone. She was evacuating the castle, and your father ran with you."

Dormir's face softened. "What else did you see?"

"An explosion, but that was it. What happened?"

He walked to a nearby flower and touched the edge of a bulbous flower petal. "My father died that day. That's also when I got this curse of sleep." He glanced at me from the corner of his eyes. "I was just a child and still remember how much my head hurt. And how much I felt betrayed by the spring stone. It was supposed to keep us safe, yet my father was killed and I received a terrible head wound." He sighed, his shoulders rising and falling. "I haven't taken any royal responsibilities because I can't bring myself to touch that stone again." His hands were tucked behind his back, but I reached out and slid my fingers into his hand, causing him to drop them at his sides.

"I know so little about the stone or it's magic. But perhaps the magic isn't what you believe it is? Perhaps the magic has another purpose that isn't protection at all?"

"I suppose that could be," Dormir relented.

I smiled up at him, then looked around the meadow. "I truly don't want to leave this."

"What if I lose you?" Dormir's unexpected question broke the companionable silence we'd fallen into.

I met his gaze.

His cheeks flushed, and he cleared his throat. "I just mean I don't want you to die."

I grinned. "You won't lose me that easily. Oh, one more thing. I learned that your people are the true holders of the throne. What if we put your family back on it?"

Dormir stared at me with wide eyes. "You truly think you could do that?"

I shrugged. "It wouldn't hurt to try. I'm going to have my mother and father teach me some battle techniques before we go since I've never exactly been a dragon before." I turned, but Dormir didn't let go of my hand. I stopped and faced him.

He stepped forward in a fluid motion, slid one arm around my waist, and entwined the other in my hair. His lips caressed mine. Dormir felt like a blanket on a chilly night under a sky of bright stars. He smelled like warm rain on a hot spring day. He tasted like fresh berries.

I rose up on my toes and threw my arms around his neck. A shiver ran through my body as if I were standing on the edge of a cliff about ready to fall. But

I took the plunge and never looked back. His tongue began a dance with mine.

I held on to his shoulders, never wanting him to pull away.

But he did, reluctantly tugging my bottom lip between his teeth.

I gasped a breath and settled back on the ground.

Dormir ran his thumb over his bottom lip. "My apologies, Your Highness." His voice was a sunrise warming me to my core.

I knew he didn't mean the apology.

I laughed silently and gave him another longing kiss. "I feel like I've known you forever," I said against his lips.

He put his hand on my cheek. "We were supposed to, you know. Had you been raised a dragon, we would have at least met each other a few times." Dormir laced our fingers together. "You should go learn now as much as you can. I'll travel with you whenever you are ready."

"Every moment we waste is a moment Gerard is closer to his goal." I sighed. "He could already be on the throne."

Dormir took my chin. "Or your family could be putting up a fight. Learn what you can." He kissed my forehead, and a wave of electricity ran from my head to my toes. He stepped back and slid his hands in his back pockets.

I danced on clouds the whole way back inside the cave, looking back at Dormir more than once, and he watched me with the same big, dopey grin on his face.

I skipped down the hallway until I found my parents' home and walked in. "Mother, are you busy?"

Her eyes lit up, and she set the book down she'd been reading. "Not at all."

"Can you help me learn how to fly? I mean, I made it here all right, but I've sort of missed out on a lifetime of practicing." I ran my fingers over the soft leather sitting chair I stood behind.

"Certainly!" Isaline rose to her feet, and we went outside.

I spent the rest of the day in a flying crash course. Mother took me up into the sky high enough that I could see the tops of mountains around us.

"The most important thing to remember when flying is that the wind is your ally. Feel how it tugs on your wings?" She held hers out flat without flapping them.

I followed her example. The air pushed under my wings, lifting me higher.

"Good. Now, look down."

I complied and gasped. "We're moving!" The mountains below dragged toward my right. Or rather, I was dragged toward my left by the wind.

"These are air currents," Mother explained. "You can fly through most of them, but some can be surprisingly strong, especially those that pull into storms, so always make sure to feel the air around you. Now, tilt your wings down. We're going to dive." She snapped her wings to her side and dropped like an arrow, nose pointed to the ground.

I'd been terrified of heights my entire life, worried I would fall. And now my mother wanted me to drop toward the ground on purpose? That pit in my stomach that dragged me toward the edge, the part of my mind that made me wonder what it would feel like if I just … let go …

I could finally do it.

I closed my wings against my back—it was as simple as dropping your arms to your sides—and fell. Air rushed over my scales, my insides quivered with delight, and the wind whistled in my ears.

"Now open your wings and catch yourself!" My mother's voice was distant. She was far below me. I watched as she flung her wings out to her sides and jerked to a sudden halt.

My attempt was far less graceful. I shot my wings out, just as I'd seen her do, but the instant I did so, I tilted sharply to the right, overcorrected, and rolled left before I finally managed to right myself.

Mother laughed, the sound like pebbles tumbling down a slope. "Not too bad for your first try. You will, of course, need more training. There's a lake this way. It will provide a soft landing for what we're going to try next." She tilted her wings to the left, and an air current carried her in that direction.

I shakily followed her, not confident in allowing the wind to carry me. Not quite yet. The clouds parted, revealing a wide rolling meadow with a lake surrounded by trees on one side and nothing but grass on the other.

"I want you to start taking risks." Mother moved her wings. This close to the ground, the wind didn't have enough strength to hold up our heavy dragon bodies any longer.

"I know it's going to be frightening for you because you've spent your entire life on the ground. In everyday flight, what I've taught you will be sufficient." Her blue eyes studied me. "But I know you want to go after this Gerard person, and that means you will probably be fighting in your dragon form as well. I must admit, teaching you to fight as a dragon in a few days' time isn't sufficient. I worry about you going into battle without enough experience."

"But it's better to go having learned *something* than knowing absolutely nothing."

She sighed and nodded. "I agree. Which is why you are going to practice some maneuvers."

Mother directed me to fly as fast as possible toward the lake and, as soon as I met up with the tree line, to spin to my right or left. My body wasn't used to being in a dragon form, let alone intentionally shifting it suddenly off-center. More than once I hit the water and spluttered to the surface.

"Again," Mother would direct.

And again I would try.

This continued until my mother finally stopped me at the shore and directed me to the still-rippling surface.

"Look at yourself."

I looked down at my reflection. Water dripped from my scales into the water, distorting my image. "I see me."

"You see you as what?" she pressed.

I looked over at her reflection to study her brown scales, the way her horns twisted away from the sides of her head toward her tail. I shifted to my own reflection. I had the same horns, the same shaped face, only I didn't have a beak nose like she had. The same blue eyes, though. We had that in common as well.

"I look similar to you?" I glanced at her.

Mother chuckled. "Yes, you do. I'm trying to give you a deeper lesson. Look again. Are you a human?"

"No," I scoffed. "Look at me." I hinted with my chin toward all of me.

"I see you. I'm trying to get you to see yourself."

I moved my lips to one side and returned my attention to my reflection. The water had calmed, and now the surface reflected the image of my dragon face.

"Elisa, you have to trust yourself as a dragon now. You grew up in a human body, that is unfortunate, but you're holding yourself back. You're afraid. What are you afraid of? Falling? You hit the water ever time. And even if you hit the ground from the height you've been flying, it would only sting or take your breath for a few minutes." She stepped closer so her side brushed mine.

"I'm afraid of failing," I admitted. The sunlight warmed my scales, and the water gradually evaporated off them. On the breeze, I smelled hot sagebrush and tree sap. I curled my claws, feeling the soil cave beneath my feet. "The woman who raised me, I was never good enough for her. I wasn't allowed to do things because I was the *crown princess*." I scoffed with bitterness. "She didn't even let me go on horseback rides unless it was my birthday or the spring celebration."

My mother's tail wrapped around mine. "You could never disappoint me, Elisa."

"You say that now. I'm bound to do *something* that—"

"Elisa."

I turned and faced my birth mother.

"You're young. You can't possibly have all of the answers now. Even I make mistakes, and I'm positive that queen has too."

"She did sort of steal me," I conceded.

Mother grinned. "That she did. And now you're going to go up there in the air and do this again. Because you can. Because you are the daughter of Isaline the Guardian and Rowen the Caretaker."

"Caretaker?" I balked.

She laughed. "He isn't fond of it, but it's stuck. He's the one who taught the trees to speak, you know. He's always had an affinity for nature, but he can tell you about that himself later. Now. Try again!"

I flew up into the air and to the rocky section on the edge of a hill. I'd been using it as a reference point to turn and fly back to the lake. I knew I wasn't a human in a dragon body. I'd always *been* a dragon.

With renewed confidence, I bolted for the lake. When my toes brushed the tops of the trees, I tilted to the right with all my might, kept my wings straight out, and turned sharply. This time, I didn't hit the surface of the water. I didn't lose my balance. I was finally able to trust in my wings, my arms and legs, and my neck and tail.

Now I knew I was a dragon, and I wasn't going to be stopped.

TWENTY-ONE

I sat in the meadow at Dormir's side, watching the morning sky lazily stretch and wake. Clouds strolled by below us like curly wool, shielding our view of the valleys below. The rising sun transformed them into a painting of fire—bright yellows fading to orange, pink, and lavender. The sun seemed to push the blanket of the night sky off and welcomed us with open arms.

Dormir rested his hand on my knee, and I had my head on his shoulder. "How did your training go yesterday? You were too tired at dinner to talk much."

"It was difficult," I admitted. "But I'm already much better at flying. Mother taught me how to roll in the air. She said it's particularly helpful when someone is throwing fireballs at me." I giggled and sat up. "I

238

also know how to turn now without losing altitude, and I can use the air currents to help me fly."

"All in one day?"

I flinched. "I'm not an expert by any means," I confessed. "But at least now I won't fall out of the sky if I have to turn."

Dormir laughed.

I shoved his shoulder and rolled my eyes. "Father is going to try and teach me how to breathe fire today."

He raised his eyebrows. "Now that would be something I would like to learn."

Dormir looked at me.

I looked at him.

We both erupted into laughter.

He had a way of making me feel completely at ease. Gerard and I never sat and talked like this, not that we were given much of an opportunity to do so. He'd been too greedy to get his hands on the spring stone and never cared about me.

The sound of boots crunching grass drew our attention behind us to my father Rowen.

He nodded his head. "Morning. Are you ready, Elisa?"

I scrambled to my feet and dusted off my trousers. "Ready as I'll ever be! How does this work, exactly?"

"We can't practice up here because of the children." He gestured to the fae boys and girls running about the meadow, climbing the trees, and swimming in the pool beneath the waterfall.

"Of course not. The meadow where Mother trained me to fly?"

"Can I come and watch?" Dormir requested.

I transformed into my green and yellow dragon form. "Climb on!"

It didn't take long for us to fly down to the meadow I was at the day before. Still, it took me a solid three hours before I was able to burp up my first fireball, and it struck a nearby tree and completely engulfed it.

Father and Dormir couldn't stifle their laughter.

I threw them both a glare. "You aren't helping."

"Fire breathing should be as natural for a dragon as flying," Father said, still chuckling between words. "Don't think too hard about it. We want to focus on the fire, not your specific powers, which is what I think you're trying to summon."

"Wait, specific power?" I looked to Dormir as if he could help.

He lifted and dropped his shoulders in a shrug.

"Every dragon has a different power. Your mother, for example, can manipulate the earth. She can summon rocks from the ground, or break the ground, and even create a golem if she has the time."

"And what about you? Mother said you taught the trees to speak."

He grinned. "I'm a nature dragon. I can do anything with the trees, but I also take care of flowers and shrubs."

"If you're both dragons of earth, are my powers going to be related?"

"Not necessarily." He pointed to Dormir with his tail. "For example, Dormir is a fae. All fae can use magic to an extent, but some are gifted to be more powerful than others, like the royal line. However, not all humans are the same, correct?"

I furrowed my brows. "I think I follow what you're saying. The stable boy at the castle, Philip, he doesn't want to be a stable master like his father. He has other skills and wants to pursue a different life."

Father beamed. "Exactly! Only with dragons and magical powers."

I giggled.

"Now, fire. It comes from your belly, not your chest. Think of a time you got really upset, where does it fester?"

"My heart?"

He shook his head. "Really mad. Mad enough to break something."

I thought back to when I tore the dining room apart, weeks ago. The anger had burned in my chest, like that time I got a severe cold ... but it festered in my stomach. That's where my roar had come from too.

I faced the still-smoldering tree and drew a breath so deep even my belly expanded. Then I let it go. The acrid taste of boiled eggs rolled over my tongue and out my mouth, and with it a stream of fire that set all of the nearest vegetation ablaze.

"Wonderful!" my father praised. "That's perfect. Now that you know how to breathe fire, let's practice with battling." He flew off into the air.

I hesitated. "You want me to breathe fire at you?" I gaped.

"How else will you learn how to attack?"

"We're going to destroy this entire meadow!"

Father turned in a lazy circle, traveling around the burning mass of trees and back to Dormir and me. "It's due for a good burn anyhow. Fires help bring new life. Just try to avoid the trees."

"Avoid the ... Father!" I instinctively pulled my wings around my face when I spotted a ball of fire hurdling toward me. It hit my wings, but they acted like a shield, and all I could feel was the heat, and then the smell like charcoal.

"Good! Now, in the air."

I gave Dormir a sideways look. Luckily, he was at a safe enough distance he was able to run and not get hurt. "We should get him to safety."

"Then two targets to keep safe. The trees and your lover."

"Father!" I whined again, but in honesty, I didn't mind his teasing. It was a relief from the royal passivity I'd had to deal with my entire life.

This was the kind of training Mother had mentioned the day before. Training for battle. I had to remember to trust my body while dodging fireballs or drop attacks from my father and then return with my own attacks.

It was frustrating. He landed almost every strike of his claw or blow of his fire, and I only managed to strike him on the tail once. Exhausted, I landed on the ground beside the lake. Most fire had disappeared into the air, but a few had struck the ground and started small fires in the driest areas of the meadow.

I panted, a twinge in my shoulder with each breath.

"We can be done for now," Father said, landing at my side. He walked into the water to cool off and get a drink. "You're doing well."

"Well? I can't even hit you!"

He shook his head. "Elisa, this is only your second day of training. You'll have a lifetime more."

"Except we're supposed to leave and stop Gerard, remember?" I pointed out.

"Of course. But you're nowhere near ready to face him." My father tilted his head, giving me a sincere look of apology.

I didn't even want to look at Dormir and see his disappointment.

After lunch, we returned to the meadow and practiced again, this time without Dormir to watch. He had to stay behind and talk with his mother about leaving to fight Gerard. I did a little better but not much.

That night, after dinner, Dormir and I walked to the waterfall.

"How much longer are we going to stay here, Elisa?" he asked. "I know you can sense the feeling of standing on the edge of a dagger, waiting to slip."

I had sensed it since we went the opposite direction of my castle and reluctantly nodded. "I do feel it. I just … don't feel ready yet. There's still so much I don't know."

He stopped and put his hand on my cheek. "There's a lot of time for both of us. But not for your kingdom or your people."

I shook my head. "Or yours." I looked up at the night sky. "Give me one more day. Just one?" I asked.

243

Reluctantly Dormir agreed, and he pulled me into his arms, warming me from the chilly mountain air.

The next day, however, a horrible blizzard attacked the mountain peak. Magic protected the meadow, but Father forbade us from doing any flight training.

"No dragon can fly in this," he explained.

So he tried to get me to practice whatever "special" magic I had. I didn't seem able to do anything. I couldn't call upon the earth, or the trees, or manipulate stone, or anything. I even tried talking to the flowers, but it didn't work. And even though Dormir only watched, I knew he was growing restless.

The next day, the storm was still at full intensity.

I went to my father, wringing my hands. "I know you said it's dangerous, but I *have* to get down to Griswil. I have to get to the castle. I should have listened to Dormir and not prolonged the inevitable."

"You couldn't have known the storm would come," he insisted, though he got to his feet from his position on the couch. "And you *did* need the training. We could practice—"

I put up my hand. "No. No, we need to go."

He sighed. "Elisa, I know you are worried, but it's like I said. You can't fly through that storm. None of us can."

"And what if that storm doesn't relent?" I demanded.

His brow furrowed. "All storms relent."

"Unless it's a magical storm. Quist told me Selina, the sorceress, she's real." I took a big breath. "What if she's causing the storm?"

Father shook his head. "Why? You know you aren't cursed, and didn't you say Quist told you Selina wasn't involved? Why would she stop you from coming down?"

I opened and shut my mouth. If Selina really wasn't after me, he was right. She would have no reason to keep us from leaving the mountains.

I slumped down into a nearby chair. "I should have left two days ago." I put my face in my hands.

Father came over and pulled me into a comforting hug. "You needed to learn how to be a dragon. You needed to know how to fly and fight. You made the right choice."

"What if I didn't?"

"But what if you did?" He let go, and I looked up at him. "This Gerard fellow seems rather intelligent. If he has taken the throne, as you suspect, he would have anticipated battle right away were you still alive. He left you for dead, and now that this much time has passed, he must feel confident that you and the faeries have all been successfully eliminated. You have the element of surprise on your side."

I started. "You're right!" I jumped to my feet. "We can use this time to plan." I paced the floor. "I think we should have others come. Of course, only if they choose to. I don't know if Gerard has his army here or not." I stopped. "If we can have dragons hide in the trees surrounding the forest, the armies of the faeries with them, I can go in and speak with Gerard. I could ask if he is willing to give up peacefully."

I didn't miss my father's look of skepticism.

"I know it's a long shot," I said before he could. "I'm still going to try. And then I can threaten him with attacking if I need to."

My father nodded. "I can speak with the dragons and see what they feel. You go speak with Dormir and his people. I know you two have grown close."

I didn't hide my smile or blush this time. I liked Dormir, and I wasn't going to be ashamed of that. He wasn't Gerard. He wasn't going to twist a dagger in my back and leave me for dead.

I spoke with Dormir and his mother.

She wasn't confident at all in the plan. "We are already so few in number and have children to protect," she said, glancing at Dormir.

He scowled. "Mother, I'm not a child anymore. I'm the future king, and … if this is the act that proves it, then please let me step up."

"But, your head—"

He tilted his chin down. "Mother." He gestured with both hands toward me. "I went out on my own and found the lost dragon."

"Accidentally," I interjected.

"Still found you!" He grinned.

I chuckled and shook my head.

"In all seriousness, though," Dormir added, "I know the risk. Elisa knows the risk."

"I just don't think I can give you an entire army."

I stepped up. "I'm not expecting an army. I'm expecting however many men and women are willing to volunteer. If it's only five, so be it. We will figure things out."

We had to or all could be lost.

TWENTY-TWO

The day we left, we had about fifty faeries, including Dormir, and four dragons: Nicholia, my parents, and myself. Everyone else stayed behind, protected in the mountaintop. I didn't know what to expect. I'd never been in battle, and reading about battles never gave anyone experience either.

Dormir rode on my back as we descended into the valley below and headed for the rightful land of the faeries. "You're quiet," he called over the wind, his cheek pressed to my neck.

"I don't know what to say. I'm practicing the conversation I might have with Gerard."

"Hm … I can't imagine one can adequately prepare for that conversation."

247

I coasted on a wind current. "I completely misread him. I believed he was different. And now the entire kingdom is paying the price."

"Not yet. He hasn't won yet, Elisa."

The forest below grew sparse as roads came into view, and small villages and towns dotted the landscape. We began our descent, and my stomach rose into my throat. Talking about being brave is one thing. *Actually* being brave is another.

When the castle came into view, I actually turned away until Dormir asked me where I was going. "I can't do this!" I gulped for breath.

How can I possibly face a man daring enough to leave a princess behind to burn? A man willing to hurt my family? No, he'd never said he'd hurt them. He said he'd lie to them. But how else would he pry the throne from my supposed mother?

Dormir rubbed his hand up my neck. "Breathe. You can do this. Remember how excited you were to show Gerard how strong you are?"

"But he could be stronger than we know! Maybe he could actually kill a dragon! He left me for dead once, remember?"

"Then what about your sisters?"

I peeked over my shoulder at Dormir.

"How do you think they feel right now? They think you're dead. If Gerard really did take the throne already, that means he's betrayed their trust too. If you aren't here to exact revenge on him, do it for your sisters."

"You're right." I redirected my attention forward. "If I don't do this for anyone else, I have to at least do it for them."

Even saying that aloud didn't appease my nerves.

We landed far enough away that no scouts from the castle could have spotted us and reported us to Gerard. The dragons with us transformed and the group continued the rest of the way on foot, dispersing into the trees as to not draw any more attention to us than necessary. Nicholia took a group toward the north end of the castle, my mother took a group eastward, my father took a group toward the western walls, and I walked beside Dormir as we approached the southern side, the entrance of the castle.

"This feels surreal," Dormir said. "My whole life I've wondered what it would take to reclaim our land. It's not that I wanted the throne," he added.

I smiled reassuringly. "I never wanted the throne either. I prepared because it was my duty. It's a lot of pressure I don't want. In case you didn't notice by now, I don't exactly handle pressure very well. I'm afraid I'll fail."

He shrugged. "Failure is inevitable. Just dust yourself off and try again."

"Yes, but this failure could cause the lives of—"

"People who stepped up knowing that was a possibility." Dormir caught my fingers. "How many times do you need me to tell you we all know the risks?"

I stopped and faced him. "That's the last time. I know it does me no good to worry, and yet I do. Thank you for being patient."

He grinned. "Always. Remember, this is for your sisters. Even if you can only get them to safety, we will all understand."

I kissed his lips and we were on our way. Barely two weeks ago I had started my transformation into a dragon, and here I was storming the castle!

The familiar sounds of the guards calling to each other as they switched their posts made my heart relax. I took a deep breath and smelled the hint of peaches in the air and knew the cook must be making some of her amazing peach jam. The castle came into view, and I recalled how Marigold and Dahlia had run with me to the wizard to have my dress changed for my birthday celebration.

My heart swelled. Dormir was right. If I did anything, I needed to do it for them.

"I can do this," I said out loud.

Dormir pulled me close and pressed his lips to my forehead. "Yes, you can. Go on." He winked. "I'll wait for your signal."

I straightened, lifted my chin, and stepped into the road. Each step I made brought me closer to the castle and to an unknown future. I studied the guards on the battlements of the castle walls. They wore our colors, but something was … off. They stood rigid, heads visible between the parapets.

I also realized I couldn't see their faces. Our guards wore helmets with their eyes and face exposed. But these helmets were different. They weren't decorated with any symbols or styles, just plain metal with narrow slits where the eyes should be, and their mouths were covered with a metal grate.

The tiny hint of comfort I'd felt was now gone. These men might have been wearing our colors, but they weren't our soldiers. I was grateful I hadn't announced my presence yet.

However, when I drew nearer the gates, one of the soldiers called down in a dull voice, "Name and purpose!"

"My name is ... Aura, and I am here to speak with the queen!" I called back at the voice.

A soldier appeared around the edge of the wall beside the gate and peered at me. He wore one of our helmets, and I recognized him from being around the castle. His eyes widened when our gazes met, and he headed for me in a brisk walk. "I'll speak with her!" he called. He came to a stop two feet a way and leaned in close before he glanced over his shoulder. "Princess, you should go. Get to safety. Prince Gerard—"

"Took the throne?" I asked in an equally low voice. "Why do you think I didn't use my name?"

He eyed me. "He's imprisoned your sisters and your parents."

"Did he say why?"

He shook his head. "Only that he was going to rule the kingdom now."

I arched my brow. "And none of the soldiers tried to stop him?"

Again, the soldier glanced over his shoulder. "He … has magic. Not like the wizard Jarrett. Not like anything I've ever seen." He faced me again. "He's dangerous, Elisa. He's turned the lowest of the guards into … into … monsters." He shook his head. "You should go while you have the chance."

I patted his arm reassuringly. "I know what I'm doing." I grinned. "I'm the dragon princess, remember?"

He didn't smile back.

"Where is he keeping my family?"

"Your parents are in the dungeons. Your sisters are in their room."

"Did you send her away?" the soldier above the gates called down.

"I want to speak with Gerard," I said as evenly as possible. "We have help. Faeries and dragons."

"Captain?" the voice hollered.

"She wishes a conference with Prince Gerard." He finally tore his gaze away from mine. I knew he didn't understand and that he was nervous for my safety, but I had to try. He motioned for me to follow, and I fell into step at his side. "You're risking a lot," he whispered.

"I know. But what kind of princess would I be if I ran away?"

He glanced at me from the corner of his eyes.

The soldiers at the doors pushed one open for me, and I stepped into the home I'd grown in. Being back was bittersweet, especially given the circumstances.

The polished wood gleamed like it always had, but the wood had taken on a dark tone.

I turned to my right and stepped into the throne room.

Gerard sat upon my mother's throne, and on his head sat a silver crown with four spires and grand designs. In one of those spires sat the spring stone. "Elisa. You're alive! What a relief!" He leapt to his feet, as if he were genuinely excited to see I hadn't burned to a crisp after all, and rushed toward me.

I put my hand out, stopping him from getting any closer. "I've come to talk with you and make a proposition."

"Oh?" He arched his brow.

I'd forgotten how attractive he was, how his smirk came so easily to his lips, how his brows shadowed his eyes. I wasn't falling for his looks or flattery this time. "You return the throne to my family, and I let you live."

Gerard blurted a laugh. "You're hardly a threat to me, dear girl."

"I am curious how you usurped the throne." I folded my arms.

He waved his hand dismissively before placing it behind his back. He walked a circle around me. "It doesn't matter. Minor details. What I do want to bring up, though, is that you and I are still engaged ..."

I watched him walk but didn't move my feet. "Not anymore. You sort of broke off our engagement when you tried to kill me."

He stopped on my opposite side and pouted. "Me? Leave you to die? I would never!"

"Gerard, I'm not playing this game," I said firmly. "Release my family. Now."

"Or what?"

"You forget I'm a dragon," I replied. I held out my arms so he could see the scales had disappeared.

His eyes moved to my face, and I knew he was looking for the horns that were also no longer there. Gerard's grin slowly faded. "So that's how you survived, hm? I imagine in your brave moment you saved the faeries as well? That's rather unfortunate." He tapped his finger to his lip and paced.

"I never said I saved them," I muttered, adverting my eyes to the floor in an attempt to lie to Gerard and appear sad they'd died. "The fire had already spread."

"Am I to believe you didn't save a single fae? Not even the boy who guided us to his home?" He arched a brow, his look full of distrust.

"This isn't your castle, Gerard," I said firmly. "You aren't the king."

He heaved a sigh and withdrew a parchment from a pocket inside his jacket. "I have a document here that says otherwise. Written in your mother's hand and signed with her seal." He held it out.

I snatched it from his fingers and read it over. Indeed, it was my mother's script. Indeed, it was her signature and seal. I scoffed and raised my brow. "You want me to believe my stubborn mother would sign over the throne? What did you do to force her to do it?"

254

Gerard shrugged his shoulders and slid his hands into the pockets of his pants. "I may have persuaded her, but only a little. It turns out she adores your sister, Marigold. Dotes on her like she's glass. Have you ever noticed that?"

He had seen the way my mother treated me the night of my birthday. Gerard had seen how she talked to me, and he knew those words would sting.

I tightened my hand into a fist, crumpling the side of the document. "What did you do to Marigold?"

"Don't worry, I'm not *that* cruel." He rolled his eyes. "I'd never torture a child." He swung his feet out as he walked back to the throne. "I merely gave her some nightmares." He raised his right hand and moved his fingers. Black smoke gathered around them, dancing like the smoke above a candle.

The hair on the back of my neck prickled. Dark magic. It had to be. Quist had said Gerard was raised in darkness. "Allow me to take Marigold and Dahlia. And then … and then you and I can talk."

"What in the forest would we possibly have to talk about?" He sat down. "You aren't exactly in a position to make demands, sweet Elisa. I have your family. You have an empty and unspecific threat." Gerard held his hand out. "The document."

"Oh, you mean this?" I narrowed my eyes at him. Ferocity trickled from my chest to my fingertips, and the document burst into flame. Had I been in another situation, it might have surprised me, but I didn't have time for that now. I dropped the burning paper to the floor, allowing it to burn to a crisp.

Gerard lowered his hand and narrowed his eyes into a glare. This was the real Gerard. The side he'd kept hidden from me. "I don't need a document. Your people don't care, and I'm already on the throne. I now run your kingdom whether you like it or not. It's best if you allow this to happen." He pressed his fingertips together.

I wanted to claw that stupid smirk off his face. "I could burn this castle to the ground with you inside of it," I sneered.

"And your family." He shrugged. "Go on." His sneer curled. "Let's see what the big scary dragon has got."

Apparently, I wasn't great at talking my way out of things. I didn't have anyone to ask or anyone to lean on for support. This was all me. The choice Quist said was mine. Whatever I did in this room would decide the future of my kingdom, the faeries, and the dragons.

He leaned forward as I weighed my options.

I knew in a foot battle, he'd win in two blows. In spite of my meager training, he was a prince, and by the way he wore himself, he knew how to handle a sword much better than I did. I'd already tried asking, and that hadn't worked.

I shook my head. "The throne isn't even Queen Rachel's to give," I said. "The throne belongs to the faeries."

Gerard pointed to the purple stone in his gaudy crown. "Why do you think I obtained the stone first? Unlike your ancestors, I didn't need to start a war to get the throne. The stone has always been a symbol of royalty. I got what I came for." He leaned back, his smug look accentuated by the stubble along his jaw. "What are you going to do about it, my beauty?"

"*Your* beauty?" I stretched my fingers and extended my claws.

"Admit it, Elisa, you're not too bright," Gerard chided. "You didn't know the truth about anything in your kingdom or about yourself, until I revealed it to you. You put your trust in me and gave up everything. *Love at first sight,* you called it. Of course, I'll still keep you as my wife. You're pretty." He motioned to one of the guards standing at the door. "Take her to my new bedroom."

I'd felt anger several times in my life.

I thought the most intense moment had been when I thought the last of the faeries had been killed, when my mother announced my engagement, or when I felt defeated in the woods. I'd felt so much anger my dragon side had tried to wake. Had I known then what I knew now, I wouldn't have held back the anger. I would have torn him apart that night.

This anger was far more intense.

The heat started in my chest, searing and aching like when your fingers get too cold and you hold them by the fire to thaw them. The heat rapidly flooded into my extremities.

One of the men grabbed my left elbow. I looked down when I realized there was no warmth to his touch. He wore no gloves, and I saw the bones of fingers holding on to me. I turned and slammed my right hand into his chest. A crackling explosion of ice radiated from the center of his chest and wrapped around him as he stumbled backward.

"Elisa, don't fight," Gerard warned.

I turned and found him standing with dark smoke swirling around both of his hands. "I will *never* be your wife. I'm not going to lie on a bed and let you take me. I'm not afraid of you. You will set my family free. You will return the spring stone to the faeries. And you will leave *my* kingdom."

Gerard shot his hand out, palm extended toward the floor. His eyes glowed orange, and the shadows in the corners of the room began to move as he whispered an incantation in a language I didn't know.

"No you don't!" I growled.

With my claws extended, I released a roar with everything I had inside of me. The same burning sensation exploded from my chest, through my throat, and out my mouth, and fire engulfed the throne room. The sound of the roar broke Gerard's concentration, and he had to clamp his hands over his ears while the chandeliers overhead trembled.

Before I was a dragon, I would have frozen in horror.

I would have stood in shock, apologized, tried to fix what I'd done.

But I had to save my kingdom from this monster of darkness.

TWENTY-THREE

While Gerard recovered, I ran from the room, slamming the door shut behind me. I knew Dormir had heard my roar, and he wouldn't have spared any time sending his men and women toward the castle.

I ran up the staircase to retrieve Marigold and Dahlia.

I'd barely made it halfway when the shadows along the wall began to move. I jumped over the first shadow that snatched at my ankle and somehow managed to avoid the second, but the third caught me off-balance, and I hit the stairs hard.

"You'd burn down your own castle with your family inside?" Gerard yelled at me from the foyer below.

"To save them from you!" I planted my hands, allowing ice to spread from them and toward the shadows, hoping they would shy away from the cold.

Instead, a tentacle of shadow wrapped around my wrist like a vine.

"Don't fight me, Elisa."

I glared down at him. "How dare you think you can own me!" The space wasn't large enough for my dragon size, but no one had told me I couldn't summon my dragon wings while in my human form. I'd already called upon my claws.

Gerard muttered a curse as my wings grew from my back.

I lifted my body away from the shadows and, with another explosion of fire on the stairs, sent the shadows screaming into hiding.

Gerard shouted in anger at me.

I flew to the top of the landing and sprinted down the hallway. I knew Gerard would be close behind, that he would somehow use his powers to find a way up, and I needed to use every spare second I had to get my sisters to safety.

I dug my feet into the rug lying on the hardwood floors in the hallway and slid to a stop in front of Dahlia and Marigold's door. I slammed my shoulder against the solid wood twice before my dragon strength broke it open.

Marigold and Dahlia screamed. They were cowered in the corner of the bedroom, wedged in the gap between the wall and Dahlia's bed.

"Are you both all right?" I asked as I ran over and knelt in front of them. "It's me."

Dahlia stared at me only a moment before she crawled over and threw her arms around me. "Elisa! You came back! You're … you're alive!"

"Gerard said you died. He said the faeries killed you," Marigold added. She wrapped her arms around my neck, and I held on to them both.

"Clearly, I'm not. We haven't much time. He's making his way here. I need you to trust me and jump out the window when I say to." I ran to the window and threw it open. When I turned and looked at my sisters, I noticed the black veins across Marigold's left arm. "What happened?"

I realized the answer as soon as I asked the question.

"Gerard," she said. "He did this to me so Mother would sign the paper and give him the throne." She cradled the arm and put on a brave face. "He said it was poison and it would kill me if she didn't. But he hasn't taken it away yet."

I shook my head and jumped out the window. Both of my sisters squealed and rushed to the opening, but I caught myself far from the ground with my wings, not letting myself transform into my full dragon. I didn't want to draw the attention of the dark soldiers. I flew back up to the window and held my arms out.

"You first," Dahlia said. She helped Marigold through and into my arms.

As I suspected, Dormir had heard the roar, but so had the others, and the faeries had rushed toward the castle with their swords drawn. However, Gerard must have called upon his black magic, because more skeleton soldiers surrounded the castle than I'd seen when I entered.

"I'll be right back for you, Dahlia!" I said.

"I know!"

I flew Marigold safely over the battlefield, though I heard twangs of arrows. I flew to where I knew my mother stood, still hidden in the woods, and landed in front of her.

I set Marigold on her feet. "This is my real mother," I explained, turning her to face the gorgeous dragon in front of her. "She'll look after you. I have to get Dahlia." I looked to my mother. "She's got some kind of magic infecting her."

"She's a dragon," Marigold said in wonder. "So you're really a dragon?" She spun and faced me, smiling like the excited child she was.

I winked and nodded. "A dragon *shifter*. There's a prophecy about me too. But that will have to wait for another time."

"What's going on at the castle?" my mother asked.

"I accidentally set the throne room on fire. Hopefully, it hasn't spread, but the entire building is made out of wood ... I have to get Dahlia." I spread my wings, this time allowing myself to transform fully into my dragon self.

"You're beautiful!" Marigold shouted from behind me.

I made it back to the castle only to see some of the faeries carrying away the injured, and one of them looked dead. My stomach sunk even further when I arrived at the castle. Dahlia wasn't at the window. I transformed back into my human form while in the air, and as I dropped, I caught myself on the ledge of the window and pulled myself in.

I froze.

Dahlia wasn't in there.

Black smoke billowed down the hall. The castle was still burning, or at least part of it was.

"Dahlia!" I shouted. I ran down the hallway only to skid to a halt when I spotted Dahlia standing at the top of the stairs.

Her beautiful blue eyes stared wide at the fire crackling below.

Gerard stood beside her, one foot propped up on the banister rail, and he had a dagger in his hand. He ran the blade deliberately down Dahlia's arm, and then his eyes flicked to me. They were dark. Full of hatred. "I warned you, Elisa," he said coldly.

I felt like such a fool. *I should have taken them both at the same time! I should have taken the time and transformed into a dragon! I could have carried them both!* I stepped forward. "Gerard, she has no part in this," I said cautiously.

"She's your sister. This is your last chance. Say no to me again ..." He turned the tip of the dagger between her shoulder blades and pressed.

Dahlia cried out. Shadows tilted her forward, toward the flames.

"Stop! Gerard, please don't hurt her!" I cried, but I didn't dare move.

"You stay with me, as my wife, and I will let your family go. But I am *not* giving up my throne."

I tightened my jaw. "You have the northern kingdoms. Why take ours?"

"Conquest, kiddo."

"Stop talking down to me!" I growled. "You're barely older!"

He raised his finger, and Dahlia screamed. "Mind your anger. We wouldn't want your sister to catch on fire right now, would we? Poor little Dahlia will burn right up."

Tears came to my eyes. "Why are you doing this?" I choked.

"You think you're the only one who wants a special destiny?" he snarled.

"I didn't *want* any of this. I didn't ask to have a prophecy about me. I didn't ask to have a purpose, to make decisions that mean life or death," I said, not daring to move.

Gerard sneered. "You were just *born* into it. I wasn't born into anything. I've had to fight my whole life for respect. My throne was taken from me long ago. *This* will make me important. *This* will make Selina proud."

"Selina?" I asked, startled. "The sorceress?"

"Is it yes or no, Elisa?"

Dahlia was still balanced precariously toward the flames, and tears streaked her dirty face. She was watching me. Waiting to see what I would do.

"You didn't have to do any of this." I held my hands out. "You could have married me without ever revealing …" I let the sentence fall.

264

"That I'm actually a cruel person? Sorry, beautiful, life isn't rainbows and butterflies," he said dryly.

I tightened my lips. "You're right. Life is about being locked up in a castle your entire life, never really having a true friend, disappointing your mother with everything you do. It's being raised by humans who've convinced you that you're cursed and you're going to turn into a monster and kill everyone you love, when in fact, you are a dragon with parents who love you. Life is about putting trust in one person, just one for the first time ... and having him leave you to die on the mountains, take your throne, and threaten to kill your sister."

Gerard scoffed. "This charming debate is over. Do I kill your sister, or do you marry me oh important dragon?"

"Please, Elisa. I don't want to die!" Dahlia sobbed.

I knew I had one shot. I ran as fast as I could to Dahlia.

Gerard growled and Dahlia began to fall.

I leapt and snatched the back of Dahlia's dress, managing to pull her back so she landed on me, and we both tumbled down the first few steps. The fire nipped at Dahlia's feet. I grinned at her.

She scrambled to her feet behind me, and I put my body between her and Gerard.

"Wrong choice," Gerard said with ice on his words.

Dahlia gasped.

I wheeled around. A shadowy sword protruded through her chest. Her blue eyes looked at me in confusion and pain, then looked down.

"No. Dahlia, no!"

The sword pulled away with a sickening squelch, revealing a skeleton soldier behind her.

Dahlia fell forward. I dropped to my knees and caught her in my arms. "Hold on. It will be all right." I pressed my hand to the wound, knowing in my heart it was useless. "I'll take you to the faeries. They will help you." I tried to get up.

"I ... love you, El," she whispered.

"No, no, no," I whimpered. "H-Hold on. You're strong. Just a little longer. I can get you outside. The fae ..." I stifled a sob and half-carried, half-dragged her a few feet.

She coughed and blood speckled my clothes. "Mm. Tell ... Marigold ... sh-she can have my ... acorns."

I choked on a laugh. Dahlia had collected acorns for years and painted them to look like woodland creatures. She had a box of them in their room and Marigold wasn't allowed to touch them.

"I will," I promised, smearing ash across my cheek with the back of my hand.

"You're the ... best big ... sister." The light in her eyes faded, her head lolled to the side, and her body went limp.

"Dahlia?" My voice cracked.

She didn't move.

I would no longer sneak off to the kitchen with her for a midnight snack because she couldn't sleep. She wouldn't roll her eyes at Mother because I was forbidden to do something. She wouldn't be there to look after Marigold and help her with writing lessons.

I clutched Dahlia's body to my chest and screamed as my heart was torn from my body. Ice exploded across the floor and walls, smothering the fire on the stairs instantly. The building shook violently. The glass in the windows exploded.

I held on to Dahlia's body as I got to my feet, glaring at Gerard. "You ... *monster*," I hissed.

For the first time all day, he looked genuinely frightened. Gerard's face had paled, and he had taken a few steps back. "I didn't mean for that to happen," he blurted. "It was just ... you were supposed to give in! You were supposed to agree—"

The comfortable and familiar tingle of scales rippled across my body.

"I have the fae," Gerard suddenly said. He motioned his hand to the hall behind him.

A shadowy pool appeared on the floor, and two skeleton figures stepped out. Between them, they carried Dormir. Dormir's blue hair was a mess, and blood poured from his nose and a wound on his cheek. His shirt was in tatters and also bloody.

"Oh good," I said. "Let him go and I'll let you live." I stepped forward, forcing Gerard back farther. I caught my reflection in a nearby mirror and saw that, while I was still human in shape, I was covered in my dragon scales, with my dragon horns on the side of my head, and my dragon wings and tail behind.

"I can kill him too," Gerard warned.

"But you won't," I growled. "Because then I'll tear you apart limb from limb." Gerard only had this last card to play. I could call his bluff.

Dormir lifted his head and his lavender eyes focused on me. I would save him. I couldn't save Dahlia, but I wouldn't let Dormir be killed too.

"Last chance before I burn you," I growled.

Gerard tightened his lips, clearly not about to admit his defeat. He faced Dormir and used words I'd never heard before while moving his hands in sharp patterns.

I ran at Gerard while he was distracted.

He finished the last word before I reached him, and dark light wrapped around Dormir.

"Elisa!" he screamed.

The darkness fell like sand, and Dormir was gone.

"What did you do?" I roared.

"Easy!" Gerard said, holding up a lantern in front of him. Inside the lantern stood Dormir, his hands pressed on the glass. "One wrong move and he dies. I would hate to drop him."

A soft rumble radiated from my chest, and I bore my teeth at the monster I'd once trusted.

I didn't know what to do. I thought I had won this, but Gerard had already *murdered* Dahlia and Dormir was about to be killed. I'd already proven I couldn't make decisions. If I had just accepted Gerard's demands, Dahlia would have still been alive. I opened my mouth, fully ready to admit defeat.

But a familiar voice said, "Yes, your sister might still be alive if you had submitted to him, but he could have killed her after you made your arrangement."

I turned and saw Quist. We stood in the meadow again, like in my vision before. I fell to my knees and sobbed. "She's gone! She died because of my selfishness!"

"You did what you thought was right." Quist crouched and touched my cheek. I looked up and saw him, a handsome man with golden hair, bright golden eyes, and a dashing smile. "You know who you are. Elisa, or Aura as you choose, the Favored Light. But you don't believe in yourself yet. You still have the dragons and the faeries nearby. You can defeat Gerard once and for all. Remember what I said about you?"

I wiped away my tears. "You said I was brave."

He nodded. "How many girls would have run to save their sister? And how many others would have given into Gerard's demands the first moment he threatened? You can do this, Aura. Call upon Tao." He pressed his lips to my forehead like my father used to when I was sick.

Warmth spread across my body.

The king and queen of Griswil had stolen me and raised me, but there had been so much good in my childhood. Mother had taught me to paint. Father had taught me to sword fight. I played with my sisters. Even now, I wasn't a different person.

Braver, perhaps, but I was still me. I knew exactly what I would do.

TWENTY-FOUR

I ran.

I picked up Dahlia's body, slid down the ice-covered stairs, and ran out the front doors and onto the battlefield of skeleton soldiers.

I opened my mouth and roared as loudly as my body would allow. I drew the attention of nearby skeletons but swiftly spread ice on the road from the main gates to the door. To my surprise, the skeletons were unable to rise up through the ice. I froze the ankles of the nearest skeletons, creating a sort of wall with their bodies to protect me from the oncoming group before I laid Dahlia gently on the surface.

My heart wrenched, looking down at her face.

Tears blinded me, but I transformed into my dragon form and roared again, then turned as the skeletons broke through and breathed fire on them.

I heard the beating wings of the dragons before they came into view. They landed on top of the skeletons and turned to me.

"I left Marigold with one of the fae. A few are injured and have set up a place of healing," my mother explained.

"Gerard killed my other sister, Dahlia." I looked in the direction of her body. "I don't care if we burn the entire castle down, but he also has Dormir and the king and queen are in the dungeon." I turned back to the dragons.

My father shook his head. "Dormir managed to get them out. He'd gone back in to help you with your sisters and didn't make it back out."

I bore my teeth. "Gerard is clever and controls the shadows and skeletons."

"He's a necromancer," Nicholia stated, swishing his tail and wiping out a flurry of skeletons behind him.

"What does that mean?"

"He can summon the dead," my father explained. "Hence, the skeletons."

"I need your help," I admitted. "I need to take Dahlia to the faeries." My words caught.

My mother rubbed her head against my neck. "Do that. We will keep the skeletons at bay and when you return we will save Dormir. Together we will end this once and for all."

I nodded and tenderly carried Dahlia in my claws. I knew I was giving Gerard time to think of something, but Dahlia deserved to rest with respect. I couldn't live with myself if Gerard turned her body into a monster too. I landed in the small clearing and set her body down. After a quick scan of the group, a good handful were wounded, and the man and woman I once called my father and mother stood holding Marigold.

I swallowed hard and stepped back. "He killed Dahlia. I haven't any time. Please take care of her." I flew back into the air, and Queen Rachel's scream of anguish followed me.

There would be proper time to mourn once Gerard was gone.

I arrived back at the castle, and the four of us entered through its main doors.

"Gerard, we need to talk!" I called.

"I suppose now isn't the time to point out the scorch marks and ice?" Rowen whispered.

"My dragon magic," I explained.

"Fire *and* ice?" he said, clearly impressed.

I smiled in spite of myself.

The lantern with Dormir inside slid up from a dark pool in the middle of the floor. The pool stretched and rippled like spilled ink. Dormir pounded against the glass with his fists and his mouth was moving as though he were yelling, but I couldn't hear what he said even with my keen dragon hearing.

I crouched into a defensive stance, not sure what to prepare myself for. "The skeletons come from the pool," I explained. "I don't know what else."

The pool continued to widen, stretching to the back corners of the walls.

"He could be summoning an army," Isaline said.

I glanced at Dormir, who was pointing to me, the pool, and then stretching his arms out and flapping them.

I furrowed my brow. "You want me to fly into the pool?" I called.

He shook his head. He stretched his arms out again and flapped them like wings, then pointed to the pool. He put his hands in front of him and moved his fingers like fire.

"Something with wings is coming from the shadows?"

He nodded vigorously, then pointed to each of us.

The inky surface rippled violently.

Nicholia gasped. "No … that's impossible!"

A nose broke the surface, then claws. Dragon claws. A dragon's mouth and face, but no scales protected it, only moving shadows that shifted like the wisp of smoke on the wind, no wind blew around us.

"A wraith dragon!" Nicholia shouted. "We cannot defeat him alone. We need all of the dragons! Rowen, go get the others!"

"It will be half a day before any of us return!" he said as the creature continued to claw its way out of the pool. "You'll be dead by then." He turned and looked through the open doors. "But I can send a message through the trees." He disappeared into the sunlight.

"Are they like us?" I asked, my eyes darting around the room for any sign of Gerard.

"They used to be, but like humans, dragons also have dark sides," Nicholia explained, making his way around the edge of the room for a different angle. "They served darkness and serve it in death. Though, unlike us, a wraith dragon can only heed the orders of their master."

"Gerard has to be somewhere near! He has to be saying an incantation! If we can stop him before he finishes, maybe the dragon won't make it out." Like a fool, I tried to run up the icy stairs, only to curse myself and fly up them instead.

"We better hurry," Rowen called, flinging the nearby door open.

The wraith dragon roared, and the sound felt like a million souls screaming in torment pierced through my chest, making my blood run cold and stealing my breath. The dragon was massive, bigger than Nicholia, and I knew he was right. Three dragons against this massive dragon—we didn't stand a chance. I hardly counted in their numbers. I didn't know how to truly fight yet, but I never imagined we would face a creature such as this.

I flung the library door open and then ran to the next door and flung that open.

"He isn't down here!" Isaline shouted.

"I can't get to the back rooms," Nicholia reported.

"I'm going to get Dormir," Rowen said.

I stopped and ran to the top of the stairs. "I'm at a better vantage!"

The wraith dragon had his entire upper body out of the hole now, and it went right through Dormir like a ghost. The dragon already filled the entire entrance of the castle and if it made it out of the hole, it would destroy the entire front of the castle.

"Act fast!" my father called.

I couldn't hesitate this time. I spread my wings behind me and jumped from the landing, hand outstretched toward Dormir. He began to sink. I could see into the void. Gray men and women with sunken faces and skeleton fingers stood in a horde, clawing at the surface as though pleading for their chance to enter the mortal realm.

I snapped my wings out at the last possible moment and plunged my hand into the darkness. I grasped Dormir's prison, but a chill ran through me like I'd never felt. The pool of darkness seized my hand and held on.

I saw my kingdom in ruins—the castle a smoldering pile of ashes, nearby homes burning or completely decimated, people lying dead in the streets, the faeries wailing for their loved ones. Bodies of dragons lay scattered among orchards or meadows.

Despair crept into my heart, and I longed to dive headfirst into the darkness. I wanted to let it swallow me up. I let myself imagine how I would feel to leave this world.

Another screaming roar from the wraith dragon broke my thoughts of misery, and I lifted my gaze to see my mother yelling at me. I blinked heavily. Everything felt so slow. She waved her hands, motioning me toward her.

Another blink and movements began to speed up. A third.

A fourth.

Finally time resumed, and I pulled the cage from the pool. I flung myself toward my mother, holding Dormir close to my chest, and collapsed against the stone floor gasping for breath.

"You completely froze!" my mother said. She grabbed me under my shoulders and dragged me into the adjoining room.

The wraith dragon reached a clawed hand out, shattering the floorboards beneath his claws as he grappled for us. I rolled to my knees and opened Dormir's cage.

The instant his feet touched the floor, he returned to his normal size. He staggered and fell to a knee.

"Dormir!" I flung my arms around him and held him tightly.

"Ow, ow, ow."

"Sorry!" I let go.

He smiled weakly, but relieved. "Just … give me a moment. Going from tiny to big …" He put his hand on his chest and rubbed hard. "And that place …" He shuddered.

"We don't have time!" My mother shoved us both as the dragon's hand burst through the doorway and barely missed us. "We need to get outside and burn this place down with Gerard inside it."

I took Dormir's hand the instant he reached for me, and we climbed out the broken window and ran outside. The faeries had returned and were battling the undead, but they had discovered my patch of ice and all stood on it, surrounded by skeletons as they fought. Those soldiers who were left from the castle fought alongside the fae.

Dormir smiled. "I wish the others had joined us."

"I can make the rest of this area ice," I said, keeping on topic. "The skeletons are starting to appear on the parapets," I pointed out.

Dormir looked at the walls. "Where's the armory? I'm a pretty good archer myself."

"That tower."

He grabbed me and crushed his lips to mine. "I know it's not the right time, but you are the most amazing woman I've ever met." He grinned and took off across the battlefield.

Nicholia was already in his dragon form, and Father was in the middle of transforming. Mother transformed the instant she was outside as well. I spread ice across the ground while Nicholia and my father flew into the air and breathed fire at the castle.

The mindless skeletons were completely oblivious to the dangers of the ice and stood stupidly as it spread up their legs, keeping them in place. The faeries cheered and easily took them out with the swipe of a scimitar or sword.

I glanced up at the parapets in time to see Dormir shooting his arrows and slaughtering even more skeletons. I wanted to stare at the way his body moved, the confidence in his gentle eyes, but we were still in the middle of a fight I wasn't sure we could win.

I transformed into my dragon and took to the skies, spreading the ice all the way around the castle. By the time I had finished, the building was already engulfed in flames. It was bittersweet. I knew it had to be done, but I had hoped we would have been able to return the beautiful structure to the fae queen, to Dormir.

I gasped, remembering Dahlia's acorns. Without hesitation, I dove through her burning window and grabbed the nightstand in which the acorns had been stored. I dropped to the ice and returned to my human form long enough to yank the drawer out and open the burnt box. I only hesitated a moment before opening the lid.

Inside, all of the acorns were in pristine condition.

I held the box close to my chest, then turned to face the castle as crackling started.

The roof collapsed, and we waited with bated breath.

The top floor collapsed.

And then nothing but fire.

"Did we do it?" Dormir called from behind me.

I looked over my shoulder. He leaned his hands on the edge of the parapet to get the safest view.

But the wraith dragon's screaming roar tore through me again, and a new kind of dread froze my bones. I faced the rubble and watched in horror as the wooden beams shifted until mighty wings spread out and the largest dragon I'd ever seen shook off the last burning pieces of the castle.

He looked directly at me.

"How do we defeat a wraith dragon?" I asked. I shoved Dahlia's treasure in my pocket and took off running up the steps to Dormir.

"I don't know," Nicholia called down to me. "Attack with all we've got?"

I nodded. "Then we attack." I stopped beside Dormir. "Shoot it with everything you have. Get your archers."

He snatched my wrist as I turned, pulled me to his chest, and kissed me. "You better come back."

"You won't lose me, remember?" I grinned. "I should be worried about you. You don't even have any armor. Give this to Marigold." I tossed the box of acorns to Dormir and transformed.

"What's this?"

"Your reason to live! You better make sure my sister gets that, or else …" I let it hang as I joined my parents and Nicholia in the sky.

The four of us dove and blasted fireballs at the dragon. They seemed to strike, but it was almost as if the smoke surrounding the dragon extinguished the flames and the blows didn't land. Darkness began to surround us, and it was only then I glanced to see the sun setting. We were losing daylight, which meant more shadows for Gerard to play with. He still hadn't shown his disgusting face.

The dragon stretched its wings as if it hadn't moved them for centuries. Mother landed on the ground a safe distance away. The earth trembled and shifted as she used her magic to manipulate the earth so it would clamp down on the dragon's feet and legs. Enormous boulders began to spring from the ground.

The wraith roared at her, then beat its mighty wings, kicking up the surrounding dirt and easily breaking its mighty claws from the earth. He opened his mouth, and a purple light exploded toward Mother.

She pulled her wings in front of her face, using them as a shield against the otherworldly fire. She gasped and beat her wings feverously, taking back to the air. "His fire burns beyond heat!" she called to us.

A crackling purple ball exploded between us, hitting me in the face like thousands of needles that pierced through my scales. I tumbled in the air but somehow managed to catch myself.

"We need to attack all at once," Nicholia said. "Follow me." He dove, then curved wide, spiraling down toward the dragon and releasing a flurry of fireballs.

Father followed, then me, exhaling as much of my breath as I possibly could at once. Mother took up the rear. The fire hit in a fury that even caused the wraith dragon to stumble, though we couldn't tell if there was any damage.

And then the dragon took to the sky.

"Look for a weak spot," my father said.

Against the night sky, the dragon appeared to be only a shadowy cloud moving across the stars.

"I can barely see him."

"Because he has no blood," Mother explained. "We can't use our eyes to see him."

No sooner had she said that then an explosion of light lit up the sky and exposed the wraith dragon's location. We all turned. Father was the closest, and he extended all four sets of claws before diving at the dragon's back. Nicholia aimed for the dragon's chest.

The dragon bit into Nicholia's neck but screamed when Nicholia's back leg hit something, and something dark began to drip.

Another ball of light came as soon as the other faded, and I turned to see Dormir standing on the ground. His hands were cupped in front of him, and floating over them was a familiar purple stone.

I grinned.

That cheeky boy had the spring stone.

I didn't know if he'd taken it from Gerard, or if Gerard had a fake one and Dormir had the real one the entire time. Whatever the truth, I was grateful for Dormir's help, and I was hopeful we could actually win this.

Nicholia tried to break free, but the wraith had a firm grip on his neck and shook his head side to side. Nicholia grunted, clawing at the wraith's chest. Father landed hard on the dragon's back, and Mother and I struck opposite sides. Only then did it drop Nicholia. The wraith wheeled his snarling head around and snapped at my father.

Nicholia tried, and failed, to extend his left wing as he hurtled toward the earth.

"I've got you! Transform!" I dove for him.

"You can't get me in time." He grimaced and tried to guide his descent with his right wing but ended up falling into a spiral.

"Trust me!" I yelled.

Nicholia's massive form shifted until he was only a man. I extended both front legs toward him and grasped at the darkness, opening and closing my claws in a blind attempt at catching him.

I missed.

My legs slammed into the earth, sending me into a tumbling roll. I dug my claws into the ground and skidded to a halt, then spun around, expecting to see Nicholia in a heap, broken and dead.

But he sat on the ground with a small group of horses around him.

I got to my feet, staggered until I got my footing, then ran toward him.

"I'm alright, Elisa," he called to me. "Apparently he is a friend of yours."

I slowed to a stop. I stared.

Tao threw his head, and a long horn reflected the light of the moon.

"You really are a unicorn," I said breathlessly.

Tao bowed, extending one leg forward. He turned his face to look in the sky.

My father roared, and I turned my gaze upward as well. The fight against the wraith dragon had moved, threatening a nearby town.

I looked at the unicorn. "Tao, can you help me get the villagers to safety?"

Tao straightened and whinnied.

He and the other unicorns took off at a swift gallop, and Nicholia motioned me to go with them, adding, "I can blow fire at the wraith from down here."

I flew to the town and landed on the edge before a group of gawking onlookers. At my sides, the unicorns stepped into the light cast from open doors and windows. Everyone in town had come out to see what the chaos was all about, and more than likely, they were too shocked by the sight of dragons to realize they were genuinely in danger.

"You need to run now! Get everyone out before it's too late!" I ordered.

"Who are you?" one of the men demanded, holding his wife to his side, his eyes wide in shock.

I transformed into their princess. "Crown Princess Elisa, or Aura the Favored Light."

They all gasped and began to murmur.

"There isn't time to explain anything. You must evacuate before—Ah!" One of the purple balls of dark magic demolished a nearby home, and the shockwave knocked us from our feet. "Get out now!" I yelled.

This time, everyone ran.

The unicorns ran about, guiding people into the woods, even allowing the townspeople to place their children on their backs.

Trusting Tao had everything in order, I transformed and headed back into the sky. Both my father and mother had wounds of their own, though none appeared to be life threatening. But there was barely any damage at all to the wraith. I imagined, to him, we were only like flies annoying a horse on a hot summer afternoon.

The wraith snatched my mother, and I slammed into his neck with all the force and strength I had. I clamped my sharp teeth on its neck and desperately tried to break his defenses, to puncture him, injure him in some way. He reached a claw up and flung me away.

Another one of Dormir's balls of light faded, but this time another didn't follow.

I looked at the ground. Gerard stood with one foot on Dormir's chest and a sword to his throat.

TWENTY-FIVE

My entire life I was raised with the belief that dragons were monsters—giant lizards with a mind to devour livestock, burn down cities, and steal treasure. I'd been told one day I would be one of those mindless monsters. What I discovered, however, was that dragons aren't monsters at all. They have a society, just like humans, are rather intelligent, but most importantly, have magic no one can predict.

As I dove for Gerard, with my sight set on saving Dormir, the speed of my dive suddenly accelerated, and when I tucked my wings against my body, I went even faster than I thought possible. I snatched Gerard with my claws and threw him into a nearby tree, then landed and put my hand on his body, keeping him in place.

He groaned and pushed against my finger before he focused on me and stopped moving.

"You're done, Gerard," I hissed.

"Wait!" He put both hands up desperately. "I can send it away! I can control it! It listens to me!"

"And what do you want in exchange?" I spat.

"The spring stone."

"Why do you care so much about it?"

He opened and closed his mouth, then shook his head. "I need it."

"For what?"

"Elisa, look out!" Dormir shouted, running across the field toward me with a severe limp. He clutched at his leg.

I looked over my shoulder in time to meet the claws that slashed across my body, lifted me into the air, and then threw me back down to the ground. My body broke trees as I rolled, and I wasn't certain the cracking wasn't only from the trees. My side screamed, and I struggled to get back to my feet, but my left leg wasn't complying. The claws struck me again, and this time my body was being crushed under the weight of the wraith's claws. The wraith hoisted me into the air and pressed one of its claws against my ribs. As it tightened its fist, the claw dug into me. My protective scales broke, and I screamed in agony as the claw buried itself deeper and deeper into my body.

You can't fail! I told myself.

I transformed. As a human, I was much smaller, which also meant I was much more difficult for the wraith to hold on to. I slipped from his grasp and fell into the void of night. I transformed back, but couldn't finish the transformation before I struck trees, though

I did manage to get to my dragon form before I struck the ground.

I lay there, gasping in pain. I didn't know where I was or where the wraith had gone. I didn't know if Gerard had killed Dormir or if Dormir needed my help.

I can't give up. Quist said I am the light.

I stumbled to my feet and staggered to the side, then fell back to my belly. I could barely stand, let alone walk.

And then came a sound I never expected to hear. The trees around me leaned, and two of them pressed against my side.

"They are coming," the trees said. "The dragons are coming."

"Hold on, Light."

"Get to your feet."

"The dragons are coming."

I took as big a breath as I could summon, and that alone caused stars of pain in my eyes. The wraith must have collapsed one of my lungs. I forced myself back to my feet. The trees were talking again. More importantly, they were talking to me. And their message was one of hope.

If the dragons really were coming, we could defeat this wraith for good.

"That's it, princess."

"Into the sky!"

I spread my wings and heeded their directions. I flew into the sky. The agony in my body pulled on me, pleading with me to stop, but I had a job to do.

The village was already engulfed in flames, and the flames were spreading to the orchards.

I scanned the skies and spotted one dragon frantically flying in a circle. They were too far away for me to see who it was, but I headed in that direction with caution. I summoned the magic to me that had brought me to Gerard so quickly, and my speed increased just as it had before. I forced it to a stop when I was close enough to slow down.

"You're all right!" Mother gasped, flying over to me. "Your father and the wraith hit the ground, but I can't find where in this darkness!"

"The trees told me the dragons are coming," I said. "If the trees are awake again, perhaps they are speaking to Father. Maybe even protecting him."

"Let's hope," she said. "If we fly over the trees, we might be able to find him. Come."

We both dropped until the tips of our wings almost brushed against the trees.

A roar echoed, followed by a series of others. I lifted my gaze, and in the distance, lights in the darkness approached. My heart leapt with joy!

"They have come!"

"The dragons are here!"

"You can disperse the darkness now!" the trees exclaimed.

"You are the light!"

I grinned at my mother, who smiled back at me.

Her gaze suddenly shifted, and she shouted, "There!" She dove, and I followed.

My father had somehow managed to get the wraith out of the sky and onto the ground. It was only when we landed nearby that I saw the wraith's wings were torn.

The wraith snatched my father's tail and dragged him near.

"Hey!" I shouted and clamped down on the wraith's tail, using its own trick to distract it.

The wraith roared at me in frustration and snapped at me.

But we had managed to distract the wraith long enough. The dragons overhead roared in unison. I flew up into the sky, soon followed by my father and mother, and then as a hoard, we attacked.

Dragons of every kind descended on the wraith, blinding him with light, striking him with lightning, burning him with fire. As a group, we broke his defenses, pierced his unseen scales. Beneath him, a pool of darkness began to form. The shimmer of it reminded me of the dark pool from whence Gerard had summoned it.

I took a breath until my ribs screamed, and with everything I had in me, I released my magic on the wraith. Light blinded the area, as bright as the afternoon sun. The rays burned into the wraith dragon and its shadows dispersed until the bones themselves peeled away like ashes on a log.

With one final defeated roar, it collapsed into the puddle of blackness and disappeared.

I joined my people as we cheered. But I knew defeating the wraith was only one piece of the problem.

The other piece was Gerard, and if he had the time, he could summon the wraith again.

"We need to get to the ruins of the castle. The faeries are there and hopefully Gerard. We need to capture him," I ordered.

Everyone flew in the direction of the castle.

To my surprise, when we arrived, Gerard sat on his knees, arms bound behind him, and Dormir held a sword to his neck. A gag was wrapped around his head, preventing him from talking. The faeries had lit torches and stood like protective sentinels.

I landed in front of Dormir and transformed. I was covered in my own blood, barely able to breathe, let alone stand, but I was ready to exact my revenge on the one who had started this all.

"You!" I snarled.

I stormed over to Gerard and snatched the sword from Dormir's hand.

"Wait, Elisa—" Dormir tried.

"You killed my sister!" I screamed and raised the sword.

Terror filled Gerard's green eyes. His pupils were dilated and he leaned back as far as he could. Fear. He was afraid. But he closed his eyes and straightened, resigning himself to his fate.

"You will always remember this moment," I heard Dormir say behind me. "How are you going to choose to remember it?"

"By law, we can kill you," I spat. "Sentence you to death for murder alone." Tears blinded me.

Gerard held his head high, his jaw clenched tightly. The muscle in his jaw flexed.

I lowered the sword and put a hand on my stomach, touching Dahlia's crusted blood on the front of my shirt. By law, I could have. When I saw Gerard helpless, frightened, and very much alone, I pitied him. He didn't have an army of men at his side to command. He had a troupe of the undead. Quist had told me he was raised in darkness, and I couldn't even pretend to imagine what that would be like as a child. Who had taught him to play with dead things? How old was he when that training began? *How* had he been trained?

How could someone raise a child to summon such creatures?

I crouched and loosened the gag. I looked Gerard in the eye. "What good is another death?" I whispered. "You've caused … so much heartache."

His lips tightened.

"But I am going to show you mercy."

Gerard's brows shifted from resignation to confusion.

"Whoever you work with, you can tell them that we are not a weak people. The humans, dragons, and faeries will work together from now on. Griswil is not weak. We have learned from our mistakes, and you will never return. If you do, I won't be so merciful. Do you understand?"

"Do you think this is wise?" Misla's voice was full of bitterness.

I looked up at her. "He's alone. Can't you see how frightened he is?"

Gerard turned his face away when Dormir met his gaze. "I … had resigned myself to death. And now you let me go?"

I nodded. "Dormir, release him."

Dormir reluctantly sliced the sword through the ropes.

Gerard stared up at me, confusion lining his brow. He slowly climbed to his feet. "Why?"

I stepped forward so only he could hear. "Because you were raised in darkness," I whispered. "And someone needs to show you the light."

Gerard's face softened.

I reached up and touched his cheek. "I hope you never forget us." I kissed his cheek and then stepped away.

The crowd parted.

Gerard looked around one final time, then limped off into the darkness.

Everyone turned to me, Crown Princess Elisa of Griswil, or Aura the Favored Light. Whichever I preferred, according to Quist.

But I could be both.

I let out a breath and shook my head. "Thank you. All of you. I propose we find somewhere to sleep tonight. We need to tend to the wounded and … and bury our dead." My throat tightened, and I put a shaking hand to my lips.

Dormir walked over to me and wrapped me in his arms. He didn't even need to say anything. He just held me while I broke down.

"You heard her." My father, Rowen, clapped his hands. "Dragons, let's make some fires to ward off the night air. The fae are tending to the wounded. Those soldiers still capable, come with me to find the people of the neighboring town and see if they're all right."

My other father and mother hesitantly approached me.

Marigold broke free and ran over. I pulled away from Dormir so I could catch my youngest sister and hold on to her as we knelt in the dirt and cried together.

The whirlwind of emotions was hardly over.

With the adrenaline gone, I found out just how badly I was wounded. I had been trying to help guide the people of Sloval to our makeshift camp when I collapsed.

Marigold struggled to pull me to my feet. "Elisa, what's wrong?"

"Just a little dizzy. That's all." I tried to get up but failed.

"Someone, help!" she yelled.

Dormir pushed his way past people and scooped me up into his arms, one arm under my knees, the other around my back. "You're as white as the moon. Are you bleeding?"

"Oh. Yeah." I touched my side, only to hiss.

"You forgot?" He raised one of his blue eyebrows. "Part of taking care of the injured includes yourself, you know," he said, sounding like a father scolding his child.

He carried me to the most brightly lit space, where faeries worked feverishly to see the wounds, burns, scratches, and bruises of all injured. The rest of the faeries had come when the rest of the dragons arrived. From what I had seen, not one had hesitated to step in and help the humans in spite of their history together.

Dormir laid me down in the dirt. "Amilee, would you mind taking a look at Elisa?"

The woman walked over and knelt at my side. "We need to take off your shirt so we can see how bad the wound is."

Dormir stood to leave, but I grabbed his fingers.

"Don't go," I asked weakly. "Please?"

Dormir smiled sheepishly and rubbed the back of his neck. "You want me here?"

"You can close your eyes." I smiled.

He chuckled and sat down before closing his eyes.

"Just don't pass out," I teased.

"I'm not injured enough to … hey."

The nurse removed my shirt, revealing a gaping wound in my side. She made a comment about how she was surprised I wasn't dead, but her voice was far away. All I saw was blackness around the edge of the wound before my stomach lurched, and then there was nothing but darkness.

TWENTY-SIX

When I woke, Dormir was sound asleep, lying on his side facing me. He used one arm for a pillow and his other was on holding my hand. I couldn't help but smile. I reached up and touched his chin and then his lips. His warm breath caressed my finger. I ran my finger down his cheek, then lowered my hand. I don't know how the gods had cursed me and blessed me at the same time.

"How do you feel?" a familiar voice asked.

I looked to my other side and was rather shocked to see Queen Rachel sitting there. "I don't have much pain right now," I answered, though I could feel the radiating pain through my side, down my leg, and up through my ribs.

"We nearly lost you." She flashed a weak, but genuine, smile. "You've been asleep for days. Your … mother and I spoke."

I watched her carefully. "Oh?"

She closed her eyes, and when she opened them, there were tears. She looked utterly exhausted, with bags under her eyes and wrinkles on her forehead. "I'm so sorry for everything we did to you. I thought we were doing what was right for our people."

I reached down and played with Dormir's fingers. The air was suddenly stifling. "What you did … was wrong. You took me from my home. My family. I should have been raised all of these years to be a dragon. I should have learned how to fly and fight. I should have been with people who loved me." I looked at her when I said the last bit.

"We *did* love you, Elisa." She took my hand. "I … had grown to love you too much. With the prophecy and Jarrett's magic, we tried to suppress your dragon side, but every now and then you would have these outbursts of anger. I thought for certain we would lose you. So I began to push you away. I thought if I did that, it would hurt less when you transformed and left us." She closed her eyes. "I was deeply wrong. And with Dahlia gone—"

"Did you have her funeral?" I asked.

"No, no, not yet. You didn't miss it." She patted my hand reassuringly.

Dormir stirred. He groaned and stretched before he opened his eyes. Immediately, he grinned and sat up. "You're awake."

I gave him a relieved smile. "Of course I am, silly."

"Did your …" He paused and glanced at Rachel. It felt weird to call her that. He cleared his throat.

"Did she already tell you they've started clearing out the debris from the castle?"

I looked around. At some point over the last few days, I had been moved onto a cot and placed under a canopy. Indeed, much of the castle was already gone, and men and women sorted through the rubble, loading up wagons and wheelbarrows.

"We would like to talk," the queen said. "I've spoken with Queen Misla as well as your real parents, and we want you present. We need to know what we are going to do moving forward."

Knowing what to do moving forward was far more difficult than I imagined. We sat around a fire while those who had once been servants of the castle cooked breakfast.

The king and queen sat with Marigold between them. I took a position at the side of my true mother with Rowen at her side, and Dormir. Dormir's mother sat beside him. I looked around at our historical group.

My eyes settled on Marigold again. It was the first time I noticed Marigold's arm wrapped and leaned to Dormir to ask about it.

"Ah, it was a dark magic spell of some kind," he responded in a low voice. "They've got an ointment on it for now, but the healers say it's easy to heal."

I sighed in relief.

"A meeting like this has never taken place," Queen Misla started. "This is wonderful for all of our people." She gave everyone a kind smile.

I nodded in agreement. I wasn't ready for this conversation. We hadn't even properly buried Dahlia yet, and my side still ached terribly, which wasn't helped at all by sitting on the hard ground.

"I assume you want to talk about who has rights to the throne," Queen Rachel jumped in.

Misla nodded. "This is Dormir, my only son and heir to the fae throne."

Dormir lowered his head in a polite bow.

My previous mother glanced at me. It wasn't exactly a secret that Dormir and I liked each other.

I cleared my throat. "I think dragons and faeries have both proved they will step in and assist in times of need. Had it not been for the dragons and faeries, Gerard would have successfully usurped the throne."

"And who knows what a necromancer would have done to the kingdom," Rowen added.

The queen sniffled with indignation. "Moving forward, who has the rights to the throne, then? The faeries? Merely because they had ancestors on this land? I too had ancestors who owned this land."

"Because they took the land out from under us," Dormir said with a frown.

"Are not all kingdoms won through battle?" she countered.

"Then should we have allowed Gerard to take Griswil?" I asked.

She tightened her lips.

"Elisa *was* raised to be the next queen," the king spoke up for the first time. The father who had raised me had always been rather passive.

"Who better to know how to run the kingdom?" Isaline asked, giving me a grin.

"A dragon on the throne?" Queen Rachel muttered. "It isn't even her birthright ..."

Marigold jumped to her feet. "Well, I don't want to be the queen. Elisa has prepared her *entire* life to run the kingdom. She knows everything. *And* she's a dragon! How cool is it that a dragon would rule Griswil? The dragons would be able to come out of hiding and help down here. Did you hear the trees whispering? That's because that guy talked to them." She pointed to Rowen, who tried—and failed—to hide a grin. "Besides, Elisa will marry Dormir, and then a fae will rule at her side. It's a win-win. Done." Marigold dusted off her hands and sat down.

I didn't even know how to respond. Dormir and I had only known each other a short time, and even then I still didn't know much about him or his people, or even his family. I glanced in his direction, and he gave me a quick wink.

"That was a short conversation," Rowen said. He got to his feet. "Who is ready for breakfast?"

"What about the humans?" Rachel interjected.

What should have been a calm hour-long conversation evolved into an all-day discussion bordering on the edge of debate. What it really boiled down to was Rachel being reluctant to give up her crown.

Finally, Nicholia intervened. "Let us put the spring stone in the center of the group. One person from each race will step forward, and whomever the spring stone glows for will rule the kingdom."

"Dormir," Misla said.

He straightened. "I don't have it. I gave the stone to you."

"No, you had it after the fight with Gerard," she insisted.

He quickly patted his pockets and met my gaze with panic.

I exhaled. "Gerard got what he ultimately came for. It appears we will have to make this decision on our own. Besides, we shouldn't rely on magical artifacts forever. If everyone feels satisfied, I will step up and take the throne. My people already know me, already expect me to take over. Rumors have already begun to spread that I am a dragon and faeries have returned." I looked at the woman who raised me. "After everything that has happened, I feel I am ready for this. I wouldn't mind some help now and then, and I certainly wouldn't expect you to live in a shack."

Much to Rachel's chagrin, a vote was taken and everyone, including Marigold and the king, voted that I should take the throne.

My first order of business was Dahlia's funeral.

Her body had been prepared and a notice was sent throughout the land. Thousands of people arrived and set up tents around what used to be the castle. Unfortunately all the royal clothing had been burned in the fire, but fortunately Misla had an extra dress. She was taller than me, so the hem dragged. I hardly felt worthy to wear such a stunning gown.

It was night-sky blue with sparkles that glittered like stars. The sleeves were sheer and long, and the neckline plunged just enough to show a little bit of cleavage. The same sheer material went down my back.

Dormir knocked on the tent post, and I turned to find him standing in the entrance, staring at me. "You look positively stunning."

I curtsied. "You clean up nicely yourself."

He was back in his royal garb with the same material as mine in his tunic. He held his hand out for me to take. "I am pleased that you have chosen to take the throne. I know it wasn't something you wanted to do."

I shook my head. "I've realized it really is what I wanted all along. I wanted to do what was right by my people, I just didn't understand how. With my mother breathing down my neck, I didn't think I would ever be able to rule how I saw fit."

"Your sister is pretty bold." He twitched his brow with a playful smile. "I like her."

"You would have loved Dahlia too." I ran my hand over my bandaged side. "I keep replaying that moment in my mind. I keep trying to find a better way ..."

Dormir put his fingers under my chin, keeping my head from lowering. "That memory will be forever burned in your mind. I wish I could take that pain away from you."

I smiled. He was the only one who didn't tell me to feel better and be happy or to stop thinking about it altogether. I leaned up and kissed his cheek. "Thank you."

"With us wearing matching clothing, someone is bound to think something's up." He winked and grinned. The slant of his lips made my stomach flutter.

I took his arm and we walked from the tent. A small stage had been built so I could address the kingdom. Dormir supported me as I walked up the steps, grimacing with each movement. When we reached the top, he stepped back.

"Good people of Griswil!" I called out over the anxious crowd. "Much has happened the past few days. I will start by explaining Prince Gerard, the man I had been engaged to." I explained how he left me for dead in the land of the faeries, burned down their homes, and returned to Griswil to obtain the throne. I explained how the dragons and faeries fought at my side to bring down the wraith dragon, and how we exiled Gerard with a promise to sentence him to death should he ever return."

I looked down at the coffin on display in front of me. It had been carved from maple wood with beautiful flowers across the top. I put my hand on my chest as the ache grabbed at me.

"Dahlia died in that battle. I tried to save her ... and failed." I sniffled.

Dormir put his hand on my back. His touch warmed me.

"Dahlia loved to ride the horses. She wanted to be a famous artist or musician. She was really good at the violin." I smiled as I recalled her playing in the library while I studied.

When I finished my speech, the queen took her turn, and then the king.

Men stepped forward and hoisted Dahlia into the back of a wagon, and the funeral procession followed it up the hill into the trees to the cemetery. Dormir stayed at my side with his arm around my shoulders and handed me a handkerchief when I needed it.

With Dahlia finally at rest with a proper memorial, work on the new castle began. Volunteers from Griswil, faeries, and even the dragons had also begun rebuilding Sloval. The spring equinox drew near, and royalty from Arington, Terricina, and Zelig would soon arrive. A celebration was just what our people needed, and it was then I would be crowned queen of Griswil.

I stood in the center of the new castle as men worked on carving the three pillars holding the staircase with scenes on one pillar for the dragons, one for the faeries, and the last for the humans. When it was completed, the castle would be more beautiful than it had ever been.

We still hadn't worked out where the dragons would live, but many of them returned to the comfort of the mountains while Nicholia scouted the Drakespine Mountains to see if there was a possibility nearer.

One beautiful day, Dormir slid his hand down my arm before entwining our fingers together. "You've done a marvelous job the last several weeks."

"As long as we all keep working together, Griswil will be the strongest it's ever been." I smiled up at him.

"With you as their queen, how could it not?"

I rolled my eyes with a playful smile. "I'm just that wonderful."

For the first time in my life, I believed it.

EPILOGUE

"You complete and utter fool!" Selina's bolt of electricity slammed into my chest.

The force threw me through the air, and my back and head cracked against the stone wall. I collapsed in a heap with a groan. "I brought back the stone," I said through gritted teeth.

"You almost didn't, *and* you almost got yourself killed. Not to mention, Griswil is now on high alert, which means they will spread the word of danger to the other kingdoms!" Her gown rustled as she paced in front of me.

I flexed my jaw. Warmth trickled down the side of my head, and I was confident my right shoulder was dislocated or broken. But I forced myself to sit up on my knees, knowing the powerful sorceress would expect as much.

"I put these plans in place for the last eighteen years. I'm *not* going to have them ruined because you get greedy." She stopped a few feet away from me. "Do you understand, Gerard?"

I nodded, but that movement alone caused me to see stars, and I put a hand on the floor to keep myself from falling over.

"You're pathetic," she spat.

I held my breath, knowing exactly how she was going to finish that sentence.

"Just like your father." She turned sharply and walked to her chair by the fire. She picked up the spring stone from the table beside it. "Still ... you managed to bring this back to me." Her voice had calmed significantly. "I suppose that deserves a lesser punishment." Selina crossed to the small table behind the couch where a tray with a steaming kettle and teacups sat waiting.

I pretended not to watch her, instead keeping my eyes locked on her raven, who was ruffled and sleeping on top of his perch on the mantle. I was trying to keep my vision in focus and trying to keep myself centered so I wouldn't pass out.

Selina poured the hot water into a teacup, plopped in a tea bag, and then opened the drawer to search for just the right additive. She plucked one of the vials and dropped two drops into the tea. She walked to me and held it out.

"Thank you," I mumbled.

"What is your plan for Terricina?" she asked. Selina walked to her raven perched beside her chair and stroked its breast. "Hopefully you won't get involved with the princess this time."

I flexed my jaw. The engagement to Princess Elisa had been *her* idea. Not mine. "She led me right to the spring stone. It worked. And no, I won't be getting involved because there isn't a princess of Terricina. He's a prince."

"Ah. Then don't get involved with the prince." Her lip curled.

Heat of humiliation burned across my neck and down my jaw. "Selina …"

"You avoided my question. I think you shall spend a night behind the black door."

I flinched, instinctively drawing my shoulders upward, though doing so caused pain to explode through my shoulder and my stomach to churn so violently I vomited.

"Gerard." Selina tutted her tongue. "Now you have to clean that up."

I licked my bottom lip and wiped a trembling hand over my chin.

Selina continued. "I heard a rumor their capital city sunk into the sea. I wonder who might have caused that?"

"I heard." I took another sip of the tea, allowing the magical concoction to begin healing my shoulder and head. "I will hire a crew and investigate myself."

She nodded. "I know a man." She walked around her chair to the desk against the wall. "James owes me. I will contact him for you. You will call him Captain *Pan*." She snickered at the name.

I eyed her. "Pan?"

"Oh yes. He *hated* being called Hook." She set down the quill, and it began to scrawl on the parchment she'd laid out. Selina turned and studied me with her lips tight. "As I said, clean up your mess." She snapped her fingers and a door in the back of the room opened. The black door.

"Mistress ... please," I begged. The teacup in my hand trembled in spite of my self-determination, and I set it on the floor away from my vomit stain.

She clicked her tongue, and the raven perked up immediately. He stretched and flew over to her waiting shoulder. Selina looked at me one last time. "Don't disappoint me again, Gerard."

"Yes, ma'am," I replied.

She left me alone in the study.

I stared at the open doorway. The shadows clawed at the doorframe, begging for something, or some*one*, to play with.

I turned away, finished my tea, and set to work cleaning up my mess. The shadows called to me, making the hair on my body prickle.

Why had Elisa let me go?

I'd been bound before her, ready to accept my death, and she'd let me go.

I dumped the dirty water and washed my hands. As I faced the darkness of the black room, I made a vow.

Next time, I wouldn't risk getting so ambitious.

THE FORGOTTEN KINGDOM SERIES

The Four Stones of Tern Tovan
(Prequel to The Forgotten Kingdom Series)

The Dragon Princess
(Sleeping Beauty Reimagined)

The Siren Princess—coming fall 2019
(Little Mermaid Reimagined)

Receive the prequel to *The Four Kingdom Series* for FREE by signing up for my newsletter: https://mailchi.mp/78ba88ee86a2/lichelleslater

ALSO BY LICHELLE SLATER

Urban Fantasy
Curse of a Djinn

Science Fiction/Fantasy
Step Right Up
Come One Come All
Prepare to be Amazed

Christmas Romance Novels
Secret Santa
Accidental Secret Santa

ABOUT THE AUTHOR

Personal dragon trainer, lover of glitter, super nerd.

Lichelle Slater lives in Salt Lake City, Utah, with her adorable King Charles, Perseus. When she's not working full-time as a special education preschool teacher, she's living in the worlds she creates and shares with readers, painting, or doing any other assortment of crafting. One thing is for certain—you'll always find a dragon in her stories.

Sign up for my newsletter here: https://mailchi.mp/78ba88ee86a2/lichelleslater

To join my Facebook reader group, go to Lichelle's Book Wyrms: https://www.facebook.com/groups/753608364988213/

FOLLOW ME HERE

Instagram
https://www.instagram.com/lichelleslater_author/

Twitter
https://twitter.com/LichelleSlater

Amazon
https://www.amazon.com/Lichelle-Slater/e/
B01MSU34EN/

Goodreads
https://www.goodreads.com/author/show/16150296.
Lichelle_Slater